MANIPULATION

EDEN WINTERS

ROCKY RIDGE BOOKS

Corruption © Eden Winters 2014
Cover art by LC Chase
Edited by Jerry L. Wheeler
Interior layout and design by P.D. Singer

ISBN-13 978-1-62622-059-1

Published by:

Rocky Ridge Books
PO Box 6922
Broomfield, CO 80021
www.RockyRidgeBooks.com

Praise for the first three Bo and Lucky novels:

Diversion is one of the strongest gay romance novels I have read... It maintains a perfect balance between romantic comedy and hot sexual tension on the one hand and a solid, fascinating, complex plot about prescription drug smuggling on the other...

—Val, ARe Cafe

Forget sleep, I had to find out how this worked out. With a fast paced and tense external plot plus a relationship moving to a new level, *Collusion* kept me turning the page until I got to the end. *Diversion,* the first Bo and Lucky book, did the same thing to me, and this is a more than worthy followup.

—Cryselle, Reviews by Jessewave

So many things go on in [*Collusion*]. Some good (Bo and Lucky), some bad (Lucky in the children's cancer ward), but there's never a dull moment. Some smiley, happy ones (Lucky's confrontation with the neighbor from hell), some tear-jerking ones (the cancer ward), but you *need* to know what's going to happen. The story pulls you along to the ultimate, beautiful conclusion.

—Mrs. Condit Reviews

I find myself hesitating, not wanting to put the limitations of a label on such a unique and revelatory series and cast of characters. I only know that I want and need more of them and the dubious path that Winters has laid out before them. It's an amazing journey and I know you will want to be here with me every step of the way.

—Scattered Thoughts and Rogue Words

Many thanks to P.D. Singer, John A., John R., Lynda B., D.H. Starr, Feliz Faber, Z. Allora, A.B. Gayle, Kayla Jameth, Becky Condit, and Will Parkinson, for handholding and critique. And to David Sullivan for his police expertise. Big hugs and lots of love to Nurse Sarah, for her medical details. I'd also like to thank the instructors at the Writer's Police Academy for helping me "get it right", especially when it comes to questions like "What does a dead body look like if it's left in a Mexican drug tunnel for six months?"

Many thanks to the readers who have asked for more of Bo and Lucky's story.

MANIPULATION

EDEN WINTERS

CHAPTER ONE

IN THROUGH the nose, out through the mouth. Pine bark rasped against Lucky's back, and the bitter scent of sap assaulted his nose. Needles nearly as long as his hand fanned out before his face, hiding him from view while allowing him to see. The sun beat down, too early in the day yet for the stifling heat due to descend around 2 p.m. A few gnats buzzed around his head. Gnats he could deal with, as long as mosquitos stayed away. And palmetto bugs. The big nasty fuckers squished underfoot and still refused to die.

He studied his quarry through the trees on the far side of the ravine. Thank his redneck upbringing for hours spent in the woods learning to lay low and observe. Once his stealth had meant the difference between a full belly of deer meat and just vegetables again. Now life and death often hung in the balance. Too many times he'd been lax and paid the price. The scars on his ankle began to itch, a reminder of one of those times.

Never again would he drop his guard. Skills were only as good as the man who used them. While he'd fully earned the "dumb redneck" label folks hung on him—and wore the epithet like a badge of honor—he wasn't above learning from his mistakes. He just wouldn't let people know he'd learned. His greatest advantage was in being underestimated.

Leaves crunched underfoot and branches shook across the way. Slow, unhurried. A sitting duck. Lucky's favorite kind.

He crouched down to wait. Twigs snapped, and his target swore, picking up the pace once he'd cleared a bramble thicket. The ruckus quieted. Ah, so he'd stopped bushwhacking and

1

discovered the old cow path winding around the pine where Lucky took shelter. Perfect.

The guy muttered to himself, too low for Lucky to hear. Didn't matter. He might as well wear a cowbell around his neck. Poor guy didn't stand a chance. Too bad Lucky didn't believe in pity.

Closer and closer. Any second now. Lucky held his breath and pulled back behind the tree. Normally he hated being short, but five feet six hid a whole lot easier than six feet.

Crunch, crunch, crunch. Last year's fallen leaves tracked every footstep. The noise stopped right behind Lucky's tree. One step. Two steps. A T-shirt clad back appeared in his view. The guy had over six inches on Lucky. Lucky had surprise. He pounced.

"Ahhhh!" The man went down and came up swinging. Nice reflexes!

Lucky danced out of reach. The guy swung again. In a flash, Lucky twisted his prey's arm behind his back, forcing him to the ground and pinning him face down in Georgia clay.

Determination changed to anger on the face of the fuming brunet now glaring over his shoulder. "Damn it, Lucky! How many times do I have to tell you? Don't fucking do that! You nearly gave me a heart attack."

Bo, Lucky's partner both on and off the job, clutched his chest with his free hand as if to prove his point.

He squirmed, but Lucky held tight. Better allow some time for Bo to cool off a bit before letting him loose. No telling what he might do.

Once Lucky'd known his partner like the back of his hand. Since their latest undercover assignment, Bo had grown unpredictable, spending more and more time in his undercover persona of Cyrus Cooper and less as Bo. And wasn't that as sexy as it was troubling?

"Hey, you're the one who was teacher's pet in all those classes." Being demoted to second best still stuck in Lucky's craw. For eight years, he'd had been the star undercover operative at the Southeastern Narcotics Bureau, until Bo waltzed right in and stole Lucky's thunder. "Think of this as practical application, something you can't pick up in a conference room." The worrisome part? The niggling doubt that he wasn't the best anymore. If he wasn't the best, someone else was better—possibly the criminal with Lucky in his sights.

He loosened his grip, and Bo nearly jerked away. Hmm... not good to release him while he still wanted to fight. Taking advantage of their position, Lucky swiped his tongue over the side of Bo's neck, and the light bite that followed earned him a moan. The right moves sent the man from pissed off to horny in no time flat. Oh yeah. Bring on those right moves.

"We're out here all alone, just the two of us. How will we pass the time?" Lucky rumbled into Bo's ear. He wasn't above using lust as a diversion. Come to think of it, Bo offered the same effective distraction for Lucky.

Releasing Bo's arm to slide his hand under Bo's shirt, Lucky breathed in deeply of his lover's favorite cologne, plus tangy undertones of sweat from Bo's early morning hike. A hint of pine, freshly mown hay from a nearby field, and a touch of moisture from the river a few yards away added to the blend. If Lucky could choose one place to call home, it'd be here. With Bo. With no job or other responsibilities, and definitely no outlaw past looming over his head.

For this, Lucky had hauled his ass out of bed early, creeping out of the cabin the moment Bo left the yard.

Bo rolled over in Lucky's now unrestraining arms, hands warm and sure as they cupped Lucky's face. Over the past few weeks while sharing a cabin in the woods on their undercover assignment, Lucky had grown used to kissing his man whenever certain they'd ducked out of surveillance range. Nothing brought a lust-filled moment to a screeching halt faster than imagining coworkers critiquing the video.

Here, out in the wild with only the faint hum of cars on a back road to break the peace, they were free to do whatever they wanted away from the cameras monitoring the cabin. And Lucky wanted Bo. Here. Now.

He didn't kiss Bo so much as devour his mouth, catching Bo's low moans as they vibrated against his tongue.

Palming the back of Bo's head, Lucky crawled up the man's body to even out the difference in their height.

Lucky vaguely noticed Bo's arms around him, pulling him close, and he peeled Bo's T-shirt up and off, pausing the kiss long enough to get the collar over his head. By feel, he shucked off Bo's nylon running shorts. Bo shifted his weight to toe off his shoes and socks. Hidden from the surrounding countryside by a stand of pines, Bo soon lay naked on the ground.

He'd added muscle over the past few months on assignment, playing the role of drug-running biker and hoisting engines in a garage, and instead of the even coloring he'd once acquired at a salon, he now sported an uneven farmer's tan on his face and the part of his arms exposed by a T-shirt while out riding his Harley Davidson. His legs were far paler than they used to be.

He still made one hell of a tempting package. Bo helped Lucky out of his jeans, boots and T. By the time he'd stripped down to nothing at all, his impressive erection pointed up toward his belly. Though short in stature, Lucky was big where it counted. He rubbed against Bo, Bo's uncut cock saying "howdy" to Lucky's circumcised flesh. They rejoined their lips, roaming their hands over each other's sweat-slicked skin.

Lucky dropped down to take Bo into his mouth, pine needles cushioning his knees. Skimming back Bo's foreskin with one hand, Lucky sealed his mouth over the purpled head, swirling his tongue over the slit to catch the drop of moisture beaded there. A taste of things to...come.

Lips stretched tight, Lucky descended, trying to accommodate Bo's hefty girth. Deep moans sounded above his head. He took his time on the upstroke and back down. Let Bo squirm a bit, grow needy. Sure enough, Bo raked his fingers through Lucky's hair, gripping the back of Lucky's head to speed the pace.

Lucky resisted enough to let the man know he didn't call *all* the shots, then abandoned his hold on Bo's cock to clutch the glorious swell of a perfect bubble-butt. He used the leverage to work Bo deeper into his throat. His own cock bobbed with his movement.

The musky scent of sweat and pre-come filled Lucky's nostrils. Oh damn, oh damn, oh damn. He found a better purchase on Bo's thigh to free up a hand for his own need.

Bo pulled away. "Not like that." He grabbed Lucky's arm, hauled him upright by sheer force, and tugged him back the way he'd come on his hike. "Here."

A bed of red clover. Right when they needed one.

Shaded by pines and oaks, the cushiony plants felt cool against Lucky's heated skin. He rolled onto his back. Bo blocked out the sun and lowered himself down, placing his shaft inches from Lucky's mouth, positioned to return the favor.

Oh, hell. Bo wrapped moist lips around Lucky's straining flesh. Lucky opened his mouth and took Bo's offering. His balls tightened when Bo ran his tongue down Lucky's length, and his brain switched off.

With his arms wrapped around Bo's upper thighs, Lucky controlled the rhythm as much as he could, pushing up his hips in time with Bo's thrusts. Bo stroked Lucky's balls, reaching a finger back to massage the place just behind.

So fucking good. Lucky relaxed his throat and took Bo deeper.

Bo alternated between dragging his tongue up and down Lucky's cock and taking the head into his mouth to slide down the length. When a tingling began deep within, Lucky grunted, leg muscles trembling. Bo backed off Lucky's cock, easing the rising tide of his orgasm. Damn him for knowing Lucky's body too well. Two could play that game.

Lucky sucked in earnest, steady strokes designed to bring Bo off quickly. When Bo gasped, "I'm close," Lucky stopped dead.

"Asshole," Bo mumbled around his mouthful.

"I've got one you can use." Lucky wasn't above using spit for lube but wasn't gonna last long enough to assume the position.

Finally Bo settled into an "I mean business" pace. Lucky matched him. Faster and faster he advanced and retreated, the taste of salty pre-come on his tongue.

Bo's rhythm faltered. Oh sweet heavens.

Pulse after pulse coated Lucky's tongue. His muscles seized and he groaned, loosing the tide into Bo's mouth. *Oh God, oh God, oh God, yeah!*

He collapsed back onto the crushed clover. Boneless. Totally spent. Overhead, a few wispy clouds wandered aimlessly across a blue sky. Bo settled next to him, resting his head on Lucky's shoulder. Out of habit, Lucky wrapped his lover in a one-armed hug without thinking, the post-sex position now as familiar as breathing.

The sun warmed Lucky's skin, the scent of crushed clover and a blue jay's cackle reminding him where he was. A moment's calm before the storm.

He'd nearly drifted off to sleep when Bo asked, "When do you think they'll recall us back to Atlanta?"

A load of reality Lucky didn't want to consider came crashing back down.

For a month now, they'd hung around Athens, Georgia, waiting for a drug supplier to revamp the pipeline they'd torn apart and once more flood the region with the synthetic bogeyman known as "bath salts", or in their case, "Corruption". But the Southeastern Narcotics Bureau couldn't leave two agents idling indefinitely. Sooner or later, they'd give up the wait, ending Lucky and Bo's idyllic summer vacation together. When the recall came, they'd once more be Simon "Lucky" Harrison, and William Patrick "Bo" Schollenberger, two agents who damned sure shouldn't be caught lying in the clover, buck naked with each other's come on their breath.

"I don't know." When the call came, it'd be too fucking soon. Lucky could stay here forever, hiking, fishing, loving Bo—not that he'd confess to the fact. Back in Atlanta, they'd pretend to be merely coworkers, sneaking around and hoping no one saw them. And chances were they'd have separate assignments, taking them away from each other for weeks on end.

Bo ran his fingers through the soft clover. "When we get back, I intend to start house hunting again. I've been thinking about the one on Sycamore. You know, with the garage? I sent you a link."

"Want me to look at it? I've done some renovations back in the day. I can see if it needs work you haven't noticed."

Bo rolled on his side, staring up at Lucky with soulful brown eyes. "Would you? I'd like that."

He'd tried to include Lucky in the house selection process before. Lucky had pretty much screamed and ran. His butt should have a permanent boot imprint from all the times he kicked himself. Of course he'd tread softly now.

"Yeah. Wouldn't want you to get stuck with a money pit." A phone rang. Oh, hell. *That phone.* Lucky shot to his feet. Now where the fuck had he left his pants? He ran barefoot back to the pine tree where he and Bo had left their clothes. Ouch! Rock! Ouch! Stick!

He hopped the remaining three yards on one foot and dove into his jeans pocket for his work phone. Oops. Wrong one. It stopped ringing the moment he pushed the button to accept the call, "Walter Smith" displayed for a second on the screen. Oh shit. What did he want? Lucky hit the redial button.

Walter picked up on the first ring. "Lucky? I hope I'm not disturbing you." Did boss man know something he shouldn't? Like two of his agents "fraternizing" against bureau policy. God, Lucky hated the word. "We need you back in Atlanta. If you haven't heard from your old friend yet, you probably won't."

Your old friend. Not *Victor Mangiardi*. The man who'd shared Lucky's bed and introduced him to the exciting world of drug trafficking, resulting in a ten year sentence and a lot of personal baggage. And the reason Lucky now answered phone calls from Walter Smith, head of the Southeastern Narcotics Bureau's Department of Diversion Prevention and Control. And Lucky's boss.

Old friend, indeed. Damn it. Wasn't nothing wrong with Lucky's memory of the night some asshole conked him over the head and threw him into a car trunk. He couldn't forget hearing "Hello, Lucky" in Victor's voice. And if Victor was still out there and not dead like the papers said, he'd have a score to settle with the man who'd thrown him under the justice bus.

"What do you want me to do?" Double damn Walter for managing to worm his way under Lucky's skin, one of a handful of folks Lucky might possibly listen to.

"Since Art's accident, he's been talking more and more about retirement." The SNB took a toll on its agents. Most wised up and hauled ass. Many died in the line of duty. Few retired. Art got broadsided by a woman on her way to a birthday party and nearly lost his life to a few wayward balloons. The informant sitting next to him hadn't been so lucky.

"Can't say that I blame him." Lucky didn't. Not really. Close calls reminded one how precious and fleeting time was. But Art's leaving would take out one of the few fellow agents Lucky trusted.

"His leaving means I need you back here to assume responsibilities for the trainees." Uh-oh. Walter was using his "Boston college professor voice." He never used that particular tone when Lucky got a say in the matter.

Bo massaged his shoulders, kneading away his rising tension. Lucky leaned back into the touch, phone clapped to his ear. "So, you haven't recovered your senses enough to figure out that me and training just don't mix?"

Walter's chuckle wafted from the phone's speaker. "Would you rather entrust all these bright young minds to Keith?"

Good point, and the one argument sure to reel Lucky in. One poor excuse for a major ass wipe per department was enough. Keith didn't need to sow the seeds of ignorance into the newbies. "When do you want me back?"

"Tie up any loose ends there today if you can and get back to Atlanta."

One day? One fucking day? He rested his free hand on top of one of Bo's. One day wasn't enough. Not that he'd clue Walter in. "I'll be there."

Bo squeezed his hand. Smart man to figure out which way the wind blew with only half of the conversation to go on. Even with the sun high overhead, storm clouds gathered on Lucky's own personal horizon. Away from Bo. Going to a home that wasn't home.

"What about Bo?" Lucky kept his tone professional. Couldn't let on that he really gave a happy damn one way or the other.

"We're keeping him in place for the time being."

Keeping him in place while a pissed off Mexican drug dealer knew his whereabouts, to either take revenge or to recruit new drug runners and rebuild his stateside distribution network. Not good when the best case scenario still meant "you're fucked."

"Are you sure that's wise, with me gone?" He normally didn't naysay the boss, but this was Bo, not so long out of rookie-hood himself, and still far too trusting for his own good.

"Keith runs surveillance on the cabin, and I don't think I have to remind you how well Bo performed in training or on his cases. He's worked with you for nearly two years. Don't you think you should trust your capabilities as a trainer? I do."

Fuck. And that's why Walter called the shots. He always managed to make sense, even when Lucky didn't want him to. "I'll leave him set up, then get my ass back to Atlanta." *Dragging my heels all the way*, didn't get said. Neither Walter nor Bo needed to hear that part.

"Good. I'll expect you in my office first thing in the morning."

The comforting hand left Lucky's shoulder the moment he hung up. When he turned around, Bo was gone.

Narrowed eyes, hard as steel, stared back at him. Cyrus Cooper, Bo's undercover persona, had taken front and center. "You're leaving." Flat. Emotionless. A statement, not a question.

Those two small words set a weight on Lucky's chest. "Yeah."

"I'll go pack your bags." The man who wore Bo's face paused long enough to put his clothes back on before trudging toward the cabin without looking back.

Lucky pulled on his jeans and rammed his feet down in his boots. He hurried after Bo while struggling into his T-shirt. "Bo, wait!"

Cyrus glared over his shoulder. "It's okay, Ricky. We knew this would happen sooner or later."

Ricky, Lucky's undercover character, not *Lucky*. In the back of Lucky's mind, a door slammed shut.

CHAPTER TWO

Boxes lined one wall of the dingy apartment, some roughly cut open with little packets spilling onto the floor. Kinda looked like the boxes Lucky had been hauling recently for Mateo Reyes' drug-dealing bikers. He put his gun away, shuffled across the room, and squatted down for a closer inspection. Yeah, the packs bore the name "Corruption".

A stomach-churning stench grew stronger the longer Lucky stayed in the apartment. Blankets covered the windows, and a single dangling light bulb didn't give off enough light. What a damned clusterfuck. Beer cans and pizza boxes filled most flat surfaces in the shoebox apartment, with fast food bags overflowing onto the floor. Bold-as-brass cockroaches scurried over the trash. Motherfucking roaches.

A uniformed cop approached. "The neighbor said he heard shots about a half-hour before you got here. The dead guy's by the window. You know him?"

"You go ahead, I've got this." Loretta Johnson, the better of Lucky's two trainees, knelt down to scoop a few packets into an evidence bag with rubber-gloved hands. Efficient, professional, and not seeming to notice the pile of human shit sitting two feet away, she just might last a year or two in this job.

Lucky pushed a few loaded trash bags out of his way to wade across the room. Sorting garbage might be a good job for his other newbie, Rookie Landry, currently retching in a corner. A body lay face-up on the floor, spread-eagled, wearing only a pair of jeans. The world's worst mermaid tattoo covered the victim's chest. What the hell made those bloody gashes on his arms? Fuck. He did know the man. "Yeah, that's the guy I'm here to meet."

There'd be no teaching his trainees how to conduct a large-scale drug buy today. A dead body took the case away from the SNB and placed it firmly in the hands of Atlanta's finest.

A pool of red fanned out from under the dead dealer. A gun lay a few feet away, and white powder covered his nose and chest.

Two more officers strode in, with a middle-aged woman in slacks and a button-down shirt, who dropped down beside the corpse. A moment later, another woman in a blue uniform clicked away with a camera. Lucky stepped back and let the forensics people work. Stiffs weren't in his job description.

The woman at his feet snapped on a pair of gloves and wrapped her hand around the dead guy's wrist. She lifted his arm and put her bespectacled nose closer than Lucky would have. "Human fingernails marks on chest and arms." She stared at the man's fingertips. "Flesh beneath the nails. The claw marks appear self-inflicted."

Fuck, the bastard had done the damage to himself.

"Corruption, see demons now!" would be a pretty good ad for the crap this man sold. He took the only out he probably thought he had at the time.

Lucky jerked his phone from his pocket and called Walter. "Our dealer's dead. Class dismissed."

So much for Drug Buying 101.

Walter sat back in his chair, which emitted a startled squeak. "All the cash and drugs were still there?"

"Yeah. He'd clawed himself up pretty good. Must've been one hell of a trip." A few months ago, an office worker had taken Corruption and wound up firing at Lucky. Grazed his arm too. "Why do people take shit that makes them either want to kill each other or themselves?"

Gone were the good old days of getting stoned and drunk. Nowadays, folks wanted bigger thrills. Dumb shits.

He'd never admit it, but Lucky's stomach had rolled right along with Landry's at the sight of the bloody gouges in the dealer's flesh.

"I've asked myself the same thing about meth and every other street drug I've ever encountered." Pushing seventy, the oldest member of the SNB had likely seen one hell of a lot. Walter reached under his bifocals to rub his eyes. "I understand Johnson behaved admirably in the field today."

"Yes, sir."

"And Landry?"

"'Useless' don't half cover it. Has the office betting pool put odds on him yet? I've got twenty bucks says he won't last six months."

"Sit, let's talk."

Not words Lucky wanted to hear. Too many unanswered questions stood between them. Over the years, they'd formed a truce that had gradually turned to grudging admiration. Walter filled in for the father who'd turned his back. Yet, recently, Walter had slipped up a bit.

A recording taken from Lucky's last case captured the voice of a man who'd returned from the grave and from Lucky's past. The normally unflappable Walter had—flapped. He had some explaining to do.

Lucky dropped down in his usual chair in front of his boss's desk. Might as well clear the air. "We found a dozen or so cases of Corruption this morning. Not much. And trolling the clubs hasn't turned up anything. As far as we know, our guy in Mexico hasn't made a move, and Bo hasn't heard anything. What's he waiting for?"

Demand was on the streets of Atlanta. They'd only cut off the supply route; they hadn't found the supplier. Sooner or later, whoever ran the show would get the brass balls to try again. A shiver ran up Lucky's spine.

What if Victor had somehow managed to escape death and even now called the shots somewhere in Mexico?

Lucky hadn't hidden during his time in prison or with the SNB. Only a couple years ago, Walter arranged Richmond Eugene Lucklighter's death and created Simon "Lucky" Harrison. If Victor wanted revenge for Lucky testifying against him, he could've settled the score a million times over.

Victor Mangiardi couldn't be alive.

A man like Victor didn't build his reputation on letting enemies go. Not even if they'd once been lovers. Yet there'd been no threat in the quiet, "Hello, Lucky" that still haunted Lucky's dreams.

"The Mexican authorities are handling the investigation south of the border." Walter yawned between words. "There's nothing more we can do at the moment unless someone makes contact, or we find another pipeline forming."

Loose ends came back to bite. Best to tie them up all neatly. "So we do nothing."

"No. We move on. Unless someone contacts Bo soon, the case is closed, and the DEA assumes control."

"Yeah, yeah. We do the grunt work, they waltz in for the easy part." Lucky stifled a sigh of relief. Finding one victim who'd put a bullet in his head to escape his own mind was enough. "What a waste."

A waste of life, time, and taxpayer money. No matter how much the government spent trying to save people from themselves, the folks in question always found new and more horrifying ways to self-destruct and wreak havoc on the world in general.

Fucking job security. It meant people died.

Only a few cars remained in the parking lot. Not much reason to hurry home without Bo there. Bo. Three damned weeks with no word. No need arousing suspicion by checking in with him when Lucky wasn't on the same case anymore. Their calls and texts were monitored, and no fucking way would he give asshole Keith any ammunition to use against him or Bo.

He headed his aging Camaro toward home. Another weekend alone. Well, not entirely.

"You've calmed down lately," his landlady said when he climbed out of the car in his front yard, computer bag thrown over one shoulder. "The cops haven't brought you home in a while."

Mrs. Griggs sat on her porch swing in a lightweight bathrobe and slippers, her normal supply of cats stretched out beside her and in her lap. As far as Lucky knew, robes, slippers, and tabbies were her only attire. She'd even showed him his side of their shared duplex in a housecoat, with a calico draped over her shoulder.

Hell, she'd only seen the cops bring him home cuffed a time or two during training exercises. And only because Keith refused to release him until he was out of the car. Stupid jerkoff.

"No, ma'am. Things've been quiet lately." Too quiet. Calm-before-the-axe-murderer-in-the-horror-flick-showed-up quiet. Goosebumps rose on Lucky's arms when he keyed the lock to his front door. Something wasn't quite right. The last time he'd gotten the heebie jeebies, he'd been watched.

He whirled around and searched the street. Two kids rode scooters on the sidewalk. The usual cars lined the street and were parked in driveways. Nothing appeared amiss.

A black and white flash shot across the porch and into the house, too fast for Lucky to stop. His heart pounded. What did he expect to find? No shots rang out—no sound came from within at all. He waved at his landlady and entered his home.

Bo wasn't there to greet him, but the house was no longer empty. Shielding his bag from his landlady's keen eyes, he slipped his .38 out. Paranoia and narcotics traveled hand-in-hand. One couldn't be too careful, especially after already *dying* once in the line of duty.

He came in the door low, ducking behind an arm chair.

"Mrrrooow?" A black and white cat held its leg in the air and paused in mid-lick of its hiney to question him. The feline sat dead center of the couch like he owned the place.

"Hello, Cat Lucky." Human Lucky threw open the entry closet to peer inside. Nothing. Not that he kept the place tidy enough to notice something missing. Also nothing in the bedroom closet, bathroom, or under the kitchen sink. Before Bo came into his life, he'd check for dust prints on furniture. Hmm...a good argument for not cleaning.

"Mrroww?" Cat Lucky asked again, twining around Lucky's ankles.

"Yeah, yeah." Lucky laid his gun on the counter and dug in the cabinet for a can of tuna. With a happy cat growling its way through his dinner, Lucky sighed and checked his home computer for e-mails while munching a peanut butter sandwich. Still nothing from Bo. Damn it.

Dear Mr. Harrison,

Please stop by Human Resources at your earliest convenience. There are some documents in need of your signature.

Human Resources? What did they want? He'd get to it when he got to it.

He scrolled through the rest of his messages. New pictures from Charlotte. Damn, how his nephews had grown. Lines showed around his sister's eyes, and a touch of gray roots peeked up from her light brown hair. No. Little sister couldn't be going gray. That meant Lucky was getting older too.

Todd and Tyler towered over her now. Damn. They'd grown up without Uncle Lucky in their lives. What were they like now? Had they made out okay without a positive male influence? Did they ever hear from the no account asshole of a father? Then again, if they had, and not in a good way, the ghost of a supposedly dead brother-in-law might have to pay a visit.

Can you believe the boys are both in high school? We miss you!

Love, Charlotte

No "we" about it. The boys thought their drug dealing uncle dead, like the rest of the family did. Only Charlotte knew the truth, and only because she was too stubborn to write her brother off like she should have done years ago when he'd first been arrested. She'd showed up day after day at his trial and always believed in him even if neither of them ever pretended Lucky's innocence for a second. She loved him anyway. She and Bo.

Bo.

Lucky called up the last e-mail he'd received from his lover months ago, an invitation to go house hunting. Bo wanted a house, a family. And for some strange reason, he wanted those things with Lucky. Well, no accounting for some people's tastes.

He clicked on the link to the house Bo'd invited him to see. "Sold" now displayed on the image. Too bad. Still, Bo wanted a house. With nothing better to do, Lucky could at least show some interest and look. He took down the Realtor's name and number.

CHAPTER THREE

Lucky surveyed the eaves of the house. No security light, no cameras. A dumb move when the downward sloping property backed up to a canal. No difficult matter to paddle silently to the dock, park the boat, and creep up the hill unnoticed in the dead of night.

He rounded the corner and eased open a window casement with little resistance. Faulty latches. Not good. Not good at all. Within five minutes, he could take out a family of six, be in the boat and halfway across the county. What the hell kind of trusting soul owned this house, anyway?

One good push opened the window enough for him to slide through. He hoisted himself inside, to land on a carpeted floor at the Realtor's feet.

Lucky stared up. The woman huffed out an aggrieved sigh and gazed down at him, hands on her hips. "I take it that's a no."

Lucky shrugged. Not his fault she'd tried to sell him another unsafe house.

She plastered on the fake grin that paled more with each property. "Let's move on to the next house, shall we?"

House number nine appealed to Lucky's inner hermit. However, there were no other houses for two miles on either side, no Starbucks for fifteen, plus an hour and a half commute to work. Even though Bo spent a good deal of time on assignment and wasn't driving in to the office much, this wouldn't do.

The woods behind the house provided shade and a good place for walks. This far out, no one around? Perfect for a meth lab, or maybe a dozen.

Lucky called up the Internet on his cell phone. "Thirty-five murders in this county last year, forty-seven drugs arrests, and fifty-nine grand thefts. What kind of slum are you trying to sell me?"

The Realtor stopped even trying to smile. Her mouth said, "Next house?" while her clenched fists and the horror in her eyes said, "Dear Lord, get me out of this realty hell!"

Lucky studied the square opening in the garage ceiling. "Where does that go?"

"To the attic. There's a lot of storage room up there." A note of pride returned to the Realtor's voice as she kicked back into saleswoman mode.

"How far does it go?"

"All the way across the house. You could even add a bonus room if you wanted."

Lucky charged through the structure, noting security system contacts on the doors and windows, but not on the attic openings in both second floor bedrooms. Hell, he might as well leave the damned door open. All anyone had to do was break into the garage and they'd have free range of the house.

He shimmied out of an uncontacted basement window and climbed a wisteria vine to enter an upper room.

Oh, hell no. Last year he'd gone up a kudzu vine to gain access to a trafficker's warehouse and cases full of poison sold as cancer drugs. He'd fallen and broken his foot and ankle escaping. As if on cue, the ankle throbbed.

The vine would have to go, and he'd have to secure the attic and basement. Still, the neighborhood was nice, and not too far from the SNB offices on Peachtree Street.

But what was that? He knelt in the master bedroom on obviously new carpet to examine a stain on the baseboard.

"Hey!" his escort shouted when he grabbed the edge of the carpet and yanked. Rust-colored stains covered the plywood underneath.

"Are you going to tell me, or do I call up copies of the police report?"

"Why don't we go to the next house?"

Sounded like a good idea. Bo didn't deserve to live in a place where traces of the former owner hid beneath carpet and paint.

Lucky sniffed and sniffed again.

"What are you doing?" Little Miss I'm-sorry-I-offered-to-show-you-houses asked.

Lucky didn't reply. He dug his phone out of his pocket and called Walter.

"Walter Smith speaking."

"Four-seventeen Magnolia Trace."

"Are you sure?"

"Positive."

"I'll send a team."

Lucky hung up and faced the Realtor. "This one is temporarily off the market for cleanup. And you better tell the next prospective buyer that this building was used as a meth lab."

"What's the code?" Lucky asked his reluctant escort, now slumped against the passenger side of his Camaro.

"I can't tell you."

"Why not?"

"Mr. Security has to ask?" She'd long since stopped smiling. Lines formed around her pursed lips.

Good point. Given time, Lucky wouldn't need her help, but now wasn't the time to test the subdivision's security measures. If and when he chose a house, he'd put the entire system through its paces. If someone wanted Bo, they'd have to get through Lucky first. And they wouldn't fucking make it. Safe. Lucky would keep him safe.

The Realtor glared. Lucky glared back. Finally, she got out of the car and clip-clopped around the hood to punch in a four-digit code. 4-4-1-7. So much for security. She closed the door a little harder than necessary when she got back in the car.

"Do they always keep the gates locked, or do they open them during the day?" The gate itself was a check in the plus column, if only the security company hadn't gotten lax.

"Always. There are only three ways in: code, clicker, or having a resident buzz you in." The woman's monotone couldn't have possibly been any flatter.

Hmm...Nice. But as Bo's current apartment proved, folks were always willing to hold the door for strangers. Still, this neighborhood beat Cornfield Central.

The gate swung open, and Lucky drove inside.

"Third road on the left." The world's most reluctant real estate agent slumped against the door again.

Mostly new two and three story homes with build-in garages, some still under construction, lined either side of the road. Garages were nice, and if Bo came home late at night, he could drive right in and not worry about who might be lurking in the bushes.

Lucky pulled into the driveway of the neighborhood equivalent of a poor cousin. No shiny windows, no wreath on the door, no well-tended flower bed. One scraggly rose bush dangled a single rose bud. Dandelions dotted the overgrown lawn.

"This house is in foreclosure, which is the only reason it's in your price range." The Realtor trudged to the door and opened the lock-box to let them inside. A motion detector hugged the ceiling just inside the front door. The carpet reeked, but more of pet odors than chemicals. Marker and crayon colored the walls. Spider web cracks ran up the sliding glass door in the great room, but it hadn't shattered.

What a dump. The Realtor gave him a strained smile. "It'd be nice if you fixed it up a bit."

On a brighter note, a gas fireplace had a granite surround. Cozy. Would Bo like a fireplace? They could stretch out on a rug in front of a blaze, Cat Lucky curled against the crook of Bo's knees where he liked to sleep when Bo stayed over.

Lucky strolled into the first bedroom. Nothing to write home about. But this might be a good spot to put Bo's treadmill and weights. A single window overlooked a half-acre backyard complete with privacy fence. So far so good, even if the carpet, paint, and a light fixture needed replacing.

"The house was custom built for a large family, with the rooms enlarged from the original plans..."

Lucky tuned out the Realtor's droning. The next bedroom rivaled Lucky's duplex for size. As with the rest of the house, he'd have to do work. The former owners had removed the ceiling light and probably a fan, leaving dangling wires. Nothing he couldn't fix. The bathroom needed a good grout cleaning, some caulk, and a new toilet tank since a crack extended the width of the current one. The hole in the cabinet door beneath the sink matched a steel-toe boot, and a round hole, roughly the size of a fist, needed patching on the sheet rock. Lucky had spent a few summers on his uncle's construction crew, and he'd patched up the family farmhouse enough to know how to swing a hammer.

He and Bo could make good use of the fireplace come winter.

Bo could pick the colors and carpet and have a house to suit his tastes, at a bargain price. Doable. Definitely.

Lucky strode down a hallway into the master bedroom and stopped in his tracks. Two separate walk-in closets with his and hers sinks in an adjoining bathroom. Jacuzzi. Cracked floor tiles. Separate shower and toilet stalls. At one time, this had been a house to be proud of.

And someone trashed the hell out of it. With Lucky's sweat and Bo's attention to detail, this place could shine again. He pictured his lover soaking in the tub, Lucky nestled against his back, or the two of them in the shower big enough for them both.

That sink cabinet was just the right height to sit on for a blowjob, or bend over for a good pounding. Oh, yeah, Bo splayed out...

The Realtor clearing her throat brought him out of his daydream.

Nice. Not that he'd let her know. He passed her, mentally ticking off items in the plus column. A small sitting area off the master bedroom had been done up in pastel colors, with blue giraffes and pink elephants. A nursery. A lump formed in Lucky's throat. Bo wanted kids one day. A crib would fit fine over by the far wall, with a mobile hanging overhead. With a bit of loving care, this room would be...

Best not to finish that thought.

He trudged back down the hall and into the kitchen. Empty holes showed where a dishwasher and refrigerator once stood. Holy fuck, granite countertops. While living with his drug lord lover, Lucky'd gotten used to the finer things in life. Although granite was a far cry from the marble that had graced Victor's home, it was also far removed from the cheap Formica Bo now used for preparing meals.

The former owners hadn't managed to remove the twin, built-in ovens, nor the indoor grill. Mmm...grilled portobello mushrooms, even on rainy days. Beyond the kitchen a glassed-in dining room waited for Bo to bring in dishes from the kitchen, to be served by the... fireplace. A second fireplace in the dining room.

Now for the moment of truth. "How much?"

"Two hundred thousand."

And another twenty for fix up. How much did Bo have for a down payment? Lucky sure couldn't swing twenty percent on his own, even if he cashed in his Harley fund, reserved for the motorcycle of his dreams.

His phone rang, and Lucky glanced at the screen. Damn, if only he could talk to Bo now. Walter's name appeared. Maybe he had questions about the meth lab report. "Harrison."

A pause, and then, "I need to see you in my office as soon as possible."

"What's up, boss man? Need me to go back over to that house? You can smell the shit the moment you walk in the door. Any drug dog—"

"This isn't about the house, Lucky. Bo is missing."

24

CHAPTER FOUR

Lucky stormed into Walter's office. To hell with knocking. "What do you mean, Bo's missing? Weren't there security cameras? What do the videos show?" An hour. In one hour, Lucky could be in Athens, at the cabin he'd shared with Bo not long ago.

Bo had to be there. Maybe he'd gone hiking and forgot to tell someone. He couldn't simply vanish. Not Mr. Responsible. But who was driving at the time? While Bo wouldn't simply take off, Cyrus might. And the last words they'd said to each other definitely hadn't been "I love you."

Maybe he'd wrecked the Harley. What if, even now, he lay mangled in a kudzu-covered ravine somewhere, breathing his last? Oh, God no. Lucky trod a circuit around the room.

"Calm down, Lucky. He wasn't taken from the cabin. Nothing is out of the ordinary there. He was last seen at Buford's Bar and Grill, talking with a member of the Cruisers who'd managed to escape charges."

The 441 Cruisers, the motorcycle gang Bo infiltrated to find the source of the Corruption coming up from Mexico. Damn them all.

Lucky's boss sat behind his desk, hands folded together over his broad belly. "The man went outside, and according to the bartender, Bo finished his meal and left casually. He gave no signs of anything wrong."

Uh-huh. Lucky stopped his pacing to lean his hip against the boss' desk. "Phone records?"

"Nothing."

Fuck, fuck, fuck, fuck, fuck. "Last contact?"

"He checked in with me two weeks ago."

"Two weeks? Two fucking weeks! And you're just now telling me?" Lucky clenched his fists to keep from hitting something. "I'm heading back to the cabin. See if I can pick up the trail."

"You'll do no such thing." Walter pinched the bridge of his nose behind his glasses. "That's one reason I didn't tell you earlier. I knew you'd go charging into God knows what."

Lucky sucked in a deep breath and let it out slowly. No need to tell the boss about Bo's being more than merely a work partner. But damn, if it would get him what he needed... "Where was he when he called?"

Walter hesitated. For a split second, something close to fear flashed across his face. "Brownsville, TX. On his way to meet the Mexican supplier."

Brownsville, not far from Harlingen, where Lucky'd picked up truckloads of Corruption.

"He what? And you let him go alone?" What was the fastest way to the border? And should Lucky pause long enough to scream at the boss before hightailing it there? "The fucking border? If he's heading into Mexico, we have no jurisdiction there."

"Lucky, we have men tracking him. Don't forget, this is a joint case with the DEA. They *do* have jurisdiction."

"Who's his handler?"

"Me."

Oh hell no, Lucky wouldn't get shunted to the side. "And me."

"No."

"No? What the fuck? Why the hell not?" Lucky clenched and unclenched his fists. That ugly framed motivation poster behind Walter's desk would give a satisfying crash if he wrenched it off the wall. "Give me one good reason why I shouldn't go after my partner." *And it better be a damn good one.*

Walter blew out his breath in a forceful rush. With a calm that belied his stiff posture, he said, "They might be using him for bait."

"Bait? Bait for what?" The hairs on the back of Lucky's neck rose.

"You gave us a recording of a man you believed to be Victor Mangiardi."

That again? "It *is* Victor."

"And if the man on the recording is Victor, don't you think he might want to settle a score against the former lover who testified against him?" Nothing in Walter's even tone said snakes should be squirming in Lucky's belly. They squirmed anyway. "We need to keep you close in case he tracks you down."

What the fuck? "Victor might be using Bo as bait, but you're using me?" Lucky would never actually hit Walter, but he wanted to. He stalked across the room to avoid temptation. "What the fucking hell have you been doing, *boss*?" He gripped the edge of a bookcase to steady himself and glared at Walter.

Walter drooped his shoulders and broke eye contact to study the papers on his desk. "I included your statement in my report, and a copy of the recording. Against my wishes, we've had you under surveillance, in case you were contacted."

A criminal. They treated him like a motherfucking criminal. "I did my time. I'm a free man now. You said so yourself. Would you have watched any other member of your precious team?" The receptionist in the lobby likely heard his shout. Oh fuck. They'd better not have video of him kissing Bo, blowing Bo, fucking Bo.

"Lucky, you've been watched for your own safety. I was advised not to tell you for this exact reason—you'd overreact."

Fuck it all to hell. "You let Bo walk right into a trap meant for me."

"No, Lucky. We left an undercover agent in a position to forward his case. He was properly monitored and checked in regularly."

"Until two weeks ago," Lucky reminded him.

How much did Walter know about Lucky and Bo's relationship? Would he fire Bo for "fraternization"? While Lucky had paid off the last years of his trafficking sentence in service to the SNB and earned his freedom, probation wouldn't end for Bo until fall. Walter was up to something, and he sure wasn't sharing with Lucky.

"You expect me to hang around here with my thumb up my ass while we have a man out there in God knows what kind of shit?" *My man!*

"Lucky, go home. I'll keep you posted on further developments. But be very careful and don't take any chances." Walter raised his tired brown eyes. "Whatever you do, act normally. If someone is following you, we don't want them suspicious, and we don't want them to close in."

Ah, hell. If someone wanted Lucky dead, he'd be dead by now. If Victor still walked the earth and wanted Lucky, he wanted him alive. But for what? "I'll watch my back. Always have, always will. And I don't need anyone's help."

"Just the same, we've got someone keeping an eye out." Walter slumped down in his chair, more defeated-looking than Lucky had ever seen him before.

"Tell me it's not Keith." Oh God, not Keith stalking Lucky and being none too discreet about who he shared his observations with.

"It's not. We've assigned Rogers. You remember Rogers, don't you? He attended training classes with you last year." A vague memory-face surfaced, an SNB computer geek who hadn't deserved Lucky remembering his name at the time.

"Keep him the hell out of my way." Lucky shot a parting glower at his boss. "Are we done?"

"Yes." Walter's manner softened. "Be careful. If you notice anything out of the ordinary, call me immediately. And take this." He reached into his desk and pulled out an oblong box, the kind the surveillance gurus kept handy. "You know how to use it?"

Lucky nodded his thanks and accepted the bug detector. It wouldn't catch more sophisticated radio frequencies, but it'd definitely find the more common models. "I do."

Walter had to get the last word in. "We'll find him, Lucky."

Lucky bobbed his head, throat too tight to let out words. He didn't look back when he crossed the floor and eased out the door, the calmest he'd ever run away.

A week. A whole fucking week since Lucky had stormed out of Walter's office, and still no word on Bo.

None Walter shared, at any rate.

"Act normal, he says." Lucky grumbled under his breath, pushing a cart around the grocery store. Bo's absence left him free to pile his cart with starches, carbs, and bacon, foods Bo frowned on. Somehow, shopping lost its fun without Bo to tease. Well, it was probably more fun for Lucky than the rookie assigned to watch him.

No point in taking advantage. Lucky stuck to Bo's preferences: Stevia instead of sugar, brown rice in place of white, and whole grain bread. He bypassed pork for turkey bacon, but loaded up on full fat cheese to go with his grits. Born and bred Southern boys didn't compromise on a true Southern staple.

The back of his neck prickled. Maybe his tail had gotten too close and needed a stealth lesson.

Lucky searched for Rookie Rogers. Two older ladies shopped together, and several families loaded carts up and down the aisles. No Rogers. Someone was watching though, no doubt about it. The goose bumps on his arms said so.

He pushed his cart toward the front of the store. A flash from the corner of his eye had him spinning. A man rounded the aisle's end cap, disappearing from sight. A man with dark hair. Something about the way he carried himself seemed familiar. Bo? A chill ran up Lucky's spine. No. Not Bo. Someone else. And it wasn't Rogers. *Get a grip, Lucky. You're seeing things.*

The express line, even with more than the maximum twenty items, got him out the door fast. He broke a few speed limits on the way to his duplex and raced up the front walk, bags dangling from his arms.

Mrs. Griggs sat in her usual spot on her front porch.

"Anybody been here?"

"Not that I've seen." She'd likely not moved from her porch swing all day. A good sign. His own personal security guard. Maybe he should get her a gun.

Armed with his .38 and the RF detector, Lucky dropped his groceries on the counter, primed the device and conducted a sweep. Nothing. He traded the gizmo for a screwdriver and the gun for a flashlight as he checked inside his light switches for any devices tapped into a power supply. Nothing. No bugs, no cameras.

Unease twisted his gut.

Bang! Holy shit! Lucky grabbed his gun and dove for the floor. He sighted on the back door.

Bang! Staying low, he followed the thumping. One, two, three...With a quick turn and jerk, he unlocked and flung the door open. He aimed, both hands around the gun.

Bang! The screen door smacked the doorframe again.

"Mrrow?" Roughly twenty pounds of cat hung from the unlatched screen.

Lucky closed his eyes and exhaled. "Damned cat, you're gonna be the death of me one day." He opened the door and let his black and white roommate saunter in, giving his furry companion an ear scratch in passing.

Cat Lucky purred and stropped Human Lucky's hand.

"Hungry, boy?" Lucky rose and opened a can of tuna. While the cat ate, Lucky retreated outside to the mailbox to find a handful of envelopes. Bill, bill, bill... A plain manila envelope with no postage stamp or return address, only the name he hadn't used in over a year: Lucklighter. His heart thudded against his ribs.

He hurried back into the house and slammed the door on the darkness outside. Should he open the envelope? Call Walter and hand it over? The RF detector sat next to the envelope when he placed the suspicious package on the counter. Nothing. Not even a blip.

Gloves. He needed gloves. He rummaged under the bathroom sink and found a pair of yellow rubber gloves Bo used for cleaning. They'd do.

Lucky slit down one side of the envelope with a steak knife, upended the envelope, and shook out a single piece of paper. Clear white fluttered to the floor. Crouching down and catching one corner, Lucky flipped the paper over with the knife.

Familiar faces, though time and age had changed them both. A young Victor Mangiardi sat at a table, holding a slice of pizza aloft. The twinkle in his eyes made Lucky's heart ache. Next to him sat another man, head thrown back in laugher. Ice water ran through Lucky's veins.

A younger, thinner Walter Smith stared back at him. He yanked off his gloves and didn't care where they fell.

Breathe in, breathe out. A weight settled on Lucky's chest. *Calm the fuck down. There's a logical explanation.* He scrutinized the photo, searching for tell-tale signs of tampering. He traced his finger over a face he'd once known as well as his own. Victor had been forty-four at his death twelve years ago. He'd be fifty-six today. In the photo, he appeared to be in his early twenties. Roughly thirty years ago, give or take, putting Walter at mid to late thirties.

Yet, Lucky couldn't mistake the two men who'd each spent years as his mentors. Walter and Victor. Together and, apparently, friendly. He shook the envelope again. Another paper scrap fluttered to the floor.

Five words, scrawled in red ink: *Be careful who you trust.*

CHAPTER FIVE

Lucky whipped his Camaro to the left. The black Ford Explorer fell in behind him. The driver didn't have Rogers' distinctive red hair, and leading a tail to the SNB offices wasn't happening. Lucky picked up his cell phone while paused at a stop light. He didn't need this shit. Especially not after a sleepless night of tossing and turning, imagining terrible things about whoever'd sent him the picture.

If Bo were here, he'd get to gloat about being right. Lucky was too damned predictable in his routines. He'd picked up his tail at the Starbucks nearest his house. The same Starbucks he stopped at every day unless Bo made coffee at home. One must pay proper respects to the gods of coffee, after all.

All Bo's fault. He should be here, humming in the kitchen way too early while making breakfast, waking Lucky up with fresh coffee and warm lips. Dear God, let Bo be okay.

Lucky glanced across the car to the manila envelope lying in the passenger seat. He'd barge into his boss's office, toss the evidence on the desk, then wait for an explanation. Walter wouldn't lie to him. Not this time. And no more half-assed truths.

He hadn't told Lucky off the bat about Bo's disappearance, and had Lucky followed without giving him a heads up. Yeah, Lucky might have showed his hand if he'd known, but what if Walter didn't speak sooner because it wasn't Victor the department worried about, but Lucky himself? This wouldn't be the first time Walter held secrets close to the vest.

Was boss man waiting around for Lucky to run back to Victor? Did the man honestly think so little of him? Granted,

Lucky came from a less than stellar background, including a trafficking conviction and a ten-year sentence, the last eight served on a work release program under Walter's watchful eye. Walter should know him by now.

Stupid, stupid, stupid! A few pats on the head and a bit of fatherly advice and Lucky discarded "Lucky Lucklighter's Survival Rules" number one: don't trust anybody. Of course, Lucky Lucklighter died, to be replaced by Simon Harrison, who'd foolishly become less cautious.

Well, time to take stock, get the old head out of the ass, and start looking out for himself. And Bo, wherever the hell he was. The light turned green, and Lucky stepped on the gas. Where was Bo now? Was he hurt? Why the fuck didn't he call? Text? Send a fucking letter? He wasn't dead. No, no, no, no, no. He couldn't be.

Lucky wouldn't let him be dead. He gripped the steering wheel so hard his palms ached, and replayed their last moments together over and over. He should have grabbed the man, held him, made sure Bo knew how much he loved him. Or better yet, he should have told Walter to fuck off and remained at the cabin.

Lucky circled the block several times to shake the suspicious vehicle. He pulled beneath the building housing the SNB and into the underground parking garage, cut a circuit around the perimeter, and parked facing the entrance. Five minutes passed while he sipped his nearly cold coffee.

The shadow of an SUV flashed by the entrance and slowed. Lucky eased the .38 out of his computer bag. Thank God his probation was over so he could carry a gun. A boxy black shape swerved into the garage. Lucky held his breath.

Loretta Johnson drove her Jeep Cherokee straight for him and parked in the next spot. Phillip, a training assistant on loan from the DEA, drove in behind her. Johnson got out first, head swiveling right and left before leaving her car. Looking for someone? In a black SUV maybe? Or maybe life in general made her paranoid.

Lucky hunched down in his seat. Phillip got out of his late-model Mustang. Huh. Either being an assistant to a high-dollar consultant paid well, or Phillip's wealthy parents still gave him an allowance. Johnson fell into step beside Phillip, her lips curled up in a smile. Damn, but Lucky would love to know what they said. Maybe he should volunteer to test out some of the newer listening devices the techie types kept. Nah. Walter probably wouldn't let him.

Phillip and Johnson stood side by side while waiting for the elevator. As the doors slid open, Johnson patted Phillip's ass, grinned, and stepped inside.

Oh ho! Fraternizing with a co-worker, was she? Wait until he told Walter. Umm...no, maybe he shouldn't since he and Bo did the same thing. Only they did it better.

He stared at the vacant spot Art used to fill. Now there was a decent agent—he'd lived long enough to retire. Lucky gazed through narrowed eyes when Keith took the spot with his Hyundai Sonata. At five past nine, Owen Landry finally arrived. Oh yeah. Lucky needed to let off steam, nice of the rookie to volunteer.

Lucky beat him to the elevator. "Nice of you to join us, Landry. Too bad you're late."

Landry jumped at Lucky's voice. "Traffic was bad, I couldn't help it."

"No excuse. Leave home earlier." The elevator doors slid open. Lucky stepped past Rookie Boy into the car and jabbed the "close door" button. The guy got an eyeful of Lucky saluting with his coffee cup as the doors closed. Being the guy's trainer kept Lucky from a middle finger salute. Let the slacker catch the next elevator. Now to find Walter and set a few things straight.

The doors opened, and the perky receptionist's smile fell when Lucky stalked her way. "I need to see Walter Smith."

Deer in headlights didn't look that scared shitless. "I...I'm sorry, Mr. Harrison. Mr. Smith isn't in."

Well, hell. "Any idea when he will be?"

The woman backed up a step. "No, sir."

What? Sure Lucky wasn't the most pleasant person in the world, but it's not like he actually whupped on anybody. Much.

Damn Walter for being gone with Lucky ready to open fire with both barrels. "Tell him I need to see him as soon as possible."

The blonde nodded. At an imagined nudge from Bo, Lucky barked, "Please," and marched off down the corridor without waiting for her reaction. Not that anyone would believe her if she told them he'd been nice.

Laughter sounded from a cube to his right, and Lucky stepped past the partition to Newbie Central, the desks occupied by Landry, Johnson, and two others. Landry, the moron, had his back to the door entertaining his cube mates, except for Johnson, who sat a few feet away typing away on her keyboard, glancing up occasionally to glare at Landry.

"What an asshole! He thinks he's so damned good! He wouldn't last a minute with DEA." Landry obviously didn't notice the horror on the faces of his audience. If he had, he would have known who stood behind him.

Johnson stopped typing, pulling her red lips back in a smile. She gave a fluttery wave.

"What?" Landry leaned further back in his chair. One day soon he'd lean back and find himself on the floor, courtesy of "the chair from Hell" only Lucky knew how to sit in without being thrown.

Lucky smacked his hand down on the leather beside Landry's head and spun the chair around, putting them nose to nose. "Did the DEA teach you to sit with your back to the door when talking about your superiors? If so, good thing they sent you to the SNB for *proper* training."

A grin and a wink from Johnson said Lucky's work here was done. She'd ensure her loose-lipped cube mate didn't live down his arrogance. Landry likely got on her nerves as badly as he did Lucky's. Poor woman. Maybe Lucky could pull some strings and find a better location for her. Transferring from

Southwestern didn't earn her a place with the wet-behind-the-ears set.

At least his run-in with the rookie relieved a bit of his stress. Lucky plopped his now-empty coffee cup on his desk to join several others, and dropped down into his chair. An empty chair sat on the other side of the cube. A cup on the desk held two pens, and a docking station waited for Bo's laptop. A stack of letters and memos occupied the "Incoming Mail" tray. Behind the desk, a Christmas cactus trailed bright green tendrils down the side of a file cabinet. Everything had a place on Bo's side of their shared cube, and everything was in its place. Except for Bo.

Lucky's eyes stung, and he rubbed at them. Damn, what he'd give for some proper sleep. Oh, who was he fooling? He'd never sleep well again until Bo lay sprawled on the other side of his bed. Bo. Tightness formed in his chest.

Put it out of your mind. Worrying's not gonna get him back any quicker.

He unpacked his laptop, checked his e-mail, and he logged into the SNB website for the latest department news.

Hmm...So the DEA had finally bumped hydrocodone combination products up from schedule III to schedule II. On a scale of I to V, with I being the most dangerous and illegal in the US, raising the rating on a drug wouldn't really deter traffickers, but they were sure to rejoice. The street value just went up.

Lucky shook his head. Talk about bass ackwards.

He entered "Victor Antonio Mangiardi" into the computer's search engine. Pages of social media sites appeared. Dang! Lots of Victor Antonio Mangiardis in the world. Hopefully, the rest weren't as lawless as the one Lucky sought.

Nothing new. He tried "Victor Mangiardi arrested," "Victor Mangiardi court," and "Victor Mangiardi trial."

"Victor Mangiardi hearing," paid off in the form of a news article he hadn't read before. He struggled to breathe even before the image came clearly into view. Victor, smiling, happy, and standing on the courthouse stairs.

The article read: *Suspected drug trafficker Victor Mangiardi appeared before Judge Tyson Levinson...*

His arraignment. This photo was taken at Victor's arraignment. But he was laughing. An image came to mind of this same man in court, in rumpled clothes, disheveled and gaunt. During all their time together, Lucky had never seen his former lover looking less than perfect. Victor had even managed to pull himself together during the flu, while Lucky had lain in bed too sick to move. The haggard appearance in court had to have been an act to win the jury's pity.

Here he was, with no apparent care in the world. Victor's lawyer stood to one side, a uniformed cop on the other. Several other people trudged behind him, none of whom Lucky recognized, except for...

Lucky jabbed the magnifying button again and again. The enlargement distorted the face, but he'd know this man anywhere. It couldn't be. It just couldn't.

Standing a few feet behind Victor Mangiardi was none other than Walter Smith.

"But I thought you needed to speak with Mr. Smith," the receptionist said as Lucky stormed past her desk.

"Something came up."

"He'll be in later this afternoon."

Lucky jabbed the down arrow button on the elevator. "I changed my mind."

Holy fuck! Walter and Victor. Walter swore there'd been no deal made to get Victor out of his charges, yet Victor didn't seem at all worried in the picture. And the reason might have been who stood behind him, both literally and figuratively.

But Victor was dead. He'd hanged himself in his cell.

All the way home Lucky dredged up details he'd sworn to forget. He'd returned from a run to find certain items missing from the house he shared with Victor, the painting of Victor's mother being the most noticeable. And damning.

Victor loved that painting.

And then there were airline tickets to Rio: one for Victor, one the feds led Lucky to believe was for another plaything Victor planned to drop Lucky for. Only after Victor died, at Lucky's own trial, did the bastards reveal the passport made out in that name, with Lucky's picture.

The feds had started closing in, and Victor planned to leave the country and take Lucky with him. As in most aspects of their relationship, he'd kept the details to himself. Besides, Lucky wouldn't have willingly run and left his family behind. Victor hadn't intended to offer a choice. Manipulative bastard.

They'd been arrested before they could leave. Or had they?

Lucky recalled the picture. What if Victor made the deal before his arrest? What if, instead of a drug trafficker and a narcotics agent, the men in the photo were merely actors? Walter made one hell of a leading man, as he'd proven time and again in boardroom showdowns.

Arranging a fake death wasn't hard; Walter had done the same for Lucky. In fact, Walter suggested the plan.

"Fuck. What if he isn't dead?" Lucky asked himself out loud. He waved an impatient hand at his landlady's greeting and marched into his house. She sat on the porch much of the day. If anyone stuck anything in the mailbox, she'd know. She had to have seen who delivered the picture yesterday. And yet she'd lied about seeing anyone. With no postmark, the mail carrier sure hadn't brought the damning piece of evidence. Never again would he trust Mrs. Griggs beyond fixing faulty plumbing and feeding cats.

He'd pack a few things, stay in a motel, and avoid all contact with the SNB until he figured out what was what. What about Bo? How did he figure into the equation? If Bo came to harm because of Walter...

Lucky dragged a duffle out of the entryway closet and charged into his bedroom. A few pairs of jeans, underwear,

T-shirts. He crossed into the bathroom for his shaving kit.

Scrawled in red marker across his bathroom mirror: "Did you miss me?"

A face appeared over his left shoulder. A blur swung down. Blackness.

CHAPTER SIX

What the fuck had crawled into Lucky's mouth and died?

Rubbing the back of his aching head didn't stop the throbbing. Where the hell was he? His stomach surged, and he rolled to his side. He'd been clobbered but also drugged. With chloral hydrate, if the dizziness and nausea were anything to go by. His former drug of choice for sleeping. No one in the US still legally made it. That didn't stop the folks he normally dealt with.

He tried stretching out. At least he wasn't tied, which usually meant no one cared if he ran 'cause he had nowhere to go. All his parts were still connected. Someone wanted him alive and fairly comfortable, judging by the softness he lay on. He wasn't gagged or blindfolded, just in the dark. In more ways than one.

Fuck. The SNB needed to start coughing up bonuses every time he got conked on the head and hauled off somewhere. At this rate, two more years with them might finance his retirement.

He hadn't been stripped, though a search of his pockets turned up nothing but lint, and his latest cheap watch was gone.

He rolled onto his back and slowly extended his arm to the right. Nothing. He shifted to the left. Again nothing. No one else's breathing reached his ear. And he still hadn't found the edges of the bed. Damned short-assed arms. He wriggled as quietly as he could, the covers beneath him still rustling at his passing.

Ha! There! An end table. He walked his fingers across the surface and up a lamp with an old-timey string pull. Okay, now to do this right.

He slid closer to the edge of the mattress, jerked the cord, and dove to the floor. Nothing. No sound at all. He peered up over the edge of the bed. Dark wood furniture—genuine antiques unless he missed his guess, the kind Victor used to like. Nothing too flashy, but sturdily made and classy, like the man himself.

A fluffy white comforter covered the bed, still bearing the imprint of Lucky's body. A simple leaf design graced the headboard, echoed in two matching chairs upholstered in black leather. He sat on ceramic tile. That leaf-embossed wallpaper wasn't the cheap kind found at hardware stores. The desk alone probably cost more than his car had when new.

Whoever'd taken him had money and class. All the folks Lucky knew with money and class wanted him dead. Yet, here he was, still breathing. And alone.

He crept out from behind the bed to better survey his surroundings and made use of an equally sumptuous bathroom off to the left. No labeled prescription bottles or other personal effects in the medicine cabinet gave any clues. Soap packs under the sink had Spanish labels, which still didn't tell him much. He'd bought shampoo at an Atlanta discounter labeled in French, and the local grocery store stocked products from other countries. Atlanta: the melting pot of the South. The words he'd learned in prison didn't cover toilet paper.

The soft purr of an air conditioner told him he was in a warm climate, but that didn't narrow it down much in summer. He could be anywhere from Montana to Cuba.

A sealed water bottle sat on the counter. He washed the crud out of his mouth with a few swallows. At least he'd been given a chance to get his bearings before facing whatever he'd be dealing with.

He didn't trust the tap water to drink, but he stripped off his dirty clothes, found a washcloth, and washed off from the sink. From his smell and how badly he'd had to piss, he'd been out for at least a day.

He hated putting his smelly jeans and T back on, but he'd been left with no other choices. Somewhat refreshed, he stepped out of the bathroom. Holy fuck.

Mama Mangiardi smiled down from a gilt frame above the desk.

The painting of Victor's mother had once hung in the living room at Victor's main home, the painting he'd removed before the world went to shit. Beneath the painting was a photo of the woman herself, holding an infant Victor, her other two children, Vincent and Victoria, clinging to her skirt. Papa Mangiardi smiled along with his family. Lucky's parents named their kids after NASCAR tracks. The Mangiardis picked a letter of the alphabet.

Victor's pictures. Victor's home? Oh, fuck.

No doubt he'd owned houses Lucky didn't know about. Lucky did know of one near Valle Hermoso in Tamaulipas, Mexico, where drug dealer Reyes grew up. Corruption. Reyes. Valle Hermoso. Victor. Damn. Victor couldn't have anything to do with that low class, tacky, crappy, punk-assed shit.

All that remained was for the man himself to show up and take his revenge for Lucky's betrayal. Lucky wouldn't be leaving here alive. He damned sure wasn't going down without a fight.

The door opened and Lucky whirled, snatching a letter opener off the desk.

"¿Señor?" A young man held a tray, fear etched on his face. Lucky put the blade down. His belly growled at the tempting scents wafting from the tray. Better to meet his doom on a full stomach.

"Set it over there." He pointed to a side table by a chair. The man placed his burden on another table, by the other chair. "Who are you?" Not that Lucky couldn't tell a flunky when he saw one.

The guy cocked his head to the side and very slowly enunciated, "No understand Ing-less."

Having been in prison with plenty of Mexican-born felons, Lucky'd heard the "don't understand English" excuse enough, many times by men who spoke the language fine but faked ignorance to snub the guards.

The man fled the room, Lucky bounding after him. The door slammed in Lucky's face. A snick of the old fashioned key lock dashed hopes of escape. Fifteen seconds. That's how long it would take Lucky to open the lock. But what would he find on the other side of the door? And maybe he shouldn't let his jailer in on the fact he could leave whenever the mood struck. Let his lock-picking skills be a surprise.

The flimsy security pretty much guaranteed Victor wasn't here. Victor knew such a poor excuse for a lock wouldn't hold Lucky—hell, he'd been the one to enhance Lucky's escape-artist skills. Could be a test. Tests. Those ranked with mornings and palmetto bugs as Lucky's least favorite things.

So, a prisoner after all. His grumbling stomach reminded him of food. At the best, it'd be just food; at the worst, he'd be poisoned or drugged again. Either way, starving wouldn't help.

He sat down and eyeballed the meal. Plantains, beans, tortillas, and some kind of green thing that would stay on the plate. And a glass of orange juice.

Yep, must be Mexico. Victor had spoken often enough about his housekeeper's penchant for local food, though he'd never brought Lucky south of the border with him. Several times they'd entertained guests from Mexico, treating them to a familiar breakfast. But no coffee? That was it. Whoever'd taken him intended torture.

Chances were few that anyone outside his immediate circle had known Victor was gay, and in some countries, he hid the fact behind paid escorts to do business. He'd presented Lucky as an "associate" to the homophobes. Yeah, as if anyone with half a brain couldn't guess the truth.

Lucky scooped up some fried plantain and beans. At least they'd fill his grumbling belly. Breakfast food. So sometime before noon, though dark shutters over the windows cut any light from outside.

He cleaned the plate except for the greenery, mopped up the drippings with tortillas, and downed the glass of juice. Oh shit. Orange juice. The same stuff Victor had once spiked for him when he couldn't sleep.

The weight of the world dragged him down. He stumbled to the bed, nearly falling twice, and collapsed, spread-eagled. The last sounds he heard were his own snores.

Lucky awoke at night, the lamp casting shadows on the walls. He didn't need darkness to tell him the time of day. Murmuring voices drifted past the closed bedroom door, most speaking in Spanish, with the occasional English word thrown in. A stack of folded clothes sat on a chair. While Lucky would love a shower and a change, his host might love a cleaned up Lucky more.

They'd bashed him over the head and carted him off to God-knew-where, they could deal with the stink.

He broke the seal on a water bottle by the bed and chugged the liquid down. Twelve years he'd been off chloral hydrate, due to periodic drug testing at work. And now someone kept serving him Mickie Finns. He'd make them pay.

Sooner or later, someone owed him some answers. He lifted up the receiver on the phone by the bed and dialed the number he'd been assigned for trouble. "¿Sí?" a woman's voice answered. Lucky replaced the phone on the cradle. A house line. No way to call Walter, not that whoever'd taken him would be stupid enough to let him contact anyone. Didn't hurt to try. The world was slam-full of stupid.

Sooner or later, he'd come face to face with his past. What would he do if Victor walked in the door right now, arms open?

Bo's face rose up in his mind. No. No, he wouldn't run to his former lover. Lucky wasn't that man anymore. Whatever he'd had with Victor was never a meeting of equals. He'd been Victor's toy, and though Victor had treated him well, the gifts, the compliments, all smacked of "Good boy!" praise one would heap on a pet.

Lucky had shared his body and life with Victor, but never himself. Not completely. With the exception of a family emergency here and there, he'd always visited his folks alone, and the few of Victor's family who'd met Lucky all looked down their noses at the undereducated redneck. Well, except for Victor's bastard of a nephew, Stephan, who'd viewed Lucky as a mere possession, or a fuck toy, and not a very good one. But the asshole had sure wanted in Lucky's pants.

He sat on the edge of the bed, awaiting his fate. What would he say, what would he do? Did Walter know he was gone? Did he care? Had he had a hand in returning a friend's toy?

With nothing better to do, Lucky rambled through the dresser drawers—all were empty, as was the closet. The room might as well have been in a hotel, if not for the expensive furnishings and painting.

A carved trinket case on the dresser caught his eye, similar to the one Victor once kept on his desk, and the only personal touch in an otherwise museum of a room. Curiosity and boredom got the better of Lucky. He opened the lid.

Oh dear God in Heaven. Lucky's heart made a quick escape attempt through his throat. With shaky fingers, he lifted up a silver Rolex, the likes of which he hadn't seen in a long, long time. Apparently the feds hadn't taken the fancy timepiece along with everything else at his arrest.

He turned the watch over, tracing the inscription with his finger: *To Lucky from Victor.*

Lucky's old watch. He needed a watch since some asshole took his, and he strapped the Rolex on his wrist easily, having had years of practice with his twenty-first birthday present. Two rings sat in the bottom of the felt-lined box, gifts Lucky hadn't worn much, along with a gold chain. The watch served a purpose, the glittery shit didn't.

The door clicked open. Lucky froze but didn't turn. Watching his back didn't help much when whatever came his way wouldn't be good.

"I see you've found your things," a deep voice rumbled. Chills danced up Lucky's spine. Damn Walter for not believing him about the recording. Or damn Walter for believing and doing nothing.

Lucky glanced up into the mirror before him. Dark hair, olive skin, soul-searing eyes. The devil himself might as well have stood at Lucky's back. Oh, holy fuck. Anything but this.

"You never answered my question," the voice from Lucky's past said.

Lucky tamped down the urge to run. He willed his wildly pounding heart to calm. Up shit creek without a paddle didn't even begin the cover his current trouble.

"What question was that?" There. He'd said the words without wavering.

His jailer grinned. "The question I asked on the mirror. Did you miss me?"

Slowly Lucky glanced over his shoulder, making eye contact. Damn but the years only served to make the bastard more beautiful. But plenty of wildlife shows he'd seen on TV proved lovely creatures were sometimes the most deadly. Cobras had nothing on the man now standing behind him. Though probably sealing his own fate, Lucky went down swinging. "Not a chance in hell...Stephan."

CHAPTER SEVEN

A cruel twist of nature blessed Stephan Mangiardi with his uncle's beauty, minus any charm. He'd always been a leech, enjoying Victor's money and treating the world as his plaything. Touches of white peeked out from his jet black hair, worn the way Victor used to. A pale imitation of someone Lucky had once admired. He'd fit right in as an over-the-top villain on Lucky's favorite soap opera. And through nature or by design, the motherfucker had Victor's rumbling baritone down pat. His voice hadn't sounded so deep twelve years ago.

"Where's Victor?" No more fucking games.

"Like you, he recently finished serving his sentence, and had business to take care of elsewhere. He's currently basking in the sun at the family villa near Naples."

Naples. The birthplace of Mama Mangiardi. Lucky's heart double-thudded and paused. "Victor hanged himself." *Steady, boy, steady.*

Stephan tutted like Lucky's grandma used to do whenever one of her grandkids did something stupid. "You better than anyone should know Uncle Victor wouldn't take his own life, and deaths can be faked." He gave Lucky a knowing smirk. "No, like you, he made a deal."

Walter had said no deals. And yet, he'd sat laughing at a table with Victor. What about his strange reaction when Lucky first mentioned hearing Victor's voice during his last case? How well did Walter know Victor? The picture of them on the courthouse stairs told its own tale.

Could Lucky trust the snake standing in the doorway? Probably not. Best to play along. He'd believe Victor still lived when he saw the man with his own eyes—which might possibly be the last thing he ever laid eyes on.

"And you've brought me here to get even." Lucky stood his ground when the serpent slithered across the floor in expensive Italian loafers. He didn't manage to hide a flinch when Stephan brought his hand up to stroke Lucky's face.

"Now why would I want to get even? You were just my uncle's little pet. Without your deserting him, Uncle Victor would never have taken me and my father into the business." Bright teeth flashed against dark skin, giving him the same smile Victor used to signal a wild night ahead. "You did us all a favor."

Fuck. If the little shit could be believed, Victor lived, Walter lied, and Lucky was up to his neck in trouble.

Well, at least Lucky wouldn't have Victor's death on his conscience any longer. But Stephan was apparently calling the shots. A festering boil on the ass of mankind.

Oh, shit. What if the fucker had taken Bo too?

He'd die. Lucky would see to it. But now Lucky had to play nice until he found out what he needed to know.

Stephan had dressed himself like Victor, in a crisp button-down shirt and tailored slacks. Too bad he lacked the grace to wear them well, giving the impression of a child in Daddy's clothes rather than the master of his own universe.

"Forgive me for keeping you cooped up in here. I had visitors, and you're not ready to see company." Stephan stepped away and waved his hand to indicate Lucky's appearance. "I had clothes sent. Why are you not wearing them?" He scrunched his nose. "And you stink."

"Whatever game you're playing, count me out."

"Oh, I think you'll play." Stephan stepped back and rammed his hands into his pockets. "Imagine my surprise when I found out that someone suspected of being an informant was actually an old acquaintance—an old acquaintance who'd been reported dead. And now going by a new name.

"Tell me, *Ricky*, did working off your sentence with the SNB change you?" Stephan's grin widened. "I think not. A hard-ass like you? I'm surprised you lasted as long as you did. And the moment you'd done your time, you couldn't wait to get back in the game, could you?

"Not only did you return to your old ways, it seems you and Reyes' Sergeant at Arms got a little friendly."

Stephan pulled a pendant from his pocket and dangled the charm from a chain. "Not very manly, is it? I wonder why a hard man like Cyrus Cooper wore such a delicate thing. Do you suppose it has meaning for him?" A hummingbird. Bo's spirit totem. The one Lucky had given him after one of their assignments.

Fuck. He'd do whatever the bastard said.

And kill him later.

Lucky lay on his bed in the dark to avoid Mama Mangiardi's accusing stare. Yeah, that's right. He'd testified against her son in court.

A lifetime ago.

Time to make a plan. First, to find out where the hell he was. Second, find Bo. Third, hightail it back to Atlanta.

But running meant leaving Stephan Mangiardi on the loose.

Footsteps sounded outside the door. Lucky dropped to the floor. Damn, he shoulda stuck a chair or something under the doorknob. He clutched the letter opener, for all the good it would do against someone who might be armed.

The door eased open. The hall light illuminated a silhouette in the doorway: tall, dark, hand on the doorframe. The figure didn't move for a moment. Lucky coiled to strike. And then, "Hey, anybody in here?"

Bo! Oh dear God. Hallelujah! Lucky dropped the letter opener.

A flip of the switch flooded the room with light. "Close the door," Lucky hissed. Chances were, closing the door wouldn't help. He'd bet anything any conversation would be recorded, if not filmed.

They stood a moment, sizing each other up, Lucky's shock mirrored in Bo's eyes. So he hadn't known Lucky was here. Could be a good thing. Could be bad.

Shoulders back, pointed chin jutted out, body tight as a bowstring. Not Bo, but Cyrus. And he probably hadn't been Bo for a very long time.

But damn. Here. The dirt smear on his cheek didn't matter, or the worn jeans and T-shirt that appeared slept in. He'd been in character as Cyrus for months now, and Cyrus didn't have Bo's finickiness about appearance. The haunted look in his eyes didn't matter, nor his sun-bronzed skin. He was here. Together, they had a chance to get out alive.

It took one hell of a lot of self-control not to tackle the man to the floor, check every inch of him, make sure he was okay. Or as okay as a man could be here.

Stephan sent him. As a reward or a reminder of what he stood to lose?

Lucky and Cyrus were fuck buddies and partners in drug dealing, in Stephan's eyes. Enough to work with. Now to act like fuck buddies. If Stephan believed Bo meant nothing, he'd serve no purpose as leverage. Oh, hell, time to stop thinking.

But thank God Bo's cover hadn't been blown.

Bo's "How'd you get here?" didn't quite mean, *I love you, I missed you, let's go home.* Lucky would take what he could get.

He rubbed the still-sore goose egg on his noggin. He owed someone big time for whacking him over the head. "I got *invited.* Hurt like a motherfucker. Does Stephan know you're here?"

"He invited...no, he ordered me here." The hardness around the man's mouth and eyes wasn't something Lucky wanted to see.

If Stephan expected a show, Lucky wouldn't disappoint, the fucking pervert. With any luck, a bit of action would cover the conversation he needed to have with his partner.

Lucky slammed Bo against the door, rising up to force his way into Bo's mouth. Bo let out a "Hmmmph?" and got with the program, nearly crushing Lucky in his arms. The softness of his lips, the subtle tilt of his head, the possessive way he invaded Lucky's mouth. Home.

The hunger Bo poured into the kiss bordered on brutal. He slipped his tongue against Lucky's, conquering, demanding. Lucky pressed his rising erection against Bo's thigh. All the while he kept his hands and fingers in motion, mapping out the well-known planes of his lover's body. The contour of his shoulders, the swell of his ass. Bo. Here. Now.

Stephan could go fuck himself.

Bo pulled away, tongue against his upper teeth to form an L. Lucky cut him off with another kiss. He replaced his mouth with a finger for Bo to suck and murmured in Bo's ear, "Cyrus, remember our first time together down by the river?" The lovely suction around Lucky's finger paused, then resumed when Bo nodded. They'd been Ricky and Cyrus, as they had to be now.

The dam of longing and worry burst. Seams ripped and buttons popped in their haste to get to the skin beneath. Lucky sealed their mouths together. Tomorrow, they might both be dead. But at this moment, they were together. He'd make the most of each second. The ferocity of Bo's kiss might have been frightening had Lucky not felt the same intense need to connect. Mouth, groin, skin to skin.

If tonight was the inmate's last meal, he'd eat his fill and then some.

He traced his fingers over familiar terrain, and the patchy strands on Bo's chest. The curls surrounding his cock were coarse, tickling Lucky's nose when he dropped to his knees and engulfed Bo's flesh with his lips. Damn. The taste, the scent, the feel of silky foreskin sliding against hardened flesh roared through him like a freight train. He clung to Bo's hips to keep himself upright.

Bo moaned above him as Lucky rolled Bo's balls in one hand and gave a gentle squeeze, just the way the man liked. Bo slid his hands beneath Lucky's arms and tugged, urging him up a moment before he body-slammed Lucky onto the mattress. The springs barely squeaked in protest. Bo climbed onto the bed, straddling Lucky's thighs and leaving a slick trail across his belly from a leaking cock.

He wrapped his fingers around them both, using nature's lubricant to slide them together. Holy fuck, Lucky wasn't going to last. When his balls drew up and the pre-orgasm tingles began, Bo leaned forward and joined them mouth to mouth. Lucky worked his fingers into his mouth along with their tongues to wet them and pushed the slickened digits against Bo's hole. Bo and Lucky both moaned when they slid inside. Tight. Hot. Heaven. Lucky wanted in. He swiped up pre-come off his belly, the only lube at hand.

"No," Bo said, his hand on Lucky's wrist. "We can't." Instead of stopping, he redoubled his efforts, jacking them both off with one long-fingered hand.

Maybe a hand job was all Bo could stand with cameras likely trained on their every move. Lucky bucked up and gripped Bo's shoulders with both hands.

"Damn, I missed you," Bo murmured against Lucky's cheek.

"I missed you too." Lucky mumbled the words against Bo's slightly musky neck, rapping the headboard against the wall to cover the words. Bo smelled of sweat and a hard day's work in the sun. No familiar cologne clung to his skin. Didn't matter. Gussied up or down and dirty, the man smelled of Bo, and burying his nose in the crook of his lover's neck and taking a sniff eased some of the pressure from Lucky's chest.

Bo shoved harder, nearly scooting Lucky up the bed. Lucky dug his heels into the mattress, scrabbling at the headboard with his fingers and matching him thrust for thrust. The pressure turned brutal, as though Bo needed to pound clear through Lucky's body. The arm he'd propped his weight on began to tremble, and he grunted on every lunge.

Harder, faster...desperate. The groan Bo let out must have started at his toes. He shuddered, eyes closed and face scrunched.

Fuck! Lucky wasn't there yet. He frantically shoved up into Bo's now-slack grip. Bo began to pulse. "Ahhh..." His grip grew slick.

Lucky locked his legs around Bo's thighs and surged against Bo's belly, keeping ragged time in his race to finish. He clung tightly, his body spasming out his desperation and loneliness along with fluid to coat his skin and mingle with Bo's.

Bo propped his weight on his arms and nuzzled noses, eyes closed and breath coming fast. Eventually his eyelids snapped open, and he gazed at Lucky with brutal intensity, as though trying to memorize his face. For the longest moment they remained still, locked in a mutual stare.

Lucky lifted his arm for a tighter embrace and caught a whiff of his own body odor.

"I think we both better hose off before a family of skunks show up, hunting their long lost cousins. The tub's a whole lot bigger than the one at the cabin." Fuck. For Bo, Lucky would have taken a shower.

"Whatever." And just like that, Cyrus returned. He eased to one side. Lucky missed the comforting weight immediately.

"C'mon. Bathroom's in here." The guy must be tired as hell to let Lucky lead him by the arm.

The Jacuzzi might be nice for future use, but the shower served Lucky's purposes for now, running water to cover any conversation. Still, best to keep the questions and answers to a minimum until he got a better feel for what they were in for. Stephan hadn't brought Bo here for nothing. He turned on the water and, under the guise of adjusting the spray, checked for cameras and bugs.

He fumbled around under the sink to locate what he needed. "Um... Cy?" He held up a bottle.

"Not that. This." Bo leaned in and chose a bottle with bubbles on the label, and then another with a smiling woman washing her hair. Oh.

Lucky grabbed a washcloth and a spongy thing. Good enough. He stepped into the shower with Bo and his finds. Bo remained still, allowing Lucky to wash him. "Don't get spoiled and expect this treatment all the time," Lucky groused.

The attempted humor didn't even earn a half smile. What the fuck was wrong with the man?

Lucky drew close enough to ask and be heard. "Why are you here?"

Bo shrugged, water sluicing over his broad shoulders. "I got a call that said to come to Stephan's *hacienda*." He tried for a smile but failed, and put his mouth by Lucky's ear to whisper, "I had no idea you were here."

"I didn't either until a while ago." *Hacienda*. Mexico.

Bo raised a brow but didn't reply.

"Where exactly are we?"

"Valle Hermoso."

Shit. Lucky'd been afraid of that.

He ran the sponge down Bo's arms. Bo let out a pained gasp when the soap hit his inner elbow. No mistaking what made those marks. "What the fuck?" For the first time, he noticed Bo's wide-blown pupils. Oh, dear God, no. Lucky grabbed the wall to keep from falling.

A tear slid down Bo's face, gone a moment later when he plunged his head beneath the shower's spray.

Who the fuck just dropped a Mazda on Lucky's chest? He grabbed Bo's wrist, taking in the marks and all they stood for. "That's it. Get dressed. We're leaving." The needle holes said, "Game over."

"No!" Bo snatched his arm out of Lucky's grasp. "We wanted to find the Mexican supplier. Well, I'm finally on the inside at the factory. No one else here knows enough about pharmaceuticals to tell me all I need know. But I'll get the information firsthand."

"What the fuck? Who's shooting shit into your veins?" Or were the marks self-inflicted? Oh, hell the fuck no.

"Stephan's been doing the same to most of the men who work for him. What makes me better, huh? And it was either roll up my sleeve or go home. He gave me no other choice." If

Bo glared any harder, he might melt lead. "I don't like being anyone's experiment, but already I've got a few names that I bet would raise some eyebrows at the SNB. When we cut the head off this snake, it's not gonna fucking grow back. We'll take them all down."

"No. It's too risky." *I won't risk you. Me, maybe. You? No.*

"Damn it, Lucky!" Bo hissed. The heat in his eyes cooled to pleading. "Don't tell me you wouldn't have made the same decision."

"Whether I would or wouldn't isn't in question." For the record, Lucky would have. Bo wasn't Lucky. "What the fuck's he giving you?"

"It's only liquid hydrocodone, for fuck's sake. It's not meth. It's not Corruption. It's not heroin. It's a simple pain killer doctors prescribe by the bucketful every day. Aren't you the one who told me you sometimes have to take a few risks?"

"When did I spew such nonsense?"

A tense smile flickered across Bo's mouth and disappeared. "I believe your exact words were, 'Sometimes you gotta do what you gotta do.'"

Oh shit. Lucky had said that. "Yeah, but I was talking about me, not you!"

Bo placed a hand against Lucky's cheek. "I have to do this, but I can't without you. Thank God you're here. Please. Help me."

Lucky turned the water up to better hide their words. "What do you need me for? Sounds like you got your plan all worked out." If only the man were still a rookie, and Lucky could call the shots. Bo had been compromised. His word alone wasn't going to sway any jury. They needed hard evidence of what the hell was going on down here. But they needed to get Bo out of here more. But where? Back to Atlanta and Walter Smith?

"You know as well as I do that a case needs an agent, a supervisor, one or more operators, and monitoring. All I have is me." Which had never really bothered Lucky before now.

"My thinking may change. I might not know when I'm in too deep. You've dealt with situations like this. You know what to watch for. Help me be the man on the inside." Bo pleaded with his eyes. "Besides, if I leave now, who's going to look out for Stephan's men? They have no idea where they're up against. Stephan might be the most ruthless man I've ever met."

No. Time to leave if Bo rolled up his sleeve every day or even self-medicated. Where did the drugs come from, and how could he be sure what he took? Hydrocodone wasn't the most addictive of drugs, but it was addictive.

In time, Bo would grow tolerant to his current dose, and have to up theo amount to get the same effect.

"Lucky." Bo dropped his voice to a husky murmur. "I need you to have my back, and not just to supervise the case. I. Need. You. Besides, you know Stephan, right? Know his weaknesses. You have a history. Twisted as he is, I think in his own way he respects you."

Respects? Now, there was news.

Why did those big brown eyes have to stare into Lucky's soul? If Bo turned away, Lucky's resolve wouldn't waver. "If I help you, will you leave when I say it's time?" Not that he'd have a choice. At the first sign of trouble, Lucky would do what it took get Bo out of here.

Bo closed his eyes, too late to break the spell. After a moment, he nodded. "Let me get all the information I can, then we'll go."

Fuck. "When we leave, you're not gonna argue with me, but check yourself in somewhere to help you deal."

Bo snapped his eyes open, sparks flaring to life in their depths. "I don't think..."

Lucky met and matched Bo's glare. "You agree or we leave tonight." If Lucky found a way, that is.

Their battle of will lasted a few seconds. "Okay, you win."

No, Lucky lost. And only time would tell how badly.

Lucky lay awake in bed, listening to Bo's barely audible snores. This wouldn't be the first time an agent did drugs to stay in character and wouldn't be the last. But those other agents weren't Bo.

You can have the coffee, Lord. Just please don't take Bo from me.

Lucky awoke to an empty bed. He glanced at the clock by the bed. Six p.m.? Holy fuck, had he ever slept. Must be all the drugs still in his system. He swiped his hand over his face. Where the hell was Bo? If they'd blown Bo's cover...

The quiet servant knocked and entered, bringing a pile of clothes. He placed them on a chair and left without saying a word. Room service. In prison. Go figure.

A prison, a beautiful prison, but instead of Durham Correctional Center orange, Lucky slid on jeans designed by someone he'd never heard of and a silk shirt, the likes of which he'd never have worn on his own. When he moved, light reflected off the shiny material, jade one moment, royal blue the next, and purple a minute later. Bo might like the darned thing. Or Charlotte. Give Lucky a Grateful Dead T-shirt, and he'd be happy. At least he got to wear his own tennis shoes, since "the little man with big feet" couldn't fit the provided loafers. Must have been Stephan's.

Tiny shoes were in proportion with what Stephan carried between his legs. Needle dick. Yeah, that explained a lot.

But Stephan wasn't getting him gussied up to hang around his room all day. He sat on the unmade bed and waited. If Stephan wanted the bed made, he could damn well make it himself. Or send a flunky.

The guy who'd brought the clothes returned and gestured for Lucky to follow. There'd better be food at the end of this trip. As if on cue, the scent of what might have been roast beef hit his nose. Lucky's stomach rumbled.

The man led the way down a long, windowless hallway to a dining room, where he pulled out a chair for Lucky to sit.

Lucky parked his ass at the long table, next to Stephan, seated at the head. Well, there went his appetite. No sign of Bo. "Where is he?" Lucky growled.

"Ah...don't be so impatient, Mr. Lucklighter? Or should I call you Ricky Getsinger?"

So, Stephan actually believed Lucky's undercover persona for his last case was how he'd been living. "Since you're determined to show off, is there anything money can buy that you don't know about me?" He'd keep the asshole talking. Maybe sooner or later, he'd spill something useful.

"You served two years of a ten year sentence at the Durham Correctional Center before making a deal. You got a new name and went into witness protection. I must admit, I lost track of you for a few years. And lo and behold, you turn up working for the Mangiardis again, though I bet you didn't even know. Tell me, Lucky, do you believe in fate?"

Fate. Lucky's fist. Stephan's face. "I don't need fate. I believe in making my own rules."

Stephan shrugged. "You exchanged a lighter sentence for testifying against my uncle's former associates. Always looking out for yourself."

Well what did you know? Stephan said "former associates." He might not be smarter, but he'd learned a few big words. Victor used large words sometimes to intimidate his rivals, but never to Lucky. He'd never talked down to Lucky.

Still, once an irritating dickwad, always an irritating dickwad. "Why am I here?"

"Because, regardless of how you've spent the last few years, you haven't changed, so no need pretending."

Glorious smells wafted from the kitchen. Lucky's mouth watered. Yesterday's beans and plantains only went so far. Meat would go a hell of a long way in keeping him from going ape shit on somebody. If only the shithead would shut up and feed him. "I've never pretended anything. Now, what do you want?"

The wolf smiled his most predatorily. "Your cooperation. You see, certain happenings in the US have opened up some new opportunities for me. Though my uncle has no further use for you..." Stephan paused long enough for the knife to plunge effectively through Lucky's innards. "...I found you amusing. I'd like to offer you a job. It seems my former *associate* lost his life in a tragic motorcycle accident."

Accident, Lucky's ass. Most likely, Stephan knew the exact time of Reyes' death and who'd been driving the car responsible.

"I'm in need of a replacement to keep the men in line."

Oh shit. That voice. The one Lucky had heard the night he'd been tossed into a trunk. It hadn't been Victor's at all, but Stephan's. Best not let on that he'd been awake at the time and recording the whole incident. Not that Walter had believed him. Shit. Walter. Of course he'd overreacted, if he'd thought Victor wasn't playing for the good guys. But if a deal had been made, who would Victor work for if not the Southeastern Narcotics Bureau? DEA? What a fucked-up turn of events.

If they had Victor, they didn't need Lucky. Time to stop the circular thinking before he popped a blood vessel.

"What kind of job? Pushing that Corruption shit you've been selling?" Corruption, a synthetic designer drug capable of turning housewives into homicidal maniacs.

"Among other things. Distribution, mostly. The same job you did for my uncle, without the perks. The big fish have left me alone because I'm a little fish, and not in the same market. And also out of respect for my uncle." A muscle twitched in Stephan's jaw.

Liar. "If you expect me to fight a war for you..."

"Oh, no. You misunderstand. You see, Nestor Sauceda is an associate of Uncle Victor's, yet he doesn't trust me. You're going to convince him to. No one will dare cross me with him as my partner."

Hell, Lucky didn't trust that slippery little bastard either. "Me? How am I gonna do that? And why would I?" Lucky had met Nestor Sauceda-Vasquez on a few occasions, always with Victor. Only Sauceda living in Mexico had kept him out of jail when Lucky started rounding up the bad apples. If

Walter Smith was a piranha disguised as a favorite uncle, Nestor came closer to a shark. A bunch of sharks. In a tornado. With disruptor cannons.

Stephan smacked his hand down on the table, then drew his fingers back to reveal Bo's pendant. "You forget yourself. I know about you. *All* about you."

In a flash, he left his chair and knelt behind Lucky, wrapping him in a rough headlock. Lucky squirmed. Stephan held fast, his breath wafting hot against Lucky's ear. "I never understood what my uncle saw in you. You're not smart or witty. You're not from a powerful family. And prettier men than you are a dime a dozen. Those who knew his tastes thought there must be more to you than meets the eye to have attracted and held his attention for so long.

"Tell me, Lucky. Have you ever wondered why my uncle never brought you here to Valle Hermoso? Why he always left you home?"

Many times Lucky had wondered why until considering the kidnapping risk. He would have been a weakness. Victor didn't allow weakness, or maybe he had, to keep Lucky around at all.

Lucky kept quiet. Stephan rattled on. "I'll tell you why. Whenever my uncle came here, he filled the place with the hottest young men he could find. The locals celebrated his arrival. It meant money would flow freely into the town, not only from his generosity, but due to the parties he held, the young beauties he hired."

Squeezing his eyes shut didn't choke off the ugly images forming in Lucky's mind. He'd never kidded himself that he was Victor's one and only. What had bothered him more was Victor keeping information to himself, always making excuses as to why Lucky had to stay behind.

Hell, if Victor came here to fuck handsome young men, Lucky of twelve years ago would have happily tagged along, had some fun, and maybe even engaged in some three or four-way action. Stephan meant to hurt Lucky with the words. Too fucking bad. "And you think he didn't invite strange men home when I was there?"

Ah, to be able to see Stephan's shocked face. "We weren't committed, and I didn't expect him to be. Just because I lived with your uncle didn't mean we picked out china patterns and talked about growing old together." Lucky had never for a moment kidded himself about the temporary nature of their relationship. And yet Victor had kept him around.

Stephan took a moment before replying, "Nestor thinks you've returned to serve me faithfully as you did my uncle. And that now that you've completed your sentence, you can't wait to pick up where you left off. You'll do everything you can to keep him believing this."

He snatched the pendant from the table and dangled the charm in front of Lucky's nose. "You escaped charges when Reyes made a mess of things in Georgia. If not, I'd have had to step in. For you and for Cyrus Cooper. You're both useful to me. For now."

Please, dear Lord let the bastard believe his own delusions.

Stephan whispered into Lucky's ear, "Tell me, Lucky. Does Mr. Cooper mean something to you? You were gorgeous together last night. But I wanted to see you fuck."

Lucky's pulse double-timed. Screw Stephan motherfucking Mangiardi for not living down to his stupid reputation. And when Lucky found the hidden camera in his room, he'd ram it straight up Stephan's ass. "Motherfucking pervert."

"But no tender love words. If he means nothing to you, mind if I have him?"

Oh fuck, oh fuck, oh fuck. *Think fast, Lucky!* He kept his voice steady. "Like I have a say. You've met the man, right?" Lucky paused to let his words sink in. "He has a mind of his own, and nothing I say or do will make any difference."

Stephan chuckled. "Too true."

Lucky's fist. Stephan's face. A match made in Lucky's fondest daydreams. He clenched his fingers. A hired tough stepped into the room and eyed Lucky up and down, arms folded across his chest. Body language for *"Go ahead, try something stupid"* needed no translation.

"Maybe I should ask again, though. Call me curious. Is Cyrus Cooper just a fuck to you?"

"You have to ask? Have you ever known me to give a damn about anyone?" But the Lucky of twelve years ago had cared. About his family, and to an extent, Victor.

"And yet you gave yourself away when you saw this." Stephan brandished the pendant. "I think you care more than you'll admit. Tell me, Lucky, does Cyrus know who you really are, or does he buy the Ricky Getsinger, ex-con bullshit? Does he know you used to raise your ass for my uncle?"

Damn, when had Stephan gotten so shrewd? He wasn't worried about Lucky or Bo by themselves, but he feared their combined forces. Last night had been a test. And since Stephan still asked questions, he hadn't yet gotten what he was after.

Recalling the undercover ops classes Lucky hadn't thought he needed but had taken at Walter's insistence, he pulled on a blanket of calm. "Ricky Getsinger is who I am now. Witness protection and all that. Folks still call me Lucky."

"And Cyrus?"

Lucky kept his gaze and voice steady. "He's a handy fuck. And he's damned good with his fists. Made a decent enforcer."

"And I believe you for now. If at any time you slip up, try to use him against me, I've no qualms at all about leaving his body in the desert. You do what I say, I'll let your fuck toy live. Simple, yes?"

Bo wouldn't be so easy to kill. Especially not with Lucky standing in the way.

The nasty palmetto bug named Stephan Mangiardi needed crushing. Now. Lucky could bluster and try to con his way out of this mess, or do what he must to keep him and Bo alive. And if he found out Walter betrayed him? No army on earth would save the man.

"What do I have to do?"

CHAPTER EIGHT

Twenty minutes in a car with Stephan, and they pulled inside a set of factory gates, no different than any other factory Lucky had visited, except all the signs were in Spanish. And the road markers they'd passed didn't mention any familiar names. He belched to remind his unwanted host who he dealt with.

They drove past the main building and parked in the back. Two heavily armed men patrolled the area and only paused a moment when Stephan strode past to enter the front door.

"Look around at the Mangiardis' family legacy." Stephan stepped lightly, shoulders back as he led Lucky down a window-lined corridor. On one side, behind protective glass, lab-coated, masked workers drew pipette samples from bottles. On the other side, robotic centrifuges spun glass beakers.

Lucky had been in enough pharmaceutical plants to recognize a functional research lab, full of equipment fit to put many US facilities to shame. Damned impressive. Must have cost a fortune.

"What is this place?"

"This factory belonged to my great-grandfather originally. Uncle Victor lost interest, moving much of his operation to the States." Stephan studied Lucky much as a chemist in the next room scrutinized drug samples. "But thanks to tight controls and business restrictions, many products have been discontinued by the USFDA or have become difficult to get." Stephan nodded toward a centrifuge. "Children's dentists would kill for a lot of chloral hydrate, as would addicts who've grown dependent." He gave Lucky a smug half smile. "The product is still in big demand both in the US and Mexico."

Yeah. The stuff did have its sedative charms. "Even I know there's not enough profit in transporting one product across the border." Although listed as a controlled substance, Lucky's former drug of choice didn't have quite as high an abuse factor as most narcotics, nor as high a price. "Too much risk for too little return. It's not expensive."

Stephan showed his teeth in a feral grim. "No risk at all, really. And supply and demand plays havoc on pricing. If people want something badly enough, they'll pay any price and be grateful."

"You're buying goodwill to push higher value sales." Not to mention putting the buyer's nuts in a vise. They'd buy what they needed, then buy more and more at higher prices to keep the rare drugs they couldn't get anywhere else. Victor had used the same tactics.

"Ah, I knew you were more than just a piece of ass to my uncle." Stephan resumed his trek down the hallway and paused before another glassed-in lab. "What do you see?"

"Just a bunch of lab rats, doing lab rat things."

"According to US restrictions, strong narcotics such as oxycodone must be made tamper resistant."

In an effort to curb addictions, the US demanded that the makers of certain pills include a crush-proof coating or other deterrent to keep the product from being crushed and snorted or injected. Which just made users more creative.

The crazy son of a bitch laughed. "Take a good look, Mr. Lucklighter. At the future, my future. Pure hydrocodone, rendered completely undetectable during most standard drug tests."

Oh, fuck. Undetectable. Just like Corruption. "There's no way you've made hydrocodone undetectable." Too many other labs had tried and failed for years.

The edges of Stephan's lips turned down, in a gesture so like his uncle's. "No, I haven't. Yet. But we're testing. And soon we'll perfect a formula. Corruption paid the bills and allowed me the time to develop the real moneymaker: Codopure. A pure, liquid hydrocodone."

Stephan used Bo as a guinea pig for this. "How do you hide what you're doing during inspections?" Lucky waved a hand at the lab. "Are you exporting to the US? I'm taking it the FDA doesn't know about your new drug."

"Ah, what's the fun in spilling all my secrets? Of course, they visit from time to time to audit some other products we'll soon be exporting. I have to give some of my researchers the day off during inspections, the ones who aren't welcome at pharmaceutical companies across the border."

"They've had their license pulled and yet you hire them."

"They get what they need, I get what I need."

"How do you manage to pass inspections at all?"

"This is merely a lab, testing product purity. Nothing out of the way happens here." Stephan's innocent expression wouldn't convince anyone.

"What kind of tests are you doing?" *Confession time, Stephan.*

"Ah, Lucky, I could tell you, but you wouldn't understand." Smug bastard.

"What makes you think I can sway Nestor into investing if you can't? And if I don't *understand*?"

"Oh, you will, Lucky, you will. That is, if you ever hope to return to the US in one piece."

Fuck. Customers weren't the only ones with their nuts in a vise. "When do we meet?"

"Soon. And Lucky?"

"Yes?"

"I don't care what you have to do. I want his support." Stephan spun on his heel and marched off down the hall.

After a moment, Lucky followed past the labs, pausing to get the lay of the land. State of the art equipment. A modern factory. Unscrupulous researchers. Whatever else he may or may not be, somewhere along the way Stephan had become a shrewd businessman.

Lucky would do best to remember that.

Lucky woke several times during the night, to lie still in the dark and listen. Of course, with Stephan right down the hall and Mama Mangiardi staring down from her frame, no damned wonder sleep wouldn't come. A glass of juice beckoned by the bed. No way in hell.

He gave up on Bo showing, rolled over, and punched his pillow. Eventually, he must have dozed off, for he awakened sometime near dawn to more clothes lying on a chair, along with a pair of sturdy work boots in the right size.

Dammit. He'd let someone come in while he slept. Not good at all.

He dressed, ran a comb through his hair, and found a toothbrush and a package with a smiling tooth on the box, so maybe toothpaste and not hemorrhoid cream.

Now to face whatever waited outside the door. Conversation and the scent of bacon steered him down the hallway into the room where he'd confronted Stephan the night before.

He shivered and bypassed the head of the table, taking his place between two men dressed as common workers. Better the evils he didn't know than the one he did. One cuffed him good naturedly on the shoulder and offered a crooked smile while the other eyed him with mistrust. Both were close enough in appearance to be brothers or maybe even twins, fairly young, and likely neither one had ever been accused of being good looking.

My, how times had changed. Victor used to surround himself with attractive men, even the straight ones, and the hired hands never ate with the boss. Only Lucky and his most highly placed employees shared such an honor.

A few more men shuffled in. One, walking three paces behind the others, lifted his brow and scrutinized Lucky like a butcher sizing up a slab of meat. Ah, making friends already.

Whatever could he have done to earn the man's interest? The way he stared, he'd want to see Lucky's teeth next. The newcomers appeared to be anywhere from late twenties to early forties, while this guy hadn't long given up the pimple cream. He'd slicked his hair back in sleek waves, and rather than short and stocky like most of his counterparts, he had the slender frame of a dancer or runner. In a breakfast table beauty contest, he'd take home the crown. With tight-fitting jeans, and a blue polo shirt, neither sporting any holes, he also dressed nicer than his coworkers. Someone of importance, whether Stephan knew the full extent or not.

At least the men sitting next to Lucky kept the guy down-table. A predator. Pure and simple. *Takes one to know one.*

As soon as the new arrivals sat down, the same man who made Lucky's bedroom food and clothes deliveries entered from a side door. He deposited a dish of beans on the table and darted back through the door to return with plantains and tortillas. His next trip produced bacon and sausage, along with hash browns. The men bowed their heads, murmured prayers, crossed themselves and tucked in. Religion and drug running. What an odd combination.

Two chairs remained empty, one at each end of the table.

A niggle of guilt scared Lucky off the bacon, especially since Bo could show up at any minute, but hash browns, beans, and plantains made a tasty meal. He paused with his glass of orange juice halfway to his lips. Surely Stephan wouldn't drug his juice during broad daylight. Juice drugging at breakfast was too B-movie villain, even for Stephan. They'd all poured from the same pitcher, so drug Lucky, drug everybody, which meant not a lot would get accomplished workwise today.

Eventually the king of the assholes himself showed in a fancy robe. His uncle had always appeared at breakfast dressed to the nines and ready to start the day's business. From his vantage point, Lucky spotted a young man slipping out of the room Stephan had exited. What was the Spanish equivalent of "boy toy?"

From what Lucky had heard from Victor, gay men weren't easily accepted in Mexico, and yet here Stephan flaunted his sexuality for all to see. He was either very bold or didn't give a rat's ass.

Stephan pasted on a nervous smile. "Ah, my friends, I see you've met Lucky. He'll be taking Hector's place."

The scowling brother crossed himself, and two of the other men shot Lucky frightened eyes and promptly glanced away. Either Lucky's reputation preceded him, or so much for hoping Hector now lounged on a beach somewhere, enjoying retirement.

Mr. Handsome kept Lucky in his sights. While the youngster wasn't too hard on the eyes, he wasn't Bo. Lucky studied the assorted men around the table. Chances were, he'd be picking them out of a lineup one day.

"Who was Hector and what did he do?" Lucky paused shoveling in hash browns long enough to ask. Victor used to make sure the housekeeper cooked Lucky's favorites every morning. Maybe he should add grits, biscuits, and gravy to a list of demands.

Stephan spoke up. No one else seemed inclined to answer. "He drove the truck."

Anyone could drive a truck. Why Lucky? Half-truths wouldn't do. Stephan's piercing gaze locked on to the empty chair. "Where is Cyrus?"

The growly guy sitting next to Lucky replied in Spanish. Lucky understood about every third word. Best not to tip his hand to his smattering of prison Spanish. Stephan spoke to the stocky bodyguard type sitting to his right. "What did he say, Oscar?"

"He said Cyrus plans to meet them at the factory. He went on ahead." The man took a bite of bacon.

Stephan twisted his lips into a pout but held his tongue. Now if only he'd make that a habit. Poor, little warped fuck had his fun pissed on and couldn't hold Bo over Lucky's head in front of the men. Boo hoo. He turned his attention back to Lucky. "I want you to teach Cyrus everything you know."

What the fuck? "Me! What do I know about Mexico?"

A murmur rose around the table. The man to his left leaned behind Lucky to whisper in Spanish to the guy on his right. His puzzled frown changed to a glower. Ah, the sweet sound of dissention in the ranks.

An oily smile appeared on Stephan's face. "Remember what's at stake." He lifted his juice glass in a toast to Lucky. The men picked up their glasses. "I trust Cyrus to show you around."

The guy who'd caught Lucky's eye as a possible threat hopped from the table while licking a juice droplet off his lip. He barked a command at the men and nodded tightly to Stephan. Oh yeah. This guy was a leader, whether Stephan gave him the power or not.

Lucky left his full glass where it was. No use taking chances.

Stephan stopped him with a raised hand. "Lucky? Look in there." He nodded toward a decorative table in the hall.

Lucky eased the drawer open. A pair of Ray-Bans lay inside. Thank heaven for small favors.

"I remember how you always wore them." A kindess? From Stephan Mangiardi? What was in it for him?

The drawer also yielded a Tamaulipas driver's license for Ricky Getsinger. So Stephan had some pull. The license was dated a month ago, and no telling where he'd gotten the picture. Lucky sure as hell didn't recognize the image.

He wouldn't say thanks; he merely dropped the sunglasses in place on his nose with a grunt of approval, shoved the license into his pocket, and followed the others out the door. The men appeared more at ease once outside, judging by their smiles and banter.

The suspicious-looking brother elbowed the other and pursed his lip out toward Lucky. The friendlier brother nodded and grinned. What the fuck was that about? The hot sun beat down, a startling contrast to the coolness of the house. Thank God for the Ray-Bans.

A high wall encompassed the yard, roughly twelve feet tall, made of the same eggshell-colored stucco as the house, with razor wire and jagged glass fragments embedded in the top. The house itself was low and squat, its single story spreading out in all directions.

The leader nodded to a pair of hard-worn silver Jeep Wranglers and crawled behind the wheel of the first while one of the brothers took the other. Lucky rode shotgun with the guy who best needed watching. Assorted other men climbed into the backs of each.

In short order, they kicked up dust on the road from the house, in the direction of the factory.

The men jabbered away in the Jeep, too fast for Lucky to decipher. He tuned them out and tried to get his bearings. It'd been dark last night, and Stephan's fast driving in his classic Jaguar didn't give Lucky much time to note landmarks. Not that there were many on this barren stretch of road, dotted here and there with the odd house. Stephan's residence outclassed any other within ten miles.

The best thing to do would be to find Bo and hightail it to the border. Then what? Lucky had entered the country illegally and held a fake ID. Without Walter's help, he'd never make it back home without getting arrested and blowing a cover he still might need. And no telling how Bo had gotten here. Besides. Lucky's hackles rose at the idea of leaving without finding the truth about Victor and making Stephan pay for what he did to Bo.

Bo had to be okay. That's all Lucky asked. Anything else they'd work out.

The factory came into view, and an armed guard opened the gate to let them through. A Kenworth rig sat backed up to one of the loading bays.

The men piled out of the Jeep the moment it parked.

A loading door slowly rose. A pair of biker boots, then ankles, calves, and knees. Lucky's breath caught. He'd recognize

72

his lover anywhere, even from the thighs down. Up and up the door rose. Bo stood inside, hand planted on the doorframe. If he'd posed, he couldn't have appeared more fuckable, an image from a wet dream. His denim jeans hugged his thighs, a thin T-shirt appeared painted on. Scruff clung to his chin. A holstered gun sat on his hip.

"Didn't expect to see you today," Bo drawled. "You here to drive the truck?"

"So I'm told." Damn, the man was good. He gave nothing away, showed no signs of being anything other than a bored foreman, on a "same shit, different day" assignment.

"She's loaded and ready to go. But first we have to wait."

Stephan's crew shuffled into the building. If Lucky had to search for a silver lining, at least most of the folks he'd met down here made him look tall. The brothers came up to Lucky's nose, and another guy stood no higher than his shoulder.

That left Mr. Take Charge, who was currently trying to stare holes through Lucky. Bo hopped down to stand near Lucky. "I see you've met Cruz," he said.

So the leader had a name. And he nodded toward Bo in deference. Smart enough to know when he'd been outclassed, at any rate. "We weren't introduced."

"Oh no? Cruz,—"

"Lucky," Lucky supplied, adding, "Cy here knew me as Ricky," in case Bo hadn't clued into Stephan's openness about Lucky's true identity. Best to cover all bases, though for all he knew the guy didn't speak a lick of English.

Cruz didn't offer his hand. Worked for Lucky. Instead he wandered over to plop down on cement steps.

Bo sidled over close enough to not be overheard. His Cyrus Cooper mask fell. "I'm glad you're here. Been wondering what you and Stephan have been up to."

"Good to see you too." Now wasn't the time to examine every inch of him, though touching might help convince Lucky the man was actually here, without the fear of cameras and recorders. Then again, how safe were they in the open? "How ya doin'?"

"Okay, under the circumstances." Bo held out his arm to show fresh marks in the crook of his elbow.

Questions tripped from Lucky's tongue before he could stop them. "How'd you get to Mexico? Did he bash you in the head and drag you down here?" If so, the asshole would pay.

"No. I came on my own. My case, remember." A muscle clenched in Bo's cheek. "I'm still Cyrus Cooper, and Stephan hasn't questioned it."

"You know we're up to our asses in alligators, right?" Having Bo at his back made those alligators less scary.

"Somehow, that's been happening a lot lately." Bo's brief flicker of a smile faded into a frown. "Only this time, nobody's reporting back to Walter. I haven't found a safe way to communicate directly since I arrived. I had to leave my phone and personal effects at the border. Stephan gave me a new phone and gun."

"Walter. A conversation for another time." Call him sappy, but what Lucky needed now was a kiss. And a hug.

Bo raised a brow but didn't press. "Have you seen Victor yet?" He murmured the words in an offhand manner, like the answer didn't matter one way or the other. The stiff set of his shoulders said otherwise. Lucky heard the unspoken, *Is he a threat?*

"No." To both questions. "Just Stephan. Have you?"

"No. None of the men have either. They just go by what Stephan says."

"Bo?" Lucky kept his voice down.

Bo's soul-deep brown eyes met Lucky's. In their depths swirled a million questions. His quiet "Yeah?" carried a hopeful note.

Lucky didn't look away, and he fought the urge to cup Bo's face in his hands. "If I do see him, he's going down. He's just one more case to solve, as far as I'm concerned."

They held their gazes for a moment, until people shuffling at the door broke them apart.

Bo waved his hand from one man to the next. "Lucky, this is Juan, Jaime, and Aureo. Oh, and Rafael and Alejandro, also known as the Garcia brothers." Bo switched to Spanish to introduce Lucky. One brother grinned with far too much enthusiasm, the other scowled, and Juan, Jaime, and Aureo smiled and spoke in unison, "*Mucho gusto.*"

Much pleasure. They might regret those words in days to come. "Yeah, nice meeting you too." Not really. The more folks Lucky met, the more he'd have to arrest.

Once they'd trooped away towards the Jeeps, Bo growled, "I know how you are about names, but these are good men for the most part, who worked for the Mangiardis before Stephan started dealing in shit. Don't disrespect them."

What? "Wasn't gonna." *Take all fun out of life, why don't ya?*

Bo's hard glare kept Lucky quiet. "Before we head out every morning, we have to see the doctor to give blood samples. That's bad enough. They don't need any shit from you."

"Let me ask you something. If they're good men, why do they get drug tested every morning?"

Bo flexed his cheek again. "It's not just for a withdrawal, but a deposit." Oh. More guinea pigs for Stephan's new wonder drug.

Lucky nodded toward Cruz. "Him too?"

"No. He's got a bad heart."

Uh-huh. Like Bo and Lucky didn't learn in class to fake medical conditions to avoid sampling the wares.

Stephan tested Codopure on his own people. As Grandpa used to say, *"There's a special place in Hell for folks like that."*

Lucky climbed into the Kenworth's cab. Bo entered on the other side. Before he could shut the door, Cruz slipped through.

Bo ignored him. "The warehouse is an hour and a half away, a few yards from the border. We need to roll."

Lucky followed the Jeeps through the gate, which the guard closed behind them. He'd keep talking to a minimum. Just because Cruz hadn't spoken English yet didn't mean he couldn't. The confident way he carried himself and the too observant eyes gave Lucky the creeps.

He cranked up the radio, but couldn't find any classic rock. Maybe closer to Texas. What he wouldn't give for his iPod and a bit of "annoy the coworkers" music. Let Cruz know from the get-go who he dealt with.

About one hour later, they passed their first set of warehouses. Bo acted as tour guide. "Cruz told me they used to unload in a tunnel around here, but it collapsed about six months ago."

Information to file away. A more convenient, but closed route? Lucky would check on the extent of the damage. If all the tunnel needed was clearing and a little wall-shoring... What the fuck? He'd only been down here a few days and already thought like a felon.

If he hadn't returned to his job with the SNB, this could have been his destiny anyway, to resort to a life of crime. It's not like he had much left to lose anymore. Particularly if he'd lost Bo along with the job he'd planned to leave behind. Okay, so he owed Walter one, even if he didn't trust the man right now.

A half hour later, they pulled into an empty warehouse. "C'mon," Bo said. "While the men unload the truck, I want to show you what we're up against."

Cruz fell into step behind them on their way out into the sunshine. Lucky breathed in lung-searing heat and wiped his already sweaty brow. At least the air-conditioned truck had provided a reprieve from the heat.

They plodded over cracked asphalt, a few scraggly weeds peeking through. A mix of old and new warehouses stood on either side of the deserted street, some with chained and locked doors, others standing wide open. One stone structure bore pitted marks from bullets while other, newer buildings had holes peppering their metal siding.

"Look around, Lucky," Bo murmured. "I pray to God this is the closest you ever come to a war zone."

"What happened here?" As if Lucky couldn't guess.

"Drug wars. From time to time the cartels battle it out." A black SUV with tinted windows rounded the corner and headed toward them. Bo and Cruz both reached for their guns but didn't pull them out. Damn but Lucky wanted his .38. With no way to fight, he'd need a place to hide if the going got rough. He spotted a narrow alley between two buildings. That's where he'd run if he had to.

The vehicle slowed but kept on going. Bo snorted out a breath. "The federal patrol uses dark SUVs, but the cartels do too. Which is why Vincent, Stephan's father, bought silver Jeeps. When the bullets fly, you don't want to be in a black Chevy Tahoe."

Cruz backed off a few paces, eyes trained on the road ahead. "I think you have a shadow." Lucky eyeballed his new nemesis. Cruz flashed a shit-eating grin.

"Don't mind him. He watches out for me, I return the favor." Bo relaxed his rigid stance but kept his hand near his sidearm.

Lucky bit off, *I think he wants to do more than watch.* "Does he speak English?" Wouldn't be the first time someone on a case had fallen for Bo. This new shadow spelled trouble.

"He claims he doesn't, but I can't be sure. He's scary smart. Anyway, I speak Spanish here. Endears me to the men." People skills, Bo's strong suit. In any language, it appeared. "Those I can't win over with kindness, I resort to the old fashioned way." He cracked his knuckles and grinned wide enough to reveal the deep dimple in one cheek. Yeah, he'd certainly established pecking order with his fists before.

His smile fell. "I suppose you've noticed that Stephan doesn't speak a lick of Spanish. It pisses the men off. He sees Mexicans as inferior. Good thing he has money. They've got no other reason to follow him. He's got a mean streak the size of Texas. Don't cross him."

"Yeah, he must be pulling in the money." The labs reeked of cash.

"Cruz said Stephan used to stay away, barely came here. His father ran the plant, mostly legal stuff. It wasn't nearly as state of the art two years ago. Stephan started spending more and more time here then." Bo paused to wipe the sweat off his brow with a bandana from his back pocket. "He and his old man argued a lot, especially when Stephan added Corruption to their product line. All of a sudden Dad takes off and leaves Junior in charge." Bo stopped to open a warehouse door and motioned Lucky in ahead of him. They climbed four flights of stairs with Cruz leading the way.

Bo grabbed Lucky's hand, delivering a quick finger squeeze. Lucky squeezed back. Not nearly enough, but all they could risk. They came out on the roof of the building. Bo mumbled, "Wait here," in Spanish. Cruz nodded and ducked back into the building.

Lucky seized the opportunity to talk openly. "Start to finish, tell me how you got here."

"A guy contacted me, told me the big man wanted to see me, and here I am. Surprised the hell out of me when I heard the name 'Mangiardi'. Especially after you thought you'd heard Victor's voice not too long ago." Bo fixed Lucky with an intense frown and glanced away. "Rumor has it that Victor's not dead and made a deal with the DEA like you did with SNB. I keep hearing his name, but no one I've talked to has actually seen him. Is he really alive?"

"I...I honestly couldn't say. I don't think Walter would lie about not making a deal, at least I'd like to think he wouldn't. Right now I'm not too sure about anything. I certainly didn't expect Stephan to be running things." Although synthetic poison like Corruption did reek of the little bastard. "I got whacked on the head, drugged, and woke up to a picture of Victor's mother staring at me. What did he want you for?"

"He's restarting the pipeline. Since I was Mateo's second-in-command, they brought me here to learn what I need to fill his role. Only, after meeting me, Stephan"—Bo spat out the name—"thought I could broker deals, too, something Mateo wasn't very good at."

Not to mention Stephan dangled Bo like a carrot in front of Lucky's nose.

Mateo Reyes had been the leader of the 441 Cruisers, the drug runners who'd infested the southeastern US with a volatile drug capable of turning mild-mannered folks violent. A scar on Lucky's arm spoke of a drugged-out secretary's bad aim.

"What does he want with me?" Stephan's explanation didn't make sense. Stephan wouldn't have gone through the trouble to bring Lucky here if not expecting a payout.

"I'm told you headed up logistics for his uncle." *His uncle*, not *Victor*. Bo's pained expression clearly asked, *What if Victor wants you back?*

Not a snowball's chance in hell. A few moments alone might convince Bo of his place in Lucky's life. Victor, living or dead, was ancient history as far as a personal relationship went. Professional? Lucky drove semis all over the country while working for Victor. "Heading up logistics" sounded more dignified than the actual job he'd done.

"With Mateo out of commission, we're the next best thing, I suppose." Mateo, not "Reyes". Yet in this case, Bo getting chummy and using first names served their purposes. After all, Cyrus Cooper was the closest thing Reyes had had to a friend, judging by what the SNB uncovered.

Why would Stephan trust Lucky to know the inner workings of his operation? He knew Lucky had cooperated with authorities, even if he hadn't clued into the continued association. Either he honestly believed the heart of a felon still beat in Lucky's chest, or he thought exposing Walter's treachery would do the trick.

But if he really believed Lucky had served his sentence and returned to his old ways, why send the picture? Unless he hadn't. He'd confessed to the message on the mirror, though. Damn. Time to cut the "whys" and "what-ifs" for a while before Lucky broke his brain.

Their vantage point gave a clear view of both sides of the border and the crossing. Bo pointed to the warehouse where they'd parked. "The tunnel goes down about forty feet, stretches nearly a quarter mile, and comes out there." He pointed to a building across the border. "The collapsed tunnel is fifty-five feet deep, and a full quarter mile long. It's been fitted with rails and rail cars, electricity, and better ventilation. It's also closer to the factory. If I ran the show, I'd be putting in some effort to make it usable again. Shelter from the heat and undetected from the ground makes it a double benefit. Stephan doesn't seem to care about how much money and effort could be saved, just warns us off. He's been spooking the men with stories of demons and ghosts."

More information to tuck away for another day. "Now we know why we never found Mateo's goods crossing the border."

Bo nodded. "Yeah. They didn't cross, they went under."

Lucky had seen some tunnels on training films but had never actually been in one before. If and when he made it back to Atlanta, he'd put the knowledge to good use. Might as well share what he'd learned with the man who'd once been his trainee. "I'm supposed to teach you all I know." Both Walter and Stephan agreed.

The corner of Bo's mouth twitched and he lowered his voice. "You mean there's more?"

Lucky growled low, "You bet your sweet ass there is." He pointed toward the border crossing. "Watch the cars."

Bo stood quietly for several moments. "What are we looking for?"

"Watch the lines and tell me what you see." While Lucky had never actually transported drugs across the border, case histories filled in what personal memories didn't supply. If you couldn't get the shit over the border yourself, you found someone who could, willing or not. The method didn't work for large quantities, but any product shipped into the US beat having the shit sitting idle on a shelf in Mexico. No one made money if the merchandise didn't move.

Beneath them, the good people of Mexico formed orderly lines to cross the border. The first car took position at the crossing, two border patrol agents approached, and the driver handed something out the window—presumably license, registration, passport or visa. Lucky had flown in during his one voluntary trip to Mexico and didn't know the border crossing drill firsthand.

The majority of the time the guards popped the trunk to check inside.

"Hey, what about the far lane?" Bo pointed to exactly what Lucky hoped he'd figure out.

"They're trusted. Most likely they live in Mexico and work in Texas, crossing the border twice a day. They know the agents and pretty much get waved on through. If we needed to move goods, I'd have you write down license plates."

"Why?"

"Those good, honest, hardworking folks?"

"Yeah?"

"If we needed them to, they'd be working for us." Likely prospects sat lined up below. Cars, pickups, vans. The Chevy S-10 wouldn't do. "Vehicles with trunks do best, and nothing new enough to have a sophisticated security system." Though Lucky hadn't met a car alarm he couldn't defeat. "Next, you'd get names and addresses, find out where they work, how often they cross here, and what time. You'd also need vehicle identification numbers."

"Then what?" Bo swiped at a trickle of sweat off his cheek.

"First, we pick someone like clockwork, nine to five, find out where they live, where they're going. You can use the VIN to get a key made. Then, one night you leave a gift in the trunk and contact whoever Stephan's got in place on the other side."

"You've given this some thought."

"Happens every day." Lucky shrugged. "Oh, you'd also need identical duffle bags. I'd use black."

"Why matching bags?"

"Sooner or later someone is gonna get caught. It's the best defense you can give them."

Bo raised an incredulous brow. "You? Worried about strangers?"

Lucky turned away. "I'm not totally heartless." And he'd also experienced prison. Bad enough when he deserved to be there. He couldn't imagine being set up and rotting away while innocent. "If the same bag turns up in different cars, when the drivers don't have any other connection, it's a tipoff that someone else is shipping the cargo. Those trusted folks aren't allowed to carry anything in their trunks for a reason, even though they'd hardly ever get checked." And in a pinch, Lucky and Bo could hide out in a trunk and cross. Or use the tunnel. No doubt Stephan posted guards, so the tunnel might be the stickier option.

They could hold hands now and make a run for the border. If Cruz didn't shoot them, they could throw themselves on the mercy of the border patrol.

Or they could stay here, find out all they could about Stephan's operation, and bring the whole enterprise crashing down. Damned responsible choices.

"About Victor." Bo didn't need words to finish the question.

"Old news. I told you. He can't cook like you."

"Jerk." A glimmer of a smile showed Bo had caught the hint.

"You flatterer, you." Lucky gave Bo the closest thing he could summon to a grin

"What do we do now?" Bo gazed at Lucky, the desire radiating from those brown eyes, even dulled by the tinted lenses of his sunglasses, making the day even hotter.

Good question. It didn't escape Lucky's attention that he'd been lured away from the action and hadn't actually seen the tunnel yet. Was that Bo's decision, or Cruz's? Lucky read people as a survival skill, and he wasn't about to place his and Bo's safety in Cruz's hands. At least not until he figured out what the guy's deal was.

CHAPTER NINE

"I want to show you something." Bo sat behind the steering wheel with Lucky in the passenger seat of one of the Jeeps. Cruz stood outside talking to the Garcias. Bo opened the glove compartment, pulled out a case, and snapped it open. "Do you know what this is?"

A hypodermic lay nestled on a bed of compressed cotton, next to a small vial of naloxone. "Overdose kit. They've started making them available to cops and first responders back home."

Bo rolled the vial in his hand. "We learned the hard way that we need one."

"Hector, the one nobody talks about?"

Bo nodded. "Stephan never tested on the guy before. I mean, he drove the truck, right? Heavy equipment and heavy drugs don't mix. But one day Hector confronted Stephan about something. The next morning, the doctors called him in with the group. A few hours later he died. And there wasn't a damned thing I could do."

Premeditated murder, in Lucky's book. He bobbed his head toward the kit. "Does Stephan know you have that?"

"No, and it's another advantage I have over him. His workers know I'll save them if I can."

"Why do they put up with that shit, being used as human guinea pigs?"

"The money, for one. These men have families, or most of them do. But Lucky?" Bo wrapped a hand around Lucky's wrist. "It's an incredible high. Think you're stupid? It makes you feel smart. Think you're weak? It makes you feel

83

strong. Think you're ugly? One dose and you're gorgeous. Some would work for the shot alone."

Lucky's hackles rose. "He uses it to control them." *And you* remained unsaid.

"Yes. Piss him off, he withholds the drug. Most of them are addicted by now. Withdrawals aren't pretty."

"And so you'd put your ass on the line to save them."

"Wouldn't you?"

What Lucky would do wasn't the point. Underneath the badass Cyrus suit was a good man named Bo. Lucky wasn't a good man. A good man could never dirty his hands enough to win against Stephan.

"Anyway, you know what an opioid overdose looks like, right?"

How could Lucky not, given both his former and current occupations? "Bloodshot eyes, pinpoint pupils, low pulse, gasping for breath."

"Among other symptoms. If that happens, give them this." Bo held up the vial. "You ever given a shot?"

"Only to goats, back home."

"Same principle. Inject into muscle, preferably the thigh. Then they need medical help within an hour. I take the kit with me, just in case, and sitting in a hot vehicle all day isn't good for the naloxone."

"Where did you get that?" Sure as hell he'd not gotten the antidote the easy way.

"They keep naloxone in the lab, and from what I've seen, they're not too careful with their inventory."

An inventory count and missing drugs brought Bo to Walter's team to begin with. He still pilfered for a good cause, and Lucky wouldn't fault him. Bo was right: Lucky would do the same. He'd just be quieter about it and find someone else to blame for the good deed.

Bo put the kit away. "Lucky?"

"Yeah?"

"Ready to see the tunnel?"

"Yes." No.

"I don't really like it down here." Bo shuddered. "Gives me the willies."

Lucky wasn't too happy either. Just the entryway where they stood was forty feet underground, and narrow. Too fucking narrow. As short as he was, even he had to stoop. One of the Garcias trundled by pushing a wheelbarrow full of cardboard cases of Corruption. Lucky plastered himself against the wall to let him by. Alejandro. The happy one.

He smiled at Lucky and winked in passing. Creepy.

Aureo came by with more boxes.

Soon they'd be hauling Codopure, once Stephan took enough orders and the testing panned out. Lucky needed to haul ass across the border and be waiting on the other side before the first shipment.

Another grinning man passed. Juan? Bo murmured something to him, and he held out his arm. "*Sí, Señor* Cooper." The guy trotted off again.

The drugs. Not only was Stephan testing, he used liquid coercion to keep the men working down here in a hand-carved pit.

He and Bo didn't go in far, mostly stood at the mouth looking down into the shaft as the men used a winch and pulley to lower the pallets, to be loaded on carts and wheeled beneath the border.

Lucky's breath came in short gasps. According to Bo, the tunnel not far from here had collapsed. Every rumble, every squeak, his brain twisted into the thunder of falling rocks and dirt. If Lucky had to work here day in and day out, he'd need drugs too.

He kept his eyes on the crew in case one of them started going into fits.

Cruz sat nearest the passenger door, rattling away to Bo. Damn. Lucky caught a word here and there, but not enough to piece the conversation together. Awkwardly crammed between the two seats, Bo had to rub Lucky's nose in his lack of a second language. Well, unless Italian counted, and the words he'd learned from Victor in bed didn't bear repeating in the light of day. Or mentioning to his lover.

He backed the truck and empty trailer up to the loading dock at the factory, and got out to stretch while most of the men plodded to the Jeeps. Bo and Cruz climbed down out of the rig, Bo muttering low and Cruz shaking his head. Bo repeated his words more firmly. Cruz glowered at Lucky from beneath lowered brows and stalked away toward the Jeeps.

"What did you say to piss him off?" Lucky might have to take notes.

"I told them to go on without us."

Bo disappeared into the building and reappeared guiding the black Harley Davidson Road King he'd been assigned by SNB for the case. Lucky got butt-ugly Malibus, Bo got Harleys. Go figure. He pushed the bike to the far side of the dock and down a loading ramp. "Get on."

No helmets, no gear. When in Mexico...

Lucky climbed on the back of the Harley, keeping a distance between his and Bo's bodies. Right now the men preferred Bo to Stephan. They might not if they knew of his involvement with a man. No telling. Normally, Lucky would say, "Screw them if they don't like it," but he wasn't about to risk Bo's position. They needed any advantages.

Bo waved the men on and they took point, the Harley growling along behind. Even on a paved road, Bo had to drop way back to avoid dust clouds.

The distance between the vehicles grew. Bo eased back on the gas to lag further behind. One hand on the throttle, he reached back with the other to briefly clasp Lucky's fingers where they rested on his thigh. Once out of sight of the Jeeps, Lucky leaned in to place his nose inches from Bo's neck. He whiffed. No cologne wafted from his lover's skin, but the scent was still pure Bo. Blindfolded, Lucky could pick the man out of a lineup by smell alone.

A bump in the road gave him the perfect opportunity to wrap his arms around his man and snug his crotch up against the ample swell of Bo's ass. Finally. Seeing but not touching all day nearly drove him mad.

His cock swelled in his jeans. He gave an experimental thrust. How he'd love to bury himself in that denim-covered mound. Bo shifted back on the seat, placing Lucky's erection more firmly in his cleft.

Oh, dear Lord! Lucky groaned and sank his teeth into his lower lip. "Don't do that," he growled between clenched teeth. "What ya want me to do, blow right here?"

The handlebar mirror showed the brilliant flash of Bo's teeth. He mouthed "Yes" and pushed back again.

Clutching Bo in a death grip, Lucky swiveled his hips forward and drew back, avoiding side to side motions to keep from tipping the bike. He swiped his tongue up the side of Bo's neck.

The Harley's scorching hot pipes couldn't compare to the heat in Lucky's groin. He worked himself against Bo's ass. A car approached and he stilled, face buried between Bo's shoulder blades. Bo's chuckle rumbled through his back.

With the car fading in the rearview, Lucky resumed his humping, forcing his hand between their bodies to shift his cock into a more comfortable position. He nearly came from the touch alone. He clasped Bo tightly to his chest and shoved harder against the firmness beneath Bo's jeans.

"Oh my God!" The vibrations from the bike between Lucky's legs worked their own magic, thrumming against his balls and the sensitive zone between his balls and his hole.

He bit a fold in Bo's T-shirt to keep from sucking up a mark on the man's neck. Out here in the open, where anyone could see, and he was about to come. Bo, with his penchant for outdoor sex, probably loved every minute.

Images formed in his head: the time he'd backed Bo into a bathroom stall, taking him in an alley behind a two-bit bar, leaning over the bike seat in a garage. The first time he'd had Bo bare. The heat, the raw power of being so totally connected.

"Uh, uh, uh," escaped him and he panted into Bo's ear. Eyes tightly shut, he came in shuddering waves. Pulse after pulse after pulse. He clung with all his might to keep from toppling from the Harley. Bo patted his thigh. Damn!

Lucky reached around to run his hand up Bo's stiffy and found a wet spot. He kept rubbing until Bo shuddered against him. One, twice, three times.

Bo grabbed Lucky's hand and laced their fingers, leaning back into Lucky's one-armed embrace. Not a car in sight. Sexed-out bliss on a motorcycle. The perfect high. Eventually Bo let go: Lucky's cue to right himself before they re-entered the strange world they'd found themselves in.

The gate stood open, a truck visible inside when Bo and Lucky reached Stephan's house. Without a word, Lucky climbed off the seat and stood beside the bike. He tried to raise one brow in question as he'd seen Bo and Walter do. No such luck. Instead he raised his sunglasses and stared at Bo's dark lenses, asking *"When will I see you again?"* without words.

Bo's wide grin was gone, replaced by Cyrus Cooper's grim determination. The moment had come and gone. Who was Bo now? Was he still Bo? Was he Cyrus? Was he an odd mix of both? Who would he be once they returned to Atlanta—if he returned to Atlanta?

Most importantly: would he still want Lucky?

And they were here, taking precious time out of their lives for a bastard like Stephan Mangiardi. Did Stephan enjoy playing with people's lives, dangling them like puppets from strings? While Victor had without a doubt called the shots in his people's lives, he didn't act like some small child with a toy in his power. He'd never risk his men. He tested his men, didn't test *on* them, and kept the good ones. The others, well Lucky was glad he didn't have to deal with Victor's outcasts.

Stephan's men reacted with fear, which wasn't the same as respect. Victor's men would have followed him to the gates of Hell. Those who wouldn't didn't last.

But Victor's men gave respect because Victor respected them, too, in a way. He respected what they did for his business, if not the individuals themselves.

Hands clasped in front of him to hide the wetness in his jeans, Lucky nodded to no one in general and fled into the house. And if he met Stephan, he just might have to kill the guy with his bare hands.

Lucky stepped out of the bathroom and jumped back inside, slamming the door. Stephan Mangiardi sat on his bed.

He wrapped a towel around his waist. Time for "Lucky enters the room" take two. "Who the hell do you think you are, busting into my room like this?"

"The owner of the house?" Stephan grinned with too many teeth. Lucky's fist could help him out with that.

"What do you want?"

"Did you have a good day?"

The pile of clothes Lucky had left in the floor were now gone. Including the stained jeans. "Do you really give a flying fuck what kind of day I had?" One perk of being here: he didn't have to be nice per Walter's instructions.

"Not really. But if we're to be partners, we should be civil, don't you agree?"

Civil. Yeah, right. "And what does your dear, sweet papa think of me as your partner?" Partners?

All emotion fled Stephan's face. "I'm in charge now. What my father thinks isn't important."

Really? So the puppy had grown up and got teeth, had he? In the old days he might have been a useless waste of skin, but Stephan had toed the line where his father was concerned, and Vincent Mangiardi had absolutely no use for Lucky Lucklighter at all, considering him a disgrace who'd led Victor astray. Homophobic asshole. As if his brother wouldn't have reduced a bed to firewood if he'd attempted to carve a notch for each male conquest.

"Interesting setup you got." It'd make Lucky feel better if the whole enterprise was falling down around Stephan's ears. It wasn't, so he must be doing some things right.

Stephan pulled himself up a bit taller. "Thank you. It wasn't easy rebuilding after my uncle's arrest."

Like Stephan had single-handedly righted any wrongs. "Look, I need to get dressed. Get the hell out of here."

"Is that any way to treat someone bringing you a present?" Stephan patted a cellphone lying on the bed. "If you're working with me, you'll need these." He held up the watch Lucky had left in the case that morning. "Don't you like it? I saved it all these years, knowing one day you'd be back."

I saved it. Not *Victor*. "You really expect me to wear something that expensive down to the tunnel?"

"I expect anyone who works for me to know their position. You're not a common laborer, you're my partner." Which might explain why Bo and Cruz led him away while most of the real work took place.

"What does your uncle think of you partnering with me?"

For one split second, Stephan furrowed his brow. "He has fond memories, but he's moved on. He likes his amusements"—Stephan scrutinized Lucky—"younger."

"I'll always be younger than you." Thirty-seven wasn't old, damn it.

"This is true. Young men have their place, but at the end of the day, grown men are better. They hold their own. And you'd never say, 'Yes, sir' and 'no, sir' to me."

"Damned right, I wouldn't."

Stephan rose and crossed the floor in bare feet to stand toe to toe with Lucky. Cologne and soap filled Lucky's senses. His instincts screamed, "Run!" but he held his ground. Stephan wasn't quite as tall as Victor, and didn't have as far to lean for his breath to caress Lucky's cheek. "Years ago I'd have happily taken you to my bed. The offer still stands. We could be more than just business partners."

Lucky fought off the urge to hurl. Bile burned this throat, Stephan backed away. If the man demanded sex in exchange for Bo's life, Lucky wouldn't say no—couldn't say no. But he'd never say yes otherwise.

"I had clothes brought for you. Get dressed. We're going out. There are people you need to meet."

Stephan made it to the door before Lucky found his voice. "If you want me for a partner, I get my own place. No more stepping out of the shower and finding you here." Best to start making demands now. If Stephan wanted his services he'd have to pay well.

His back to Lucky, and his hand on the doorknob, Stephan replied, "You're safer here. We have enemies."

"I don't care. The other men don't stay here, do they? I don't notice Cyrus hanging around."

Even from where he was standing, Lucky couldn't miss Stephan's fingers tightening on the doorknob. "No. A man like Cyrus needs his own space."

"If he takes his chances, so will I."

Stephan didn't move for a moment or two. "I'll...think about it."

"I pick the place, you don't have a key, and you don't get to install cameras or recorders, got that? If I'm going to be your partner, you'll treat me as an equal."

"Now, wait a..."

"Or I go straight to Nestor." Not that Lucky could find the man, even if he wanted to.

The bluff found its mark. "You have my word."

Stephan's word meant less than nothing. "Tomorrow. I get a place tomorrow."

"I'll have someone show you around." Stephan stepped into the hall and closed the door behind him. He didn't click the lock. Maybe he intended to give Lucky the illusion of freedom, even with the shackle of Bo's fate firmly clasped around his ankle.

***

Lucky tuned out Stephan's small talk attempts to glance into the side mirror at Cruz and Bo following in the Jeep. His fingers still stung from the girl who'd come in to give him a manicure—a first, and last, if he had his way. She'd seemed so sweet at first, the little sadist, before gouging and poking at his fingers.

The new clothes scratched too. Every now and then he'd get gussied up at Walter's command, usually to meet with pharmaceutical bigwigs or whenever called to testify at hearings, kept to a minimum to protect his identity. The suit he wore probably cost three times as much as the one in his closet back home. Stephan's likely cost even more. He sure as hell intended to impress someone.

At the border Stephan handed over their IDs. He laughed and chatted with the border guards like old friends, and they crossed into Texas. One split second, that's all it would take for Lucky to open the door and jump. With any luck, he'd be on his feet and running before Stephan caught up with him.

"If you're thinking of giving me the slip while you're here, let me remind you that I found you before, I'll find you again. And next time I won't be offering a partnership. And don't forget how fast I can make Cyrus Cooper disappear."

Lucky would see Stephan dead or behind bars. He'd lived his life staring over his shoulder. One way or another, he'd never look back again when this was done.

And he'd never, ever let Bo hear of Stephan's threats.

They drove to the warehouse Bo had pointed out earlier to pick up two cases. As he'd figured, two armed guards kept watch on the US side of the tunnel, though from what Bo had said, the entrance wasn't easily found.

From there they drove into Brownsville and pulled into the parking lot of what appeared to be an upscale restaurant. The Jeep parked in a nearby spot. Even with his beard scruff and buzzed hair, Bo cleaned up nice, and he didn't appear nearly as awkward in his business getup as Lucky felt.

Cruz dressed more casually, in black slacks and body-hugging shirt, showing off his slender frame. He leaned hipshot against the Jaguar while Lucky, Bo, and Stephan headed for the restaurant. Maybe Lucky would bring him a doggie bag.

Bo carried an iPad. Stephan carried a few vials from the cases they'd picked up.

Back in the day, Lucky had met many types of people in his line of work, but no one in the restaurant seemed the stereotypical villain. Of course, one of the most conniving drug lords he'd put out of business recently had been a lady doctor who'd come across all Southern charm, and he'd stopped black market racketeers who could have passed for soccer parents. It took all kinds.

Stephan led them to an out of the way table where two men sat. The older wore a wedding band and a suit to rival Stephan's. His brown hair held a touch of gray. The younger man sported bleached blond hair and bleached teeth, with smooth, shiny nails. Lucky clenched his fists to hide his own recent manicure.

"Rufus, Conner, I'd like you to meet my partner, Lucky Lucklighter, and you know Cyrus." Lucky shook their hands. Bo smiled and nodded. The blond smiled back, a little wider than absolutely necessary.

They sat down at Rufus's invitation, the older man acting as spokesman. "I took the liberty of ordering wine. I hope you approve."

A waiter appeared and poured them all glasses one third full. Lucky sipped with caution. He'd never be accused of being a connoisseur, but the stuff tasted of a huge price tag.

"Did you bring the samples?" Rufus practically salivated once the waiter departed.

Stephan withdrew the vials from his pocket.

Mr. Too-friendly-with-Bo-for-his-own-good snatched one of the glass bottles. "And this is undetectable. You're sure?"

Bo pulled a stack of papers from his iPad case and slid them across the table. The two buyers put their heads together. "Amino acid based, huh? So when it's cleaved, the parts you get are things that are there anyway and a small molecule that could be easily found if anyone thought to look for it. Interesting. So, you'd fool basic tests, but nothing sophisticated." Judging by Rufus's raised brows and disbelieving expression, they were well on their way to making a sale.

They placed their orders when the waiter returned, and to his credit, Bo didn't bat an eyelash at Lucky's choice of prime rib. Never let it be said that Lucky was a cheap date, particularly if Stephan, or the two wannabe drug dealers, picked up the tab.

Bo ordered vegetable lasagna. One thing about being on the wrong side of the law—Lucky and Bo ate like kings.

"How much of this can we get?" the blond asked over the salad course.

Bo tapped a bit on his iPad and turned the screen around. "Two cases tonight and plenty more where that came from." The buyers needed to practice their poker faces. They gave too much away with their open mouths and wide eyes.

"How much?"

Again Bo tapped out numbers and turned the iPad around. The buyers chewed on the figures while chewing on their steaks, occasionally stopping to murmur to each other. Smooth hands, expensive clothes, absolutely zero business savvy. If Lucky had to guess, he's say these men were both doctors, either looking to supply their patients with drugs too heavily regulated in the States, or planning a sideline business. Either way, Lucky would be back for them after he took care of Stephan.

As the meal progressed, the buyers spent more and more time in private conversation. Over chocolate mousse, Rufus announced, "You have a deal."

Stephan regarded Bo with a shark smile. "Cyrus? Standard arrangement."

Bo pulled his chair closer to share the iPad screen.

Standard arrangement for many Mexican/US drug deals consisted of a broker and peso exchange. The buyers would give a broker US currency. The broker, in turn, would purchase American-made goods, to be brought into Mexico and sold there. The resulting pesos would find their way into Stephan's bank account, deposited in increments small enough not to draw undue attention when combined with the factory's doctored figures from legitimate drug sales.

No fuss, no muss, and no large amounts of cash to carry.

And if the drugs weren't yet fully tested? Let the buyer beware.

"You test on your own men." Lucky wasn't near as inclined to silence on the way back to Stephan's. He'd love to be in the Jeep, with Bo. Time enough later.

"What's wrong, Lucky? You weren't nearly so squeamish back in your younger days. I pay them well. They never complain." Daylight giving way to darkness didn't quite hide the genuine shock on Stephan's face. Did he honestly believe handing out paychecks gave him the right to turn his workers into addicts?

Yeah, tell that to Hector, the guy nobody talked about. "You're not shooting anything into my arm."

"Lucky, you're my partner, not a laborer. I wouldn't dream of it."

"Cruz?" No one was fucking safe with Captain Crazy at the wheel.

"The doctor says Cruz has a medical condition, making him unsuitable for testing."

Yeah, Bo had said the same thing, a bad heart. Lucky would love to know the details, but didn't ask.

"How's testing done? What kind of controls?" He wouldn't outright ask about Bo and let Stephan read too much into it.

"Some of the men are given Codopure, others a placebo. Some are alternated. Cyrus is given a low, consistent dosage for comparison. The doctor takes blood samples every morning and gives them a shot. Some he gives more than others, to test proper dosage."

Like the poor slob who'd gotten too much. "You know some countries might approve this drug, right?"

Stephan snorted. "And they wouldn't give me near as much as I'll get from street dealers in New York and Chicago."

Money. The ultimate decision maker.

"Pretty smart idea." Feeding Stephan's ego might earn him more information.

Stephan took his eyes off the road long enough to flash Lucky an open-mouthed gawk. "Thank you. It's something I've been working on for a long time. Even before my father...retired."

Just a tiny pause, a fraction of a second. But there all the same.

Stephan must have interpreted Lucky's silence as permission to keep crowing. "If there's one thing I've learned, it's that people will do just about anything to get high. As an escape from reality. As a coping mechanism to deal with mundane concerns in their pitiful lives." His lips turned up in a smug little smile. A smile Lucky wanted to bitch slap off the man's face. "Whatever the reason, I don't care. This product puts me at the top of the food chain. Can you imagine? Using every day, never worrying about drug tests. It's beautiful."

Lord help the poor souls on board a plane with a hopped-up captain, or on an operating table with a surgeon who'd taken a little pick-me-up.

For a few months, the frontliners on the war on drugs might cheer the dropping number of overdoses due to oxycodone and heroin. Yeah, folks had rejoiced over King Kong's death too... before Godzilla arrived.

A glass of orange juice waited on Lucky's nightstand. No fucking way, no matter how badly he'd kill for a good night's sleep. He poured the juice down the sink.

He'd no sooner gotten into bed when his door opened and closed. Tomorrow he was so out of here.

He rolled over to turn on the light and ran smack into a warm body. "You!" He yanked the lamp cord and scuttled backward. Stephan grinned at him, a moment before descending.

"What the h..." Lucky planted his hands against Stephan's naked chest and shoved.

Stephan pulled back in surprise, narrowing his eyes. "I see you didn't drink the nightcap I left for you."

"I don't need help sleeping." Or to wake up spread-eagled with Stephan or whoever else staring down at him.

"You used to."

He did now, truth be told, unless Bo occupied the other side of the bed. "Not anymore."

"It doesn't matter. I'm here, you're here. Let's have some fun."

Wide pupils, more deranged than usual? "You been sampling the goods?"

"And what if I have? You should try them." Stephan's maniacal smile wouldn't have been out of place on an axe murderer's face.

"Your uncle never touched the product."

The mention of Victor stopped Stephan cold. "Victor, Victor, Victor! Why do you always have to drag my uncle into this? He's gone! You'll never see him again. I'm here. Me! Don't expect me to believe that you wanted him for anything besides his money. Did he ever offer you more than a place in his bed? Did he offer you a partnership?"

Stephan bounded out of bed and stalked across the floor. He'd be about the same age now that Victor had been the last time Lucky laid eyes on the man. But Victor had worked out, taken care of himself. A spare tire rounded Stephan's middle. The erect cock he'd brushed against Lucky's leg earlier now hung limp down between his legs.

Yep. Needle dick. Got it in one.

"You'll want me. Sooner or later, you'll come begging."

The door slammed after Stephan's retreating back. And that explained the power of the drug: it made humans believe they were gods. Lucky stuck a chair under the doorknob and climbed back into bed. For four hours he tossed and turned. He should've wedged a chair under the door earlier and drunk the damned juice.

CHAPTER TEN

"FOUND ME a place yet?" Lucky issued his challenge at breakfast in front of all the men.

"Not yet. But I'm looking." Stephan looked like hell was more like it, with his bleary eyes and dark circles.

Lucky got the same answer the next day. Stephan stopped showing up at breakfast. Worked for Lucky. But without money or access to his US accounts that wouldn't tip his hand, and no income coming in, he couldn't exactly find a place on his own. And moving in with Bo might get someone killed. So much for the "partnership" if he stayed broke. Dependent is right where Stephan wanted him to be.

On Saturday, he stepped out of the house to find Bo waiting. Creepy Cruz was nowhere in sight.

"Your watch dog off chasing his tail?"

"It's our day off. I came to get you." Bo leaned against the still-pinging Harley, tanned arms folded across his chest and eyes hidden behind dark shades. All thighs should look so good in denim. He'd taken time to trim his facial scruff. Worn jeans didn't conceal his ample package.

Time to pause and savor the image.

Those jeans would look mighty fine bunched around Bo's ankles. Bo, leaning over the bike seat while Lucky pounded into him from behind. Damn. Lucky feasted his eyes on a wet dream come to life, and all Bo got for scenery was...a shrimp of an ex-con named Lucky.

"Nice watch," Bo grumbled when Lucky approached.

"This old thing?" Yeah, best not dwell too much on the watch Stephan insisted he wear today. No doubt containing

99

a tracker of some sort. He'd once worn Victor's gift proudly. Now it felt more like a shackle. "I got it from a street vendor in Tijuana." First stray dog he spotted got a fancy new collar.

"You've never been to Tijuana."

"Details, details." Lucky stopped by the bike. "You gonna let me drive?"

"Did you get a license?"

"As a matter of fact..."

"Do you know where we're going?"

"Well, no."

"You have the keys?" Bo jangled a key ring before Lucky's nose.

Lucky made a grab, but Bo snatched the keys away, lips pulled back to show his gleaming teeth. Without another word, Bo slipped onto the driver's seat and fired up the bike. Oh, well, another battle lost. Lucky donned his shades, hopped on the bike, and held on. Bo had taken a bit of effort with his appearance today, and even dabbed on cologne. Nice.

Wind in his hair, sun kissing his face, Lucky relaxed against the backrest. Years ago, he'd ridden without a helmet, back in the days when he'd thought himself indestructible. Nothing compared to being helmetless, though he'd known too many people who'd exchanged their lives for the freedom. Now, without the helmet, he felt naked, exposed, especially since his dirty blond hair made him stand out in these parts.

Bo seemed to fit in anywhere. Drop him in the middle of a drug-smuggling biker gang, he'd become Sergeant at Arms. Toss him into a park with a group of coworkers for a picnic, and ten minutes later they'd be oohing and aahing over his potato salad.

And down here where gringos were regarded with suspicion, thanks to Stephan and folks like him, Bo spoke Spanish and lugged cases along with the lowest man on the totem pole. *"Sí, Señor* Cooper." If only Bo could work his magic on Stephan without tangling himself up in the spider's web.

They drove in the direction of the factory. Once out of sight of the house, Bo rested his free hand on Lucky's thigh, a familiar gesture from rides gone by. At a crossroads, he veered right instead of left.

He slowed to a stop in front of a rundown garage on the edge of a small town, vaguely reminiscent of the place they'd busted a few months ago, where Bo had worked as a mechanic for Mateo Reyes. Nothing as fancy as a garage door opener here. Bo hopped off and opened the padlock on the bay door, raised the metal panel, then motioned Lucky forward.

Oh goody, he got to drive for a full twenty feet. But yeah, leaving the Harley outside in this neighborhood likely meant later finding a husk, stripped down for parts.

The garage bay held the distinct aroma of old oil and decades of car exhaust. Lucky breathed deeply. Ah. Home.

Bo stepped outside and closed the door. The lock clicked into place. He reappeared through a side door.

"It's not much, but it's home." He paused, hand behind him still gripping the door handle. Before Lucky's eyes, Cy Cooper's cockiness bled away. One side of Bo's mouth lifted, quivered a bit, then dropped again, along with his troubled gaze. "Damn, but I've missed being able to hold you without worrying who might be watching."

He was in Lucky's arms in an instant. With nearly crushing force, he pulled Lucky to his chest, tipped Lucky's head back, and plundered his mouth. He tasted of green tea. Yes, definitely home.

Bo, in his arms. Lucky latched on. If a man with a gun suddenly appeared, they'd both be dead, 'cause damned if he would let go.

With a ferocity that bordered on violence, Bo plunged his tongue into Lucky's mouth, one hand on the back of Lucky's head. Lucky answered stroke for stroke. Outside the door a thousand challenges screamed their names, but here, now, nothing else mattered but the sweet slide of Bo's hand under

Lucky's shirt, skimming the fabric up and off his body. Lucky's boots proved a challenge and stayed on. Two pair of shades fell to the floor, along with Lucky's doubts.

Bo attacked Lucky's jeans, dropping the fabric and himself to the floor. He engulfed Lucky's cock in the welcome heat of his mouth. His whiskers rasped against Lucky's skin, and he stared up, the picture of lust and decadence.

Oh, dear Lord! Lucky grabbed at the short strands of Bo's hair to keep himself upright. His knees refused to hold his weight.

Bo slid down Lucky's cock, his lips coming within a hair's breadth of Lucky's groin. Familiar tension built inside. Lucky groaned at the loss when Bo withdrew. A moment later Bo returned, releasing a moan of his own.

"I missed this," Lucky said. *I missed you, I nearly lost my mind without you.*

What did Bo's "Hmmmph" mean? Oh. He seized Lucky's ass with both hands and plunged deeper, holding Lucky in his throat while he swallowed. Fuck!

No way in hell could Lucky last.

"That can't be comfortable." It took all of his willpower to drag Bo up off the floor. The concrete couldn't be good for his knees. Bo sealed their mouths together and, pushing and pulling, danced them toward the back of the garage. With his jeans around his ankles, Lucky barely avoided hitting the floor. With some blind fumbling he managed to open a door, and they stepped into what had probably once been a storage room, now converted into a living area.

A single bed took up a good portion of the space. One minute Lucky gazed down at white sheets, the next he stared at peeling paint hanging from the ceiling. Bo's pounce blocked the view. For a moment their gazes locked. Bo descended. The bliss of mouth on mouth lost none of its fire for its slow exploration. Lucky slid his tongue against his lover's in a scorching tango as hot as the arid land outside. Damn! Category Five Hurricane Bo. Lucky's favorite storm.

"Mmmm..." Lucky toed at his laced up boots without breaking their lip lock, then tried again, then again. Damned things wouldn't budge.

Bo pulled away. "Allow me." With deft fingers, he untied, unlaced, and removed the boots. They *thunked* when they hit the floor. Lucky's jeans and boxers landed on top of the pile a moment later.

Lucky ran his fingers over Bo's shoulders and tasted the saltiness of Bo's neck. Skimmed his hands over taut muscle. Hiked a leg over Bo's thighs. The smile on Bo's face put the sun to shame a second before he reclaimed Lucky's mouth.

Weeks of pent up need begged Lucky to flip Bo over and drive home. He swiped his tongue against his lover's.

Bo had other ideas. Language lessons weren't needed to recognize the package Bo retrieved from under the bed. The squish of lube against Lucky's hole announced the man's intentions.

Lucky relaxed, accepting the fingers breaching him. Bo's lips curled upward. Lucky rocked against Bo's hand, urging him on, but Bo wouldn't be hurried. With excruciating slowness, he worked Lucky open.

Lucky let loose a grunt when Bo found his gland. Bo grinned and repeated the gesture. "Get on with it," Lucky growled. Wait. Was that ripping sound a condom pack? What the hell?

Bo lined up his cock and slowly sank in, pausing every few seconds to back out and plunge a little deeper. The tease. At last, he sank in completely. Full. Lucky slowly exhaled, forcing his body not to fight. The initial sharp bite lessened. Time for more.

He bucked up, impaling himself completely before withdrawing. Bo wrapped his arms around Lucky, braced his weight on his elbows, and shoved.

Hot damn! They established a rhythm, their squeezed-together abs giving Lucky's cock a stroking. The bed shook, squealed, and threatened to collapse. Cheap-assed piece of shit. Let it fall—they'd screw on the floor.

In, out, Bo advanced and retreated, building the flames deep inside. "Ah, ah, ah," Lucky exhaled with each forceful thrust.

He cupped Bo's ass to feel the muscles flex. "Yeah, that's right. Oh, yeah, right there."

Wrapping his arms about Bo's back, he bucked up to get what he needed. Sweat-slicked skin against his palms, harsh breathing, the slick/slide of their bodies joining. "Harder!" Lucky moaned. Harder, faster.

Forget who they were or pretended to be. Forget they were so far from home. He poured what words couldn't express into a kiss.

He clenched around Bo, desperate to wipe everything away but this moment, this..."Oh my God!"

Electricity shot through him, consuming him, nerve endings exploding. Bo cried out and collapsed onto Lucky's chest.

Lucky awoke with a start some time later to find Bo standing over him, a plate in each hand giving off the heavenly scent of adobo and cilantro. "I walked to the cantina down the street to get us lunch. A hot plate and canned chili isn't good enough for company." He sat the plates on the wooden box he used for an end table, and dug into a dorm-sized refrigerator for two beers.

They sat on the bed to eat. "You never told me what happened with Walter." Bo rolled a tortilla around grilled veggies.

"We haven't been alone much." And telling someone else made the betrayal more real, particularly if Bo believed as Lucky did.

"We may not be now, but we're as close as we're gonna get, and I haven't seen any signs yet of bugs or cameras. Plant them in this neighborhood, and they'll be stolen, along with anything else not nailed down."

Lucky took a bite of tamale, more to stall for time than to fill his belly. He washed down his mouthful with Corona. "I found a picture of Victor and Walter at a restaurant, taken about thirty years ago." No need mentioning the note: *Be careful who you trust.*

"So? Maybe it was an innocent lunch. It's a small world, you know. Who sent it?"

"In all the time I've known the man, he's never once mentioned having met Victor." And Walter damned well should have. "I don't know where it came from. I thought Stephan at first, but he would have bragged. Besides, there's more."

"Like what?"

"Walter said he hadn't made any deals with Victor, but a news article showed him walking behind Victor on the courthouse steps. Victor was laughing, like he wasn't worried at all." The image burned into Lucky's mind, his former lover acting like he didn't have a prison sentence hanging over his head.

"Has it occurred to you that maybe Walter was in court for a different reason and happened to be using the steps at the same time?" Bo sopped up his plate with a piece of tortilla.

Honestly? No. "But—"

"But nothing. I don't like the hold he has over me anymore than you did, but he's fair, he's honest, and he gave me a second chance when no one else would. Right now we need him. When all this is over, you have to sit down and talk to him, tell him what you've found out, and see how he acts. I think you know the man better than you're letting on." Bo dropped his fork onto his plate with a *clink*.

"You're not supposed to talk sense to me, you're supposed to be on my side." Yeah, so Lucky pouted. Big deal.

Bo silently scolded Lucky with a raised brow and narrowed eyes. Pretty damned effective.

"Hey! I was gonna talk to him about the picture when I found out about the courthouse thing. I didn't wait around. As soon as I got home, someone brained me, and here I am."

"He really does care about you, you know that, right?" Bo might as well have learned his brow-raised scrutiny from Walter himself.

But did the boss care for Lucky the man, the agent, or the link to Victor?

"I'm sure Johnson misses you. I think she's grown attached."

First Alejandro Garcia grinning every chance he got, now Johnson? "Folks need to quit." Why the hell grow attached to Lucky? He made a reputation of being grouchy, opinionated, and in general not very nice. How Bo put up with him was anyone's guess.

"Walter would be proud of us, but he'd want us to be careful. If we're in danger, I think he'd tell us to head for the border."

Lucky didn't run with his tail tucked between his legs. Ever. He might make an exception this time, for Bo's sake.

"I want inside the factory, but all I get to see is the infirmary and loading docks." Bo rose and busied himself washing his plate in a tiny sink.

"I toured the lab, but not the factory floor." And only because Stephan wanted to impress Lucky.

Bo leaned against the sink and stared out a tiny window. "I'd love a shot at their records. Who sells them raw materials, their customer list. Maybe after you win Stephan's trust, he'll give you access."

The price would be too high. "Maybe." What had Lucky told Bo of his former association with Stephan? No need to rile the man unnecessarily. Particularly if Lucky resorted to desperate measures to keep Bo safe.

"At the restaurant, he referred to you as his partner. Is that true?" Bo didn't turn around. Maybe he didn't want to see the truth in Lucky's eyes.

"That's what he says, though I don't know why. He also wants Nestor Sauceda as a partner, and thinks I can get the guy to cooperate."

Bo whistled low and turned around. "I've heard of Sauceda. Powerful man. Head of one of the oldest crime families in these parts."

Lucky nodded. "He was a friend of Victor's. I don't know why Stephan thinks I can win him over. I'm not exactly known for my charm."

"No. And that's probably why he wants you. A man like Nestor sees through bullshit, and has no time for smooth lies. If he's dealing with you, he knows exactly what he's getting. You say what you think and mean what you say."

"Most people just say I'm a rude asshole."

Crossing back to the bed where Lucky sat, Bo leaned down, putting them eye to eye. "Don't kid yourself. There's something solid and dependable about knowing where you stand with someone. And knowing they'll tell you the truth, even if you don't want to hear it. You're also loyal to a fault to anyone who's earned it."

Lucky had good points? Could that be what Bo saw in him?

"Nestor would appreciate a man like you, especially after dealing with Stephan, who talks out of both side of his face." A crease formed between Bo's brows. "When are you supposed to meet with him, or have you already?"

"I haven't, and Stephan said Nestor acts on his own time."

"Yeah, from what I've heard, that's true. He'll see you when he's good and damned ready, and not a moment before."

"How much longer do you reckon this will take before we get to go home?" Too damned long for Lucky's tastes.

"I don't know. I wish we could send a report to Walter. He knows where I am, but I haven't been able to let him know you're here. Have you?"

"No." Especially not while Lucky didn't know if Walter were friend or foe. He finished his meal slowly. Sooner or later, he'd have to return to Stephan. He'd put the moment off as long as he could.

Bo's apartment, hardly deserving of the word, wasn't much to look at, but seemed to serve the purpose. At odds with the rundown garage, neatly folded clothes sat on a low shelf, and assorted toiletries lined the cement block window sill. A window unit air conditioner kept the room livable, but barely.

The sink, floor drain, and exposed toilet took up one corner, a rickety table and hotplate another. Lucky'd seen bigger cells. He'd lived in bigger cells.

"Why are you living here? Aren't there better places?"

"Yeah." Bo took Lucky's empty plate to the sink. Running water muffled his voice. "Cruz picked this for me. It's a safe place to park the bike, and his grandmother owns it. Rent's cheap, and no one around here answers to Stephan, though I can't be too sure. But I can tap into a neighbors' unsecured Internet connection. When it's working." He grinned and flopped back down on the bed. "Not that I dare send a report to Walter. No telling who might intercept. And I know good and damned well Stephan monitors the phone he gave me."

What? Bo? Stealing Internet? "Who are you and what have you done with Bo?"

The grin fell. "We've had this conversation. Sometimes I'm Bo, sometimes I'm Cyrus, sometimes I'm a combination of both, and other times I don't know who the hell I am." Pain clouded his eyes. "When this is over, I'm not sure who I'll be."

Lucky feared the same thing. "Stephan promised me my own place but keeps making excuses, and it's not like I can go to the bank and use my ATM card."

"Is he bothering you?"

Damn, Bo got all growly for him. Nice. "He's a pain in the ass, but nothing I can't handle." Best to keep the "kicking the son of a bitch out of bed" incident quiet.

"I don't like you being there with him, but the closer you are, the more you'll find out."

Yeah, though lately Lucky hadn't learned anything beyond how many guys Stephan rotated through his bedroom door—four. "He's crazy, you know."

"Without a doubt. But we need to stop him before he spreads the crazy too far. Yesterday when the doctors tested the men, they found no trace of the drug. Even after they'd just been dosed. Codopure is ready to ship."

Oh fuck. "And he's still testing?"

"It's how he controls them. He's not giving up that hold. Besides, the doctors are studying long-term effects. Like they give a happy damn."

They stayed in bed for most of the day, alternately talking and napping. When shadows stretched across the walls, Bo took Lucky back to Stephan's.

So easy. Just aim the bike north and keep going 'til *Welcome to Texas* came into view. Lucky would bullshit their way over the border or call Walter in a pinch. They'd be back in Atlanta by tomorrow night.

And Stephan would still be here, packing crates of poison to follow Lucky to the good old US of A. No. Not on his watch. He swung his leg over the bike and gave Bo's shoulder a quick squeeze. They exchanged a smile and Bo roared off into the evening.

Stephan was waiting inside the house. His scrunched face screamed of distaste, but he didn't say anything when Lucky came creeping in.

Smart man.

That night Lucky once more jammed a chair under the doorknob and poured out his nightcap of orange juice and chloral hydrate. A workout. That's what he needed. Burpees and side planks until he fell over served as poor substitutes for a quick fix in a bottle.

The doorknob rattled a few minutes after Lucky went to bed. He smiled. Lucky one, Stephan zero.

The next morning Stephan marched up to the guys milling around the factory loading dock waiting for Alejandro. What the hell was he doing here? The guys backed away. All but Bo.

"Hey, boss." Somehow Bo, in full Cyrus mode, made "boss" into an insult.

Stephan reached into Bo's holster and withdrew his gun. "You won't be needing this." He shot Lucky a triumphant smirk and stalked off.

Bastard.

CHAPTER ELEVEN

Alejandro grinned while pinning his brother to the ground, only to get rolled over and pinned himself a moment later. Jaime and Juan cheered them on. Lucky had bet his money on Alejandro as soon as the brothers' all day sniping came to a head after finishing work.

The Garcias alternately hugged each other or scuffled, much like Lucky's younger two brothers, Dover and Daytona. They'd beat each other to a pulp, but no one else better touch either one of them.

Rafael stood and held out his hand. Alejandro reached out and, at the last minute, clasped Rafael's hand in both of his and tugged. Rafael landed in a heap in the dirt. Alejandro dashed away, chortling, Rafael hot on his heels.

Where were Dover and Daytona now? What were they doing? Did they ever think of better times with their older brother? Lucky used to take them hunting and fishing. Taught them to drive the tractor. Talked them through their first broken hearts. And had busted their asses when he'd caught them smoking pot behind the barn.

He hadn't laid eyes on them in twelve years, not since they were eighteen and nineteen. God, they were in their thirties now.

Even before they thought him dead, they'd quit speaking to him. And after all these years, Lucky never found out exactly why. Not that he hadn't given them plenty of reasons. Smoking a joint behind the barn couldn't compare with a trafficking conviction.

The Garcia brothers returned, arms around each other's shoulders and friends again. Just like Dover and Daytona.

Don't look back, Lucky, it only brings you pain.

"We're finished here, let's head for the house." Stephan's house, or rather, Victor's. Not Bo's and certainly not Lucky's. They had nowhere else to go, and Lucky couldn't stand being reminded of how his choices had cost him his family.

No use hanging around the factory when he and Bo weren't invited past the warehouse area. How Lucky would love a peek inside the doctor's office for a chance to pilfer some records. But the invite meant rolling up his sleeve. No. Definitely not, and what little information Bo got didn't amount to much.

He'd also love to go back to Bo's place, but Bo might have to pay dearly for another afternoon together if Stephan found out. The jealous bastard.

The mere thought of being in the same room, or even the same zip code as Stephan made lunch threaten to reappear. He'd promised Lucky his own place and didn't seem inclined to follow through. Like Stephan stood a chance of scoring if Lucky stayed close.

"I'll drive." Bo fished the Jeep keys from his pocket.

"No, I will." Lucky snatched the keys and danced away from Bo's swat.

Rafael growled. Growled? Alejandro wore the same adoring expression he did every time he stared at Lucky. A breeze caught Lucky in the upwind. He winced in advance of a snoot full of sweaty man and whiffed cologne instead. Alejandro smelled...pretty? The squat little guy murmured too low for Lucky to hear, setting his cohort to chuckling.

"What did he say?" Nobody made jokes at Lucky's expense.

Bo joined the laughter. "Give me the keys and I'll tell you."

Lucky attempted to wipe the grin off Bo's face with a glower. His plan fell short.

Bo held out his hand. Alejandro said something just out of hearing. Lucky dropped the keys into Bo's outstretched palm. Jerk.

"You've got an admirer. He loves your hair, and says you're a fine looking man." Bo unlocked the Jeep door with an unnecessary flourish.

"He did not!" Lucky shifted his gaze from Bo to Alejandro, who gave him a kissy face. Oh, crap. Maybe he did. At least he rode in the other Jeep and gained a ten minute head start while Bo waited for Cruz to climb into the back of theirs.

They'd gone about eight miles from the factory when a quick glance in the side mirror showed a tail. The late model Ford made no suspicious moves and didn't seem out of the ordinary. Yet it followed them just the same. "See him?" Lucky asked. Just because it wasn't a black SUV didn't mean it wasn't cartel-related.

"Yeah. He fell in behind us about five miles back." Bo flicked his gaze to the rearview mirror and back to the road. He pushed the accelerator down, leaving the Ford. The car lagged behind for mere moments, then caught up. Instead of tailing them like before, the vehicle flew by as another came up from the rear.

The front car swerved in a spray of dust. Bo slammed on the brakes. "Hold on!" He whipped the steering wheel to the left. The Jeep spun and tilted onto two wheels. Fuck! Lucky grabbed the dash with both hands. Tires squealed, and Bo stomped the gas. He hit the brakes when a truck cut them off.

The rear car blocked them from behind, three vehicles surrounding them.

"Cruz!" Damn, what Lucky wouldn't give for his gun. "Bo, tell him to get on that precious cell phone of his and start calling for help. And where the hell's his gun?" Lucky wouldn't use his phone. No doubt it was bugged all to shit, like Bo's. Too bad he'd left the handy little anti-bugging tool Walter gave him on the counter back home.

Bo fumbled under the seat and came up with a tire tool. Fuck Stephan Mangiardi for leaving them unarmed, except for Cruz, who might take them both out just for boredom and hatred of Americans.

A fourth car approached, a so-new-it-sparkled Mercedes E250. Beautiful and classy, it was the closest thing to a Sherman tank on the road. Lucky would be willing to bet the thing was damned near bulletproof. The car pulled up a few yards away and stopped. The back door swung open.

He spun in the seat to find Cruz grinning. In perfect, unaccented English, the sorry asswipe said, "Here's where you get out, *amigo*."

Lucky added Cruz's name to his shit list. He climbed out of the Jeep and approached the Mercedes. Squirming, wriggling dread gathered in the pit of his stomach. Footsteps sounded behind him.

"I'm coming with you." Bo's voice didn't waver. It wasn't a question.

"No, B...Cy. Stay here. Whoever it is, they want me." He'd love to add "where you'll be safe," but this waking nightmare offered no safety. Lucky swallowed more than a mouthful of dust.

The footsteps grew louder until Bo stood at his side. "Then I'm dying to meet them. We have so much in common, 'cause I want you too." The cocky smile might be a recent addition to Bo's repertoire of facial expressions, but The Dimple, that damned, sweet-assed dimple, said, *"I go where you go."* In the cold hard light of day, the simple gesture might end both their lives.

Hell, if he'd known Bo would follow, he'd have clobbered Cruz and run a long time ago.

"Remember, it's your choice." Lucky forced extra bluster into his words, though Bo's steady presence brought a ray of light to a gloomy world. Unless Lucky missed his guess, the moment he got in that car, he'd be in the presence of some lackey, either after information or determined to send Lucky back to Stephan with a message—one body part at a time. And he'd gladly take any punishment if whoever waited believed Bo wasn't worth their time.

Walking slowly might postpone the inevitable. For a while.

Darkly tinted windows hid anyone inside the car. The sweltering sun showed no mercy. Sweat trickled down from Lucky's brow, and his T-shirt clung to his back. He stepped in front of Bo. He made a smaller target, but any bullets coming out the door were bound to have Lucky's name on them anyway. A lone figure in the backseat came into view.

Bright teeth against sun-leathered features. An outstretched hand. Dark hair and brows shot with gray. A sixty-ish Hispanic man who'd appear relatively harmless in any other situation, yet who radiated power the way Victor had. "Welcome to my country, Mr. Lucklighter." Nestor Sauceda-Vasquez. The big fucking kahuna himself.

Lucky shook his hand, if only because he couldn't think of a reason not to. Nestor stared far longer than necessary, but not with ruthless appraisal. "You always had a rugged charm. I'm glad to see you haven't lost it."

Breathing deeply didn't bring any calm. Lucky longed to scrub his sweaty palms against his jeans. Holy shit. Entering the lion's den with Bo in tow. If he got out of this alive, he'd have to give up something. He didn't drink much, didn't smoke, needed his cussing, had already given up caffeine. Please, Lord, don't ask him to sacrifice sex.

Lucky forced a smile, recalling kicking Nestor's butt at poker in Victor's living room fifteen years ago. "You've gone to a lot of trouble for a rematch, haven't you?" The last time they'd played Five Card Draw, Lucky had walked away a thousand dollars richer. Nestor's loss bought Christmas presents for the Lucklighter brothers that year.

"Oh, I've learned my lesson, my friend. I'll never play cards with you again. 'Lucky' is more than your name." A hint of an accent caressed the words. Charlotte would have been enthralled. Nestor had quite the reputation as a ladies' man. Money and power turned even ugly men handsome, not that Nestor was hard on the eyes. In his own territory, he appeared relaxed, in charge.

Nestor released Lucky's hand, slid across the backseat, and patted the spot he'd vacated. Oh well, no hope for it now, Lucky crawled into the car, followed by Bo. Bo's presence made a comforting weight against his side, helping him face whatever came next. It wouldn't be pretty.

The man had played nice on Victor's turf. Now, he had home field advantage.

Their unwanted host tapped the headrest in front of him, and the car pulled away. "Where are your manners, Lucky? Introduce me to your friend." Nestor saved him the trouble. "Nice to meet you, Mr. Cooper. I've heard many things about you."

"From Stephan, or from Cruz? And is Stephan aware of Cruz being on your payroll?" Bo's words snapped like a bullwhip.

Nestor barked what might have been a laugh but sounded more like a hacking cough. Years of hard living must be catching up with the man. "Now, what good would he do me if Stephan knew who held his leash?"

None at all, actually. Bo sat ramrod straight, a touch of wariness in his eyes, wearing Cyrus Cooper's suspicion like a scuffed leather jacket. Good.

Mr. Big Shot Drug Lord needed to peel his eyes off Lucky's man. Now. Regardless of his womanizer reputation, he'd indulged in the occasional hired man while visiting Victor. "Why go through all this to see me?" Might as well get this show on the road, and divert attention away from Bo.

"Now, Lucky. We can't talk business in a car. How...uncivilized. Don't you remember the wonderful dinners we used to share? Tell me, whatever became of Victor's cook? What was her name? Rosa?"

"Linda."

"Ah, yes. Rosa was his housekeeper here. He never brought you to his grandfather's house, did he?"

Only pure force of will kept Lucky from grinding his teeth together. "You know full well he didn't." Maybe grabbing the guy around the throat and giving him a good shake or two would rattle loose where they were going or why, but without a doubt, the driver kept a gun handy. Cruz followed in the Jeep like a good little pet.

He'd get his payback later.

One question burned on Lucky's tongue, one he wouldn't ask with Bo around. He drummed his fingers on his thighs and fought the urge to grab Bo's hand and send a "we're in this together" message of his own. Only, Bo shouldn't be here. This entire mess fell directly on Lucky's head, traceable back to the biggest mistake of his life when he'd tried to steal a car from the wrong man. The road to his ruin started at a vintage Mercedes Roadster and ambled down to Hell, courtesy of Victor Mangiardi.

Concrete block walls and tile roofs emerged from the vastness of nothing, a town of sorts. The buildings, like the warehouse on the border, bore signs of skirmishes—gray gouges showing in terracotta walls. A stop sign had more bullet holes than metal.

The car stopped in front of a cantina.

"This looks familiar," Lucky muttered.

"It should," Bo hissed. "I live about a block away." Oh. *That* cantina.

A child of about seven sat alone in the lot. He bounced to his feet when the driver opened his door and got out, babbling in rapid-fire Spanish. The driver gave a curt command, and the boy scurried off.

"Don't be so hard on the young ones, Miguel," Nestor said, emerging from the vehicle. He called the kid back and placed a coin in his palm. The kid grinned and ran off.

The heavenly aroma of cooking meat met them on the sidewalk and invited them inside. Nestor opened the cantina door and waved them in, then led the way past a bar where three men sat watching soccer on a TV above the bar.

He stopped and turned, palm out. "Mr. Cooper. I'd prefer you stayed down here. I need to speak with Mr. Lucklighter alone."

Bo locked eyes with the viper. After a moment, he dipped his chin, never breaking eye contact. He didn't comment on the use of Lucky's real name. No need to dig a deeper hole.

Like Victor, Nestor had ways of knowing things and seeing through bullshit. It was a wonder he allowed Stephan to draw breath...or Lucky. Either they both served some kind of purpose, or soon they'd be little more than inked words in an obituary column. And unlike when Walter killed him, this time Lucky would be dead for real, his body never found.

Bo flashed Lucky a quick "be careful" glance, and slid his gaze away. Cruz hoisted himself onto a stool at the bar, already eyeing the soccer game. Bo sauntered over to a nearby table and sat with his back to the wall, facing the stairs. "You need me, holler." He crossed his arms over his chest and leaned his chair back on two legs, staring at Nestor so hard one of their heads should burst into flames. An enforcer. Just like he'd been for the Cruisers.

"Come, Lucky." One side of Nestor's mouth lifted in a bemused smirk when he fixed his eyes on Bo. "We have many things to talk about." As they climbed the stairs out of earshot of Bo, he added, "Loyalty, I like that. Tell me, what have you done to deserve such respect from a hard man like Cyrus Cooper?"

What, indeed? "I lay my cards on the table and never try to bullshit him." Not much, anyway. Whether as Cyrus Cooper or Bo Schollenberger, Bo didn't tolerate bullshit. Or lies. Or wet towels on the bathroom floor.

The upper floor held four long tables and possibly served as a party room. Lucky and Nestor were the only diners. Despite the circumstances, Lucky's stomach grumbled. The little breakfast he'd eaten had long since burned off.

A woman appeared with a tray and set a bottle of water and one of beer in front of each man. Nestor spoke to her in quiet Spanish, patted her arm, and gave her a toothy smile. The lady, her hair shot with age, grinned, and a flush crept up her cheeks.

She turned to Lucky. "Luck-key?"

He gave her a sidewise regard and nodded. How the hell did she know his name? She said something in Spanish, patted his cheek and smiled. All he made out were the words "son" and "happy."

"What's that all about?" Lucky asked Nestor.

"She hopes you like her cooking." Nestor didn't even tear his eyes away from the woman while answering.

She giggled and backed away, darting down the stairs faster than a woman of her years should be able to move.

"Graciela and I go way back." Nestor's lascivious smile dimmed to polite affection. "She was quite the looker back in her day. Still is, in my eyes."

"If you brought me here to brag about your old conquests..."

All mirth left the man. "Bite your tongue. The woman had eyes for only one man, undeserving as he was. Her misguided devotion outlived him."

Not for Nestor's but for the woman's sake, Lucky offered a quiet, "I'm sorry." Damn, but Bo was rubbing off on him. And not in the fun, leads-to-sticky-skin way.

The hard lines of the man's face softened. "I forget what a tough guy you were. Serving time behind bars hasn't mellowed you. Then again, some of my best men learned all they needed to about fighting and survival in US prisons."

Lucky had learned some of those same lessons himself, courtesy of the Durham Correctional Center. Years spent as an outsider looking in at the Southeastern Narcotics Bureau also added to his education.

"I hope you don't mind, but seeing this is your first trip to Valle Hermoso area and you're unfamiliar with local tastes, I took the liberty of ordering for us." Nestor turned his lips up in a sneer. "What most Americans call Mexican food is an insult to fine cooks like Graciela."

The woman returned with a young girl of about twelve at her heels, both carrying trays. With well-practiced movements, they silently transferred dishes to the table. The tray of sizzling meat captured Lucky's full attention, the veggies adding a side note that maybe Bo would get fed too.

Before he chowed down, he asked, "How about the men downstairs?" No need to single out Bo, though he had no love at all for Cruz. The bastard could survive on his own ego for all Lucky cared.

"Your friend is being attended as well. You've never experienced my hospitality, though Victor considered me an excellent host."

And a deadly one. In 2011 a local shootout had left several gang members, along with one Mexican cop, dead. That gang soon left the area. Nestor remained. Go figure.

Wait. He'd said "considered" not "considers." Did Nestor speaking of Victor in the past tense mean anything, or just that he hadn't seen the man recently?

If death waited at the end of the meal, better to go on a full stomach. Lucky ate. Damn! Spiced meat rolled up into tortillas made a fine meal, though the beer he washed the offering down with left something to be desired. He even tasted the vegetables to satisfy his curiosity. And maybe Bo.

Only after the woman retrieved the empty dishes did the conversation progress beyond, "Oh, you must try the gorditas," and "Graciela makes excellent salsa."

"Now." Nestor wiped his mouth with a napkin and dropped it on the table, a gesture Lucky had witnessed many times at Victor's, ending the meal and starting business. At Victor's, however, Lucky would quietly make his exit to wait upstairs for a recap of the conversation.

This time, he didn't move.

"I thought it best if we talked without Stephan overhearing." Nestor took a sip of his beer, eyes trained on Lucky's face.

If he expected Lucky to jump to Stephan's defense, he was in for a long wait. "I tend to agree."

"You don't trust him? Your own partner?"

"The partnership is his idea." Lucky would rather go into business with a palmetto bug.

"Then why are you here? What's in this for you?"

How much could Lucky say and expect to walk out of this mess with his and Bo's lives? "Let's just say he's offered me a deal I couldn't turn down."

"Oh, I see." And Nestor probably did. "So, your loyalties lie with..."

"Myself. As they always have."

Nestor let out a snort. "I think I know you better than that. You forget. I knew you when you were with Victor. I envied him your loyalty much as I envy you the loyalty of the man downstairs. Cyrus's trust is not easily won, I'm guessing, and neither is yours."

Anything Lucky said might be too much. He gave his reply with an unwavering gaze. What secrets did Nestor hope to uncover with his probing stare? In the end, Lucky shrugged.

"Victor only trusted a handful of men. Two sit at this table." Where was Nestor going with this conversation?

When Lucky stayed silent, Nestor continued, "I think, perhaps, I should trust you too. At least until you prove I can't. Now, recent States' legislation is cutting into profits, while the DEA is opening new doors."

Not what Lucky expected to hear. Apparently, he'd passed some kind of test. And it wasn't in his best interest to lose Nestor's trust, if he actually had it. "You brought me here to discuss legal pot? It's only a few states."

Again the disarming smile attempted to lull the unsuspecting. It might have worked on Lucky once upon a time. Possibly around age three. "Yes. And already I'm losing money, as are the other cartels."

"Hey, wasn't my fault. And there's not a damned thing I can do about it."

Nestor waved a dismissive hand. "It was only a matter of time. However, now I'm left with the need to diversify, find new ways to protect my profit margins."

"What's that got to do with me?"

"Stephan's proposal." The way he snarled "Stephan" left no doubt as to how little Nestor thought of the man, as if the earlier name calling wasn't clue enough. Lucky tended to agree. "We're here, where you can be totally honest with me. Don't say the words he put in your mouth."

It wouldn't do for Lucky to show too much of his hand just yet, or let on how much he'd learned. But he wasn't the only one capable of finding things out. "When have I ever said what someone else wanted me to?"

Nestor laughed, a deep, genuine sound. "I see why Victor liked you so much. You don't flatter, and you don't kiss up. You're your own man. I like that too. Now, in your time with the Southeastern Narcotics Bureau, what have you heard of a pure hydrocodone such as Stephan described?"

Lucky nearly dropped his beer. He fixed his eyes on Nestor's inquisitive gaze, seeing all he needed to. Nestor'd discovered how Lucky spent his last few years, and likely knew Lucky still drew an SNB paycheck. Hell, he probably knew what color boxers Lucky had on.

With any luck, he'd found jack shit on Bo.

The blast from Lucky's past ended their staring contest. "It's safest for you to assume you have no secrets from me and speak freely. Now, about the hydrocodone."

Lucky inhaled deeply to regain his composure. Nestor knew Lucky's background, and used intel for cash. Once spent, he'd not have it again. He wouldn't tell Stephan. Stephan wasn't worth the cost.

Might as well answer honestly. "The FDA just approved such a thing, in pill form." Pill form, but not tamper-resistant, like other easily abused painkillers, ratcheting up the potential for overdose.

The manufacturers might as well have offered powdered form, ready to snort or melt and shoot up.

And what did the US do? Make overdose kits like the one in the Jeep's glove box more readily available. Sometimes Lucky didn't understand his government.

Nestor rested his elbows on the table, steepling his fingers, the gesture so like Walter's, Lucky's heart ached for the mentor he'd known and trusted. And who possibly had been playing him all along. "And have his researchers actually managed to combine the properties of hydrocodone with the ability to remain undetectable during simple drug tests like his synthetic drug?"

Soon people would be dropping like flies and no one knowing why unless they really looked. "Yes."

"And he has buyers?"

"Yes. I met with some the other night in Brownsville."

A furrow appeared on Nestor's forehead. "What's the price point?"

"Cheaper than heroin. The US will never know what hit it."

"Do you remember the child downstairs begging for money?"

"Yeah." Vaguely.

"The boy and his father were on their way to the market and found themselves caught in the crossfire of two rival cartels. The child watched his father bleed to death on the sidewalk. And do you know why?"

The old man's eyes nearly pierced Lucky's soul. Lucky shook his head.

"Drugs. The US wants to blame the cartels, but you know who's at fault? There wouldn't be a supply without demand. Every American who's ever rolled up a dollar bill adds to the problem. Without demand, there'd be no need for us."

What? Nestor spoke against his own profession. The hypocrite. Or maybe he'd seen the errors of his ways.

"Too many lives have been lost. Too much blood spilled." Nestor seemed to be talking more to some unseen ghost than Lucky.

"You could always go legit." Lucky couldn't envision Nestor as anything other than a drug lord. "Or retire."

"Men in my line of work don't retire. When we get old, we're killed by someone who wants the life we're tired of living."

Somehow, Lucky couldn't see this man giving up without a fight. "Then go down swinging."

"I plan to. Is this product ready for shipment now?" Nestor didn't act like someone on the verge of investing an ass load of money. He might as well have been talking about the weather.

Lucky schooled the tremor from his voice. If Nestor and Stephan had their way, and he survived to tell the tale, soon the SNB would soon be battling a new enemy. "He's taken orders."

"Is this substance liquid or pill form?"

"All liquid, fast acting." Needle tracks in the men's arms. An OD kit in the truck. The man Lucky replaced that no one spoke of without crossing themselves. "He's testing on his own men."

"Who better? Although, personally, I have few in my employ I'd sacrifice in such a way."

Fuck. "Why are you so interested in something Stephan has? You're not seriously considering working with him, are you?"

"My friend, he's looking for investors. I'm looking to make a profit. This is business. If what he says is true, I want in on the action. With the DEA rescheduling certain narcotics, the market opens wide. And if Stephan has lied, well, as his nearest rival, I'd take it upon myself to see he doesn't lie again."

Nestor spoke calmly, as though a man's life—a lot of men's lives—didn't hang in the balance.

"And where do I fit in?" Lucky didn't understand chess, despite Victor's many attempts to teach him, but he felt a certain kinship to pawns.

The most dangerous man Lucky had ever met leaned in and nearly whispered, "Tell me, Lucky, what do you believe happened to Victor Mangiardi?"

Now true motives were coming out. If Nestor held Lucky responsible for testifying against a friend it'd be "*Adios*, Lucky!" With either nothing to lose or too much at stake, Lucky answered honestly. "The papers say he hung himself in his cell. But that doesn't sound like Victor. With his connections and his money, why didn't he make a deal?"

"Why, indeed. If Stephan is to be believed, his uncle did make a deal, much as you did."

"You don't believe him?"

"I have no reason to believe him. But Victor was a friend, and to have no contact with a friend for twelve years doesn't seem right, regardless of the reasons." Nestor tightened his hands into fists on the table, the knuckles turning white. He wasn't telling all he feared.

More than Mexican spices inspired the sinking feeling in Lucky's gut. "You don't believe he's alive."

"I don't believe he took his own life."

Should Lucky be happy or sad? Hell, he'd work out the details later. "Why?"

"Because if he made a deal for his freedom, they'd demand evidence against more than the pissants they arrested."

Hey! Lucky had given those names!

Nestor stared directly into Lucky's eyes. "If he really wanted someone's good graces, he'd have given them me."

"You don't think he'd protect you out of friendship?"

"If our roles were reversed, he'd expect no less of me."

Yes, trafficking was a pretty cutthroat business, with family members turning against each other to save their own skins.

And yet Lucky's testimony had helped put Victor behind bars to begin with.

Criminal minds must think alike. Nestor voiced Lucky's fear. "Your testimony didn't affect the outcome. Victor knew what was coming and took too much time getting out. And yes, he *was* in negotiations for a deal. Either way, he wouldn't have killed himself. He had too many plans for his retirement."

Negotiations for a deal? The Walter-meter swung back toward "guilty". Wait. What? "Retirement?" What the fuck? Victor never mentioned retiring to Lucky. Sure he'd been selling off properties, but he'd never mentioned leaving the business.

"He planned to pay one last business call on Rio before settling into a life of relative leisure traveling, maintaining his home base, and one legitimate business here."

"I didn't know." And yet, the Feds had found two tickets to Rio at Victor's arrest, and a doctored passport for Lucky, proving Victor intended to take Lucky with him.

For weeks building up to the arrest, Victor had acted strangely. Keeping secrets. Lucky had mentally packed his bags to make way for whoever else Victor wanted to move in. He'd never dreamed he'd meant enough to the man to be a part of his plans. "He knew the heat was coming and planned to get out first."

"Yes. He was concerned about you. He feared you wouldn't leave your family, even to save yourself."

A very good point. "Doesn't matter now." Lucky had lost his family and his self-respect all on the same day. Victor lost his freedom. And his life. Maybe. Possibly. Who the fuck knew at this point?

"Victor didn't do anything by half-measures, did he?" Again Nestor used past tense.

Lucky still being alive could only mean one thing: somehow he figured into Nestor's plans. "I still don't get where I fit into this."

"Stephan says he collected you at his uncle's request."

"What do you believe?"

"The little *pendejo* listens to no one but himself. If he chose now to bring you here, it's for his own purposes."

Chose now? "He only found out I was still alive a few months ago."

Again, a penetrating stare said Nestor knew more than he let on. "Don't think for a minute that I didn't know where you were at any given time. The men you handed over were careless, sloppy. You did me a personal favor in getting rid of them, and I have no grievances against you. But as a favor to Victor, I watched from afar and know more about you than Stephan does, *Mr. Harrison.*"

Lucky's proudest moment had to be not even blinking at Nestor's admission, though his heart slammed against his ribs. Nestor knew. Knew everything. He might not be the only one, but he was the most powerful. "Loyalty only goes so far. If you watched me, it's because there was something in it for you."

"I still haven't perfected my poker face with you, have I?" Nestor gave a little chuckle.

126

The cards were on the table. With no aces up Lucky's sleeve. "You're not afraid I'll go back to the US and turn on you?"

"For forty years, your country's authorities have wanted me." Nestor rolled his shoulders in a half-hearted shrug. "And yet here I am."

Damn. Why couldn't the bastard be a moron and walk into his own noose?

Nestor traded twinkling eyes for pursed lips and beetled brows. "I should warn you that Stephan has a lot of missing relatives."

"What do you mean?"

Nestor stared at his hands. After a moment he visibly relaxed. When he raised his gaze, determination gleamed in his eyes. "After Victor's arrest, the US government seized his properties there, and Stephan and his father came to Valle Hermoso. They evicted the tenants from Victor's house, fired his managers, and took over the factory themselves."

"Who were the tenants?"

"Victor's father had a mistress who bore him three children. Two boys and a girl. Victor allowed them to stay in the home."

Victor had half-brothers and a sister? "He never mentioned them."

"He worried for their safety, but make no mistake, he called the lady 'Mama' and paid for his sibling's education."

Steel bands loosened in Lucky's chest. "All this time, when he visited here, it was them he came to see, right?"

"Yes."

And each time Victor had left without taking Lucky had rankled. Fuck. Lucky would have liked to meet the family. That is, if they didn't treat him like dirt, as the rest of the Mangiardis did. "Why did Vincent toss them out?"

"He and Victoria never accepted their father's second family. Called the kids bastards. Victor cherished them." That was Victor. Family meant the world to him. A family, not orgies, had brought Victor to Mexico alone.

"But Vincent and Stephan stood to inherit, right?"

"Maybe. You see, a United States citizen cannot own property on Mexican soil in restricted areas, they can merely lease, which is why Victor's grandfather took a Mexican bride after his first wife died. Victor was born in Mexico City and held dual citizenship, Vincent and Stephan did not, so Victor inherited, and increased his wealth on both sides of the border. He left his American holdings to them and named other beneficiaries for Mexico."

And here Stephan had bragged for years about one day inheriting everything. "Who?"

"I cannot say, but I don't believe it was Vincent or Stephan. It couldn't be. And yet, though Vincent was half the businessman his brother was and preferred legitimate trade, he took control and eked out a living here. That is, until recently." Nestor stared at something on the far wall that Lucky couldn't see. "Money was getting tight, a few setbacks at the factory. Vincent started giving his son more and more leeway. Then six months ago, we had an appointment, Vincent and I. He never called or showed. Stephan sent apologies, saying his father had to leave suddenly to tend to his ailing sister."

Vincent and Victoria could both rot in Hell for all Lucky cared. They'd always sneered and looked down their noses whenever they'd visited, and even whined to Victor to kick Lucky out. Lucky finally resorted to escaping to his parents' house whenever they came to call—whenever they wanted money. Not a bit of love lost there.

"And you haven't heard from him since."

"No, I haven't. And in this day of cell phones and text messages, silence can only mean one thing."

Even Lucky wouldn't figure Stephan had enough balls to actually kill someone. "You think he killed his own father?"

"What do you believe? Vincent visited his warehouse on the border to find Stephan dealing in the kinds of merchandise he wouldn't touch. The hydrocodone project started as a way to provide inexpensive sedatives to the US, and turned into what you see now, created by unscrupulous men. And then... Vincent goes away." Nestor swept a hand out. "If Stephan has harmed him in any way, he'll pay. As a favor to Victor." Nestor downed the last of his beer.

Fuck. If what Nestor said was true, Stephan really had lost his damned mind. No telling what he might do.

What a hell of a lot to process. And now Lucky had to go back and face the bastard. He hadn't cared for Vincent, but he cared even less for Stephan. "What do you want me to do?"

"Do what you do so well, Mr. Lucklighter. Watch your back."

"Can I ask one more question?"

"You can ask. I can't promise an answer you'll like."

"If you knew where I was all these years, and left me alone for Victor's sake, why didn't anyone else take me out?"

"That's easy. One, you'd likely be a hard man to kill, and two, your life hinged on the outside chance Victor still lived. No one wanted to anger him. Plus, Walter Smith doesn't take insults lightly. To kill one of his people would be to write one's own death warrant."

Drug lords feared Walter Smith. Good to know. And added another layer to an already complex man.

"Now, if you'll excuse me, I have another appointment. Cruz will drive you home." Nestor rose from his chair.

"What about Stephan?"

"What about him?"

"The partnership?"

"While his inviting you into business makes the offer more palatable, tell him...I'm not yet persuaded."

Graciela waited at the bottom of the stairs, chatting with Bo. She laughed and patted her graying hair at something he said. Yeah, he had that effect on people, no matter in what language. Had them eating from his hand in no time flat.

"Graciela." Nestor motioned her over with a wave of his hand.

"¿Sí?" Her smile grew wider with each footstep.

He spoke quiet Spanish. Lucky understood "Stephan Mangiardi."

Thunderclouds wiped away the woman's smile. She spat and crossed herself. "Diablo!" she cried.

Now that's one Spanish word Lucky did know: Devil.

And he still hadn't gotten a yes. Nestor met and held Lucky's gaze. "If the dog proves rabid, put him down."

Lucky strode out the cantina door and snatched the keys from Cruz's hand in the parking lot.

"Hey!"

"Hey, yourself, you lowlife maggot!" Lucky grasped him by the shoulder, spun him around, and slammed him against the Jeep.

"Lucky, don't!" Bo grabbed Lucky's arm before he could swing his fist toward Cruz's mouth. "We need him. He's our link to Nestor and..." Bo whipped Lucky around to face half a dozen men, scowls on their faces and arms folded across their chests.

As pissed as he was, Lucky could take them all.

"No, Lucky." Bo put his lips close to Lucky's ear. "I've got a better idea."

Bo drove the Jeep while Lucky watched Cruz grow smaller and smaller in the side mirror. The son of a bitch could find his own way home. "Now, you gonna tell me what Nestor said?"

Lucky's anger still needed a target. Where was a gym when he needed one? "Lots of talk that went nowhere. I think the old man's lonely for someone else who knew Victor. I also think he was feeling me out."

"Why?"

"I don't know, but I probably won't like the answer."

CHAPTER TWELVE

"What is this?" Lucky scowled at the tinfoil package on the seat of the Kenworth, warm to the touch.

"Your admirer sent you cheese tamales." Cruz grinned a bit wider than necessary.

"What the fuck?" Lucky glared over his shoulder. Alejandro waved and hopped into the Jeep, keeping him away from Lucky for a while.

Bo climbed in the truck. "Oh, something smells good. What you got there?"

"Tamales," Cruz said, taunting Lucky with a smirk. If he said one more word... Lucky liked Cruz even less now that he spoke English. And still owed him an ass-whooping over the Nestor deal.

"Oh, I'm hungry. Didn't feel like eating much this morning." Bo grabbed the tinfoil.

Lucky hadn't either, what with Stephan shooting daggers at him and Bo with his eyes over the breakfast table.

"There's no meat in there, right?" Bo sniffed.

"Cheese and chilis," Cruz replied.

Lucky said, "Help yourself."

Bo peeled back a corn husk to take a bite. "Oh, damn, that's good. Who made these?"

"Alejandro did." No telling what kind of cook Alejandro was. Never in a million years would Lucky admit why the man made them, that is, if Cruz told the truth.

"Tell him thanks, these are great!" Bo grabbed another tamale.

About halfway to the warehouse, Lucky's hunger got the best of him. He ventured a bite of tamale. Oh, hell yeah! At least he'd managed to attract another good cook.

Lucky schlepped cases to keep from losing his mind while waiting for the crew to unload the truck. Bo, or rather Cyrus, stood shirtless at the top of the tunnel shaft, shouting orders down to the workers, most of whom had also abandoned their shirts before disappearing underground.

One wolf whistle out of Alejandro and Lucky put his T-shirt back on. He shivered, even in the heat, watching Bo hovering over the tunnel's entrance.

Brrr. No fucking way would Lucky get close to the tunnel again. Once was enough. How the hell did the guys stand being down in the belly of the earth, when a collapse could happen at any moment? Hell, they'd probably worked in the old tunnel before the cave in.

Bo trudged across the concrete floor to pull a water bottle out of a cooler sitting on the tailgate of one of the Jeeps. "Want one?"

Lucky nodded.

"Here you go." Lucky ran a forefinger over Bo's palm while taking the water. The hardness in Bo's eyes gave no indication of familiarity. Sometimes he played his role too well, getting lost in being Cyrus Cooper and stuffing Bo Schollenberger deep down inside.

"*Jefe! Jefe!*" Rafael popped out the tunnel entrance and barreled toward Bo.

Lucky recognized the word "boss." The men never called Bo "boss," they called him Cyrus. Must be trouble. Oh shit! Boss! Stephan better not hear those words.

Rafael grabbed Bo's hand and tugged him toward the tunnel.

"Lucky!" Bo shouted. "Go get the kit."

Oh damn.

Lucky dove for Bo's discarded shirt and fished the syringe box out of the pocket while racing toward the tunnel. Bo joined Rafael to man the pulley and raised the platform out of the hole in the ground. Juan lay still on the platform, Alejandro at his side.

Bo hoisted the still form onto the concrete floor while dropping to his knees. Two fingers at Juan's neck, he lowered his head, ear positioned over the victim's nose. "Weak pulse, labored breath." He pried an eyelid open. "Lucky, give me the kit."

Lucky tore open an alcohol wipe while Cruz jerked Juan's pants down. Bo grabbed the wet gauze pad, made a cursory swipe over Juan's thigh, and plunged the needle home. He sat back on his haunches.

Several times he checked his patient, while the Garcias and Cruz looked on. Juan opened his eyes and blinked hard a few times. Bo *whoosh*ed out a breath. Alejandro grinned and clapped him on the back.

"Cruz?" Bo's shorter shadow stepped up. Bo spoke to him a few moments. Cruz and the Garcias carried Juan to the Jeep, settled him in, and Cruz pulled the Jeep from the building and out of sight.

Bo watched them leave, arm around Lucky to guide him out of hearing range of the men. "He's going to the hospital. The shot only works for about an hour. He could be okay, but better to be safe."

"What would Stephan say about your heroics?"

"I don't give a flying fuck what that shithead thinks. A man's life is at stake. That means something to me." Bo pounded his chest with one hand. If Stephan walked in the building right then, Bo might have torn him apart. "I'm tired of that son of a bitch and his doctors playing God with people's lives."

Lucky's breath hitched at the sight of pure loathing painted across Bo's face. "We need to find all the dirt there is on the useless piece of shit and take care of business. Otherwise, I'm going to take a gun and put him out of everyone's misery." Bo whirled and stalked off, barking orders at the crew hovering by the second Jeep.

Dread pooled in Lucky's stomach.

That night, sleep wouldn't come. He could spend another night staring at the ceiling or brace the door and drink the damned juice.

Just once couldn't hurt. Could it?

***

Cruz drove the Jeep, with Bo and Lucky in back. Lucky drove his foot nearly through the floorboard. The asshole got a little crazy, fishtailing and screeching tires for no apparent reason. They left the road completely to kick up a dust cloud. Cruz spun a doughnut in the sand, grinning like an idiot all the time.

"It's his favorite pastime," Bo remarked in casual tones when an aggressive spin slammed him full force into Lucky. "Fucking with the gringos."

Lucky leaned up to eyeball Cruz. "You're pissed because of Texas, ain't ya? Well, I personally don't have a dog in that fight. Mexico can have the whole damned state back."

Cruz grinned wider and gunned the gas. Asshole.

Bo pressed his leg more firmly against Lucky's and gave him a 'pick your battles' glare. "He's upset over what happened to Juan. So am I. He may be Nestor's man, but he cares about the guys. We all have our own ways of dealing with things when we feel helpless. Cut him some slack and don't take it personal."

Yeah, right. If the shit hit the fan with Stephan, Cruz might, just might, get word to Nestor. Who'd do who knew what? Oh yeah, nothing screwed up about this operation. Nothing at all. And if it came right down to it, Cruz would probably tell Stephan all he wanted to know about Lucky to save his own skin. As long as he had Bo's back...

Lucky grabbed an "oh shit" handle that'd seen one "oh shit" too many—yeah, he was a wimp—and stared out the window at low-growing scrub and dusty plains. Walter had said there was no deal and insisted Victor was dead. But could Walter be trusted?

Nestor believed Victor and Vincent both dead and said a deal had been in the works. But could Nestor be trusted?

Graciela claimed Stephan Mangiardi was the devil. Now, *her* Lucky believed.

Cruz ran into the house the moment they arrived. "How do you say 'weasel' in Spanish?" Lucky huffed under his breath.

"*Comadreja*," Bo replied as he breezed on past. "But since he speaks English, I vote to keep calling him weasel." Instead of the house, Bo headed for his big, black Harley Road King, so out of place amidst the hodgepodge of cars, most of which screamed, "laborer." The last time Lucky set eyes on a pickup so dilapidated and rusted out, it had rested on cinder blocks in his grandfather's pasture.

He stepped double-time to match Bo's longer strides. "Will I see you tonight?"

"This morning Stephan said he'd see me tomorrow. It was an order." More softly Bo said, "Take care of yourself. If you need me, you know where to find me."

Yeah, right. Like Stephan would hand over the keys to his Jag.

The bookend brothers slithered into the truck cab while the other men piled into the bed.

Bo fired up the Harley, adjusted his shades, and took off in a cloud of dust without a backward glance—or a helmet. But given where they were, and the men bouncing around in the back of a truck, he'd have marked himself as a wuss for obeying Georgia law. Damn, and Lucky had hundreds of questions to ask without Cruz's eager ears, now that he knew the bastard understood.

The truck drove right into Bo's dust. Lucky could stand in the yard and cough, or go into the house.

He took a deep breath and stared at the door. Stephan likely waited inside. Cruz opened the door and trotted out, flashing a wide grin before climbing into a late model Toyota.

He should be sitting in the back of the truck. Then maybe the brothers would hit a bump, and he'd fly out.

The door beckoned. Lucky approached his doom.

"Diablo" didn't meet him at the door, so he traipsed down the hallway to his room. Spending half the day with clothes sticking to him left him with the need for a shower.

He stepped from the bathroom to find Stephan Mangiardi lounging in a chair by the bed, and promptly returned for a towel. One Mangiardi ogling his junk was enough for this lifetime, and Stephan seemed to be making this a habit.

One deep breath. Then another. Lucky braved entering his room. "Like what you saw?"

"I'm still trying to figure out why my uncle kept you around so many years." Stephan stretched like a lazy cat. The black and white tuxedo kitty at Lucky's house deserved better than being compared to this piece of shit. Maybe Stephan was a rat. And please let Mrs. Griggs be looking out for Cat Lucky.

"He called me 'restful.'"

"Restful? Angry badgers are more restful."

Possibly, but being surrounded by scorpions all day warped a man's mind. To most, Victor presented too much danger to offer any peace, and yet, Lucky had found him restful too. In a way. He didn't bullshit or talk in circles. Like Lucky, he spoke his mind. "Are you here for a reason?"

"Now, now. Is that the way to treat the man giving you a fresh start?"

"Fresh? Smells like shit to me. You conk me on the head, drug my ass, and haul me down to some God-forsaken place that ain't even got decent trees. Then expect me to work for you without money, a car, or even my own place."

Instead of recoiling, Stephan smiled. "I think I may see what Uncle Victor wanted with you after all. No matter how outmatched you are, you never give up fighting, do you?" He swung one pant-clad leg over the arm of the chair. While everyone in his employ wore the clothes of a working man,

Stephan decked himself out like he'd somewhere important to go—and those loafers hadn't come cheap.

"If your uncle wants to talk to me, he can damn well do it himself. So you can get the hell out of this room or let me go."

The smile fled Stephan's face. "Don't think for a minute that Uncle Victor hasn't replaced you twelve times over in the past twelve years. I believe you recall that he liked his fucks young."

Yes, he did. And many a time Lucky had heard wagers of how long Victor would keep him around once he'd hit twenty-five. Back then, deep down, each whisper cut straight to his heart.

Now? Everything he needed rode off on a motorcycle about a half hour ago. "I'm my own man, always have been, always will be. I knew that, Victor knew that. Either one of us was free to go whenever we wanted to."

"But you've not been lonely, have you?" The smile returned, a twisted, oily thing, suitable for back alley drug dealers with a knife aimed at your back. "He's a bit rough around the edges, but I like Cyrus Cooper's dangerous edge." Stephan exaggerated a shiver.

"Yeah, I'm surprised he hasn't cut out your liver yet and eaten it for breakfast or fed it to a dog."

Stephan barked a laugh. "Tell me, how can a man as hard as Cyrus be a vegetarian?"

Some people just begged to be messed with. "He had to eat a man once."

Ah, what a lovely shade of green. Stephan's grin vanished. "He what?"

Think, man, think! "You heard me. He went hiking. Has he mentioned that he likes to hike?"

"He has."

"Did he tell you about the avalanche out in Wyoming?" They did have avalanches in Wyoming, right? "Well, his buddy died instantly, but out there, cut off for days, he could have starved to death if he hadn't..."

Stephan held out a hand, looking greener by the minute. Gullible wuss. "I get the picture."

Oh hell no. The bastard wasn't getting off easy. "You gotta be careful, 'cause sometimes he has flashbacks, ya know? You might wake up with his teeth in you." Lucky winked. "Gotta keep him away from the tender bits, if you get my drift. That's what he ate first. Easier to chew off without a knife, he says."

Well, from the way Stephan's Adam's apple bobbed, he might be on the verge of losing his lunch, and any plans to seduce Bo just got waylaid. Nice. Only Stephan would fall for this shit. For a man in his forties who ran a huge drug ring under the guise of a legal business, he was still such a child at times.

And this man might have killed his own father? Why? The Stephan of twelve years ago was a boot licker, groveling at the feet of the rich, powerful Victor Mangiardi, and a sharp bark from Vincent brought the dog to heel.

If Lucky could get away tonight, he already had enough charges on Stephan to put him away for a while, but not permanently. He needed to find a dead body. The way to do that was to win the bastard's trust. Trust was for wimps. Thank God, Stephan fit the bill.

"Actually, I'm here to remind you what you stand to lose." Stephan's smirk promised no good.

"What do you mean by that?" The only thing he stood to lose was Bo.

"You'll find out soon enough."

Lucky had a bigger cell than the last time he'd been imprisoned. With a nice bed, a Jacuzzi, and a chair shoved under the door handle. And no way to get word to Walter, if he'd even wanted to.

Charlotte. Up in Spokane. His anchor. When he got out of this mess, he'd quit procrastinating, go see her and the boys.

Surely his nephews were old enough by now to understand why their uncle wasn't really dead.

Richmond Eugene Lucklighter. Faking death and changing his name to Simon "Lucky" Harrison hadn't prevented Nestor from finding him anyway. Why did Walter even bother with the whole process if he'd been sharing information with the enemy? Nothing made sense.

Lucky gazed into the dresser mirror at the rich furnishings of his room, then at himself.

"I'm Richmond Eugene Lucklighter." His reflection agreed. Yes. If he ever got out of here, damn Simon Harrison. He'd use the name his parents had given him. No evil stalking him came close to the Mangiardi family. He didn't belong here any more than he had in Victor's home or life. Where did he belong?

In a cabin in the woods, next to a river. With Bo.

"I'm here to remind you what you stand to lose."

Lucky would tear Stephan apart with his bare hands if he harmed Bo in any way.

The doorknob turned and he whirled, grabbing the letter opener again as he hit the light switch. Damn but he needed better weapons. That bastard Stephan better not think of invading Lucky's space. "Go away and leave me the fuck alone."

Years ago Stephan had harassed Lucky at every opportunity. *"What's the difference between one dick and another in the dark?"* he'd asked.

"The dick it's attached to," Lucky always answered.

The handle stopped turning and footsteps led away from the door.

CHAPTER THIRTEEN

Once again Stephan sat on Lucky's bed when he came out of the shower. Screw it. He didn't even bother with a towel, he merely grabbed a pair of jeans and slid them on commando. Bastard must have gotten in through the window. "Do you want something?"

Stephan rubbed a hand over his crotch. "I might."

Fuck no. "Something you stand a snowball's chance in Hell of getting?"

"Nestor called. He's still considering my offer of an interest in the new product line in exchange for protection and backing."

What kind of game was Nestor playing? "So?"

Stephan smile appeared strained. "You're a condition of our association. He refuses to deal with me. Only you. And I need his backing to keep the supply route open between the factory and the border. Others want their share of the take."

Ah, so it wasn't only Stephan's drugs Nestor intended to protect. One day, if they met on opposite sides of the law, Lucky might have a problem. At the moment, with Bo at stake, he'd worry about tomorrow when it got here. "You're testing on Cyrus. I want it stopped."

"Only a low dose. I know you think I'm stupid, but I wouldn't risk my foreman."

"I don't care. I want it stopped. Now. I won't have someone in charge that I can't trust. And I can't trust him if he's high."

Nestor's backing gave Lucky courage. He stalked over to the bed. Stephan flinched but wiped the fear from his face.

141

"Nestor'll only deal with me? Good! 'Cause I only deal with Cyrus. If anything happens to him, I'm leaving, got it?"

He didn't give the man time to answer. He jerked the chair from under the doorknob and strode out of the room before he put his fist through a face way too much like Victor's.

Jaime set one of his boxes down on a cart and turned an ashen face to Lucky. He swayed on his feet and grabbed Lucky's shoulder.

"Jaime, buddy? You okay?" Lucky shifted the case he carried to one side to wrap an arm around the suddenly limp man. Crap. Lucky dropped the box to ease Jaime to the floor. "Cyrus! Cy, get over here!"

Bo came running. "What's wrong?"

"It's Jaime."

Bo dropped to his knees and took over, rolling Jaime onto his back. Sweat sheened the worker's face. He pushed Bo away, turned over onto his hands and knees, and threw up.

Lucky jumped back while Alejandro rushed forward with a bottle of water.

Bo made eye contact over Alejandro's bent back. "Withdrawals."

No, a threat from Stephan.

The shit had gone on long enough. If Stephan wanted to send messages, he needed to talk, not harm his own workers. Lucky entered the house on a mission. Time to act like a full partner if that's what it took to protect the men. No more Stephan calling the shots.

"Why couldn't you just listen to me?" Stephan's angry shout echoed through the house.

What the hell? Lucky stopped his stomping and crept toward

the far end of the hall. If Stephan planned to beat up his latest boy toy, he'd have to go through Lucky first. Hell, if the man even shouted at the cook, Lucky would kick his ass.

"None of this would have happened if you'd have listened to me. But no! You knew best. You always knew best, you arrogant son of a bitch."

Stephan's bedroom door stood partially open. Lucky flattened himself against the wall and peered inside.

"It's all your fault! You made me do it!"

Lucky maneuvered to see more of the room.

The room was empty, except for Stephan. Not good.

If the dog is rabid, put him down.

And if Lucky simply slunk off back to the border, no telling what would happen to the guys he was becoming dangerously attached to. Fuck Bo's "learn their names" crap. But Jaime was a good hard worker who never complained. He didn't deserve to roll in the dust puking his guts out, like Juan didn't deserve to nearly die of an overdose.

The kitchen was deserted, so he helped himself to a butcher knife and crept back down to his room. He shoved a chair under the doorknob, secured the window, and downed his nightcap. A few hours. A few hours to escape this nightmare. That's all he asked. And a gun. Or a rabies shot. He slept with the knife clutched in his fist.

Stephan appeared bright-eyed at breakfast, though a young man limped from his room. "Today is a big day," he announced.

Lucky took the bait. "Why's that?"

"Today we begin shipping the Codopure."

Oh shit. Shoulda put him down last night.

But...the bigger Stephan's operation grew, the more attention he'd draw. And without Nestor's support, sooner or later, someone would notice.

CHAPTER FOURTEEN

The men lugged cartons all day, unknowing or uncaring what they now hauled over the border. Alejandro fussed like a mother hen over Jaime, and no longer smiled while he worked. Bo crawled down inside of himself, too, barely speaking but to give directions.

Cruz worked the pulley like a man possessed, lost in his own thoughts.

The gloom and doom vibe followed them into the evening.

Wary eyes met Lucky's over the dinner table. Bo divided his attention between Stephan and Lucky, mumbling all the while to Cruz.

Stephan strutted and preened. All his little deranged dreams were coming true, until Bo and Lucky got a chance to form a plan.

The normal glass of juice sat on the nightstand. Lucky was through taking chances but still needed sleep. He pulled out the bottle he'd taken from the warehouse and an individual serving of orange juice he'd snagged from the local store with the meager pocket money Stephan doled out. Enough cash to keep him fed, but not enough to leave on.

Juan hadn't come back to work and Jaime was a bit shaky, and the remaining men had to take up the slack. Lucky and Bo didn't need a gym to keep fit—they worked their asses off hauling boxes down to the open tunnel for the brothers to push across the border on carts. They needed the closed tunnel open again. Its rail system would make their lives so much easier.

"Tired" didn't come close to describing how Lucky felt. If he didn't get a good night's sleep, he just might find a bridge to jump off.

"In the field, you do what you must," he heard his boss say. But first to bar the door and latch the window.

He took a dose with the juice, not enough to addle him, but enough to get some rest. "You do what you gotta," he toasted himself and settled beneath the covers. This probably wasn't what Walter had in mind.

"You arrogant bastard!" penetrated Lucky's drug-aided sleep. What the fuck? Pants half on, he hopped down the hallway to Stephan's office, tugging up the denim. He stopped short.

"What gives you the right—" A resounding slap cut off Stephan's words.

"Shut up. Listen!" another voice shrieked.

Stephan's fuck of the evening stood trembling in the hallway, with a fat tear rolling down his face. "Please, *señor,*" he said in heavily accented English. "I want to go home. Please take me home. Don't let those men find me here."

The unmistakable click of a gun cocking reached Lucky's ears. Yeah, take the kid home. Good idea. He'd hotwire a car if he had to. "Which way?"

The boy—not a boy, but younger than most of Lucky's socks—grabbed Lucky's arm and pulled him in the opposite direction.

A shout of "Now wait a damned minute you—" from the office hastened his steps. Whoever and whatever went on in there, Lucky wanted no part of it.

"Who's in there?" he asked.

Frightened eyes stared back at him. "I don't know. They don't like him"—the kid nodded toward the office—"and want him gone. Or for him to give them money."

Yeah, sooner or later opportunists were bound to show up. Nestor needed to either piss or get off the pot with this partnership deal. Promises weren't helping.

In a moment of calm, bawling tires rent the night. Anguished cries froze Lucky's blood. "Aureo!" The gates squealed open. Not good at this hour.

The boy's eyes widened. "Come!" He darted down a hallway Lucky hadn't seen before. Lucky followed his guide out a side door.

Both Jeeps skidded to stop in the courtyard, barely missing the sobbing guard. He knelt beside a bloody lump, illuminated in two sets of headlights. "Aureo!" the man cried again.

The front door slammed. Two men sauntered across the yard. They didn't display guns, they didn't have to. One look said they were forces to be reckoned with. One stalked up, kicked the body, and spat on the guard.

Cruz and Bo jumped from the Jeeps. Oh shit. Now was not the time for heroics. Lucky darted toward Bo. The kicker got right up in Bo's face. Oh, hell the fuck no. Lucky charged. His tackle knocked the man back into the dirt.

"You will pay for that, my friend," the man shouted.

"Put it on my tab." Lucky pulled back his fist and let fly.

The man's head snapped back. Hands grabbed him, but Lucky fought. About time he got to do something other than sit around with his thumb up his ass, waiting for the right time to make a bust. He swung, but a pair of arms held him tighter than iron bands. "No, Lucky. Now's not the time." Bo tightened his grip.

The man stood, dusted himself off, and marched out of the gate to a waiting car, clutching his jaw. He pulled a knife from his pocket and reached down to something tied to the bumper. A rope. From the bumper to the bloody lump's leg. Oh, dear God. He sneered. "A warning."

Two door slams later, the car pulled away.

"Lucky!" Stephan snarled from the porch. "I don't care if you have to suck his dick, get Nestor on board. Now!" He waved a hand at the man lying in the yard. "And...get rid of that!" His heels clicked when he whirled and ran back in the house. Coward.

"Aureo, Aureo," the guard moaned.

Oh fuck it all. Lucky dove to the man's side. Dark eyes stared at him and blinked. "B... Cyrus! This man's still alive."

Bo joined him on the ground, shoving his fingers into Aureo's neck and leaning down to listen to his chest. He straightened. "We have to get him to a hospital, now. Cruz! I need you!"

Lucky looked for an undamaged body part to grab and help haul the guy up. Parts of Aureo's leg stuck out that shouldn't have.

"Here, let me." Bo scooped the man up like he weighed nothing and bustled him to the first Jeep.

"I'm coming too." Lucky climbed into the back, sinking to the floorboard to give the injured man room on the seat.

"Ride up front," Bo said. "He needs me back here in case something goes wrong."

Lucky further broke the already broken "oh shit" handle when Cruz took off.

"What happened?" Bo's voice was a faint murmur over the roar of the engine.

"Two men paid Stephan a call. Stephan's latest boy toy..." Crap. The kid! Surely someone took him home. No sense worrying now. The other Jeep followed, no doubt carrying the distraught guard. A lot of folks 'round these parts seemed to be kin.

"How did you happen to be here?" Lucky glanced from Bo to Cruz and back again.

Bo stiffened. "After I left here, I got word that two guys grabbed Aureo out of a bar. Cruz and I went looking. We were coming back when we saw the car—" Bo made a retching noise. "We saw the car dragging something. It wasn't 'til it pulled up at Stephan's that we saw what."

There were at least three people in the car. Three asses Lucky owed a stomping.

"Lucky?"

"Yeah?"

"What do you remember of CPR?"

Lucky slipped between the seats to the back. "One-one

148

thousand." Hands laced together, he compressed Aureo's chest. Bones crackled under his hands.

"Easy," Bo said. "At thirty, stop and I'll breathe."

After five minutes, they switched off. Bo murmured, "Hang in there, buddy."

Aureo didn't answer. Thank God. If Lucky had a syringe full of Stephan's magic elixir, he'd have dosed the man. In the low light of the Jeep's interior light, he gazed at a bloody mess of a face, scraped arms and legs, muscles showing in places through tattered clothes. This man's life would never be the same—if he lived.

"One and two!" Bo bobbed up and down in the back seat, fighting for a man he barely knew.

"One and two!'

Bo stopped, and Lucky delivered two breaths. *Breathe, damn it, breathe!*

In a blur they worked. Cruz stopped the Jeep and other hands took over. A solemn doctor delivered the news with a shake of his head.

Bo would have been howling about the injustice of it all and mourning the loss of a friend. Instead, Cyrus stared with dry eyes at the sheet-covered gurney. No emotion. Nothing at all showed on his face. "Let's go home."

"I can't. If I go back to Stephan's tonight, I might just beat him to death."

Another death racked up to Stephan's indifference, added to the unfortunate Hector and the nameless man Lucky had found in an Atlanta apartment. And Mateo Reyes, and possibly Vincent Mangiardi. How many more had to die? They should take what intel they'd gathered and call the case done. But if they did, chances were Stephan would track them down or run. That couldn't happen. The man needed to pay for his crimes.

Bo placed an arm around Lucky's tired shoulders. Chest compressions made one hell of a workout. A living Aureo would make another ten hours of spaghetti arms worth the effort.

"Then come home with me. We need to talk. Cruz can drop us off and pick us up in the morning."

In the future, a showdown with Stephan loomed. Not tonight. Not on too little sleep and too much adrenaline letdown. "Good idea." An hour or so in Bo's arms wouldn't erase the horror of the night, but it sure as hell beat an hour or so *not* in Bo's arms.

"No gloves, no mask, and blood all over us. Our first responder coach would have our asses." Bo led the way into his living area. He kicked aside a chair by the sink to expose the drain set directly in the floor. He turned the taps in the sink and pulled out a handheld shower nozzle. "Get your clothes off. We need soap and water."

No curtains, no door. The best Lucky could hope for was not to splash the bed. Bo held the sprayer up, soaked him down, and handed him a bar of soap. At least the thin gray sliver smelled nice. Rusty water ran down Lucky's body from the blood he'd smeared from his hands to his face. He lathered himself up with his fingers, then worked soap onto Bo's lightly furred chest.

Bo exhaled slowly. The day's stress couldn't have been easy. Bo had cared for Aureo, like he did for any man working with him. If not for Bo, Lucky would have just called him Shorty and not bothered to learn anything about him to keep a professional distance. But the distance Lucky tried to maintain didn't lessen the heartache. A man who'd had a life and people who loved him died tonight. Lucky didn't get close to folks for a reason. One way or another, caring led to pain.

"How well did you know the guy?"

"Not very. The guard's his brother. His wife is eight months pregnant with their third child." Bo let out another ragged breath. "They killed a man horribly to send a message. A motherfucking message!" He grabbed the soap and hurled the bar across the room. It bounced back to land at his feet. "And then Stephan wants us to *get rid of that*! Sometimes I hate the human race."

Join the club. Lucky hated most humans most of the time. "I need you to promise me something."

"What?"

"Promise me we'll never have a night like this one again." Lucky didn't bother drying off. He hobbled over to the bed, dripping wet.

He awoke in the night to the sound of gentle sobs. Without a word, he wrapped himself around his lover. Together they'd mourn the fallen man.

Lucky studied Nestor with new eyes. Like Stephan, he held the power of life or death in his hands. What was it like to say the word and a man died or lived?

"A man was dragged to death last night, as a warning to Stephan."

"And what do you want me to do?" Nestor cocked his head to the side.

The son of a bitch had to ask? "Make it stop."

"Make what stop? The death? The threats? Stephan?"

"All of the above."

"Done."

Wait! What? "Just like that. All this time you haven't given an answer and now you say yes. Why?"

"Because you asked for someone other than yourself and Stephan. I do believe Victor would be proud. I merely waited until you asked me for help and meant it."

Sorry bastard. "You're as bad as Stephan."

Nestor jerked upright in his chair. He brought his fist crashing down on the table. Knives and forks clattered. "Do not ever, ever compare me to such a monster. You think you know me. You know nothing."

Drug dealer, money launderer, cartel kingpin, murderer, either directly or indirectly, if anyone who'd ever taken the poison Nestor sold fatally overdosed.

Nestor dropped his voice to conversational level. "If you don't like Stephan, and don't agree with his leadership, take it."

What the fuck? "What do you mean, 'take it'?"

Nestor leaned across the table, fixing Lucky with his unblinking, soul-dark stare. "Exactly what I said. His men have no love for him. No loyalty. He looks down on them. They're coming to respect you and Cyrus."

"I could never..."

"Maybe not alone, but with Cyrus at your side, you'll have a loyal force. He won't back down from a challenge, and neither will you. You forget, I've played poker with you. The fact you stayed with Victor so long speaks of your strength."

"I wasn't born to this life." Lucky waved a hand, meant to include Nestor's organization and not the cantina where they sat. "I'm a farmer's son from North Carolina."

"And an accident of birth made me the son of a marijuana smuggler. An accident of death made me his heir." Nestor heaved out a sigh, his years etched into his face. "I was an art student. Doted on by my mother and sent to the States to further my education. No need for me to learn the family business, with three older brothers already working for my father." His eyes clouded. He blinked the sorrow away, forming his face into an unreadable mask. "I was away at school when I heard the news. An upstart, very much like Stephan, killed my father and brothers."

He paused from sipping his beer, lips twisted with bitterness. Lines deepened around his mouth and eyes. "I gave up my dreams and returned home, to head my family. I meted out justice." He sipped again.

Meted out justice. The closest he'd likely come to a murder confession. And here Lucky'd considered Nestor born to violence and shady deals. He'd seemed such a relentless man at times, yet he'd relaxed when he'd been a guest at Victor's home.

"Then I married a wealthy, powerful man's daughter. He offered to back me. Together we conquered our rivals. In the end my only son was used against me. His killers paid for his death. His mother's madness I couldn't avenge. She killed herself."

Lucky watched the man's hand encircling a beer bottle. An artist's hands, not a killer's. And yet, when he'd had to, he hadn't shrunk back, and spoke so casually of loss of life. Nestor wasn't given a choice. Lucky had chosen his own wrong path. "I'm sorry." Didn't happen often, but what could he do?

"I don't dwell on what I can't change. I focus on what I can. Our marriage was arranged, but in time my wife and I grew to be...friends. I miss her wise advice. And she gave me my boy."

No talk of love. Lucky's parents had disowned him, yet they'd clung to one another, even if Daddy didn't often say the word "love." He'd showed it often enough, a bunch of wild-flowers picked from a field. A heated gaze. A kiss as he headed out the door.

"What about your art?"

"I still paint sometimes, as a hobby. It helps me deal with my life. I believe you've seen my greatest work."

"Mama Mangiardi." The painting in Lucky's room. The one Victor had cherished and fought his siblings for. He'd only been three when his mother died. Perhaps he'd valued the work as much for the artist as the subject.

"A gift for Victor's twentieth birthday, painted from an old photo. To hide our relationship, I presented the painting to the family."

"You were lovers."

"A long time ago. He had to hide who he was here. His grandfather and father didn't deal heavily in illicit trade, but on occasion needed my brokerage services. I took young Victor under my wing." He shrugged. "As I've heard you Americans say, 'Shit happens.'"

Yeah, shit happened sometimes. The men Victor took to his bed when Lucky wasn't around hadn't bothered him much, and he'd never mentioned having ever been in love. The wistful way he'd studied the painting sometimes and even raised a glass of brandy in toast made sense now.

Instead of jealousy, the truth about Nestor inspired kinship. "He loved you."

"I like to think so. I believe you might call it 'puppy love.' I taught him how to be ruthless. But I also taught him respect for Mexican culture. Together we toured museums, attended plays. And when his father died, I helped him establish himself and redefine his business. Mostly in the States. He kept himself above reproach here."

"He trafficked illegal drugs."

"But he wasn't violent and didn't join in the power struggles. He wanted to protect his family. He'd have done anything for his family." Nestor would likely defend Victor to the death. Maybe the love went both ways.

Nestor rubbed at his eyes with a fingertip. "He grew into a truly great man. Merciless when he needed to be, yet still loving and patient. His business didn't define him as it does so many others. Victor never lost touch with who he was. Even I've strayed on occasion." Lucky swallowed back against the lump forming in his throat. Nestor spoke fondly of Victor. Yes, there'd been true feelings between them.

"And you don't believe he's alive."

"Do you see him here?" Nestor's hand wave did indicate the cantina. "I believe he loved you as much as he did me, if not more. If he was here, he'd ask me to watch over you, help you. For an old friend, I do this."

Nestor offered what few could refuse. After all, for years Lucky had learned from Victor, though not everything. Nestor could fill in the gaps. *What the fuck am I thinking? I'm a narcotics agent, not a drug lord.* Another agent who'd disappeared and been presumed dead came to mind. On a later raid the man turned up, alive and well, running his own smuggling ring. Sometimes the lure of money and power became too much to ignore.

While undercover, Lucky met with similar temptations: flashy cars, pockets full of cash. In the end, he traded in high dollar living for his ancient Camaro and rented duplex. With the kind of money to be made down here, he could afford to build Bo a mansion instead of rooting around for a decent fixer-upper.

And yet, even without the threat of the SNB hunting him down, he couldn't. "That's a kind offer, but I can't."

Nestor patted his hand. "I know. Victor always said your big heart would be the ruin of you. But you want Stephan to pay for his sins. I understand, and I'll help in any way I can."

"Thanks." Lucky stood from the table to end their meeting. Time to tear Stephan down.

"Lucky?"

"Yeah?"

"Make no mistake. I loved Victor too. I regret never telling him so."

Victor, running gentle fingers over an oil-painted canvas. His excitement when he announced an old friend coming to visit. The way he'd encouraged Lucky and Nestor to get to know one another and smiled when Lucky met with Nestor's approval.

"He knew."

CHAPTER FIFTEEN

The holes in Bo's arm needed to go. And take his pissy-ass attitude with them. "What?" he shouted when Lucky glared. The strutting, the bravado, all Cyrus, times ten. No sign of Bo. At least until the four p.m. crash and burn. And if they stayed out late, a bad case of the shakes.

What a fucking old cycle. How much of it was real? Stephan said he'd given Bo a low dose. Yet, Stephan and the truth didn't often travel hand in hand.

Oh, for five minutes alone with the dickhead from Hell. A hammer to the head. Running over him with Daddy's tractor. Using him for target practice. The man needed killing.

Meeting buyers across the border, handing out samples, some at fancy restaurants, others in clubs or even back alley locations. Those things didn't belong in the life Lucky had spent the last twelve years building for himself. Twelve years of keeping his nose clean, tossed down the tubes by Stephan Fucking Mangiardi.

Stephan walked ahead, out of earshot. Cruz stayed with the cars. Once more they entered the steakhouse to meet with upscale dealers who resembled accountants more than street pushers.

The meeting went as all others before. Men in business suits scrutinized reports, asked the same old questions, transferred money into accounts.

The meal ended, and the men rose from their seats, Bo carrying a takeout tray for Cruz. He passed the Styrofoam to Lucky and smiled. "Excuse me, I see an old friend."

Stephan dipped his chin and kept walking, busy chatting with his new customers. Lucky paused. Who had Bo seen? Bo

157

approached a table, body hiding the occupants. He hugged a woman in greeting, her face appearing over Bo's shoulder.

Loretta Johnson.

Halla-fucking-lujah.

"You still haven't told me what Johnson said last night. Or how she found us." Lucky leaned against the side of the loaded eighteen-wheeler.

"After what happened with Aureo, I risked sending an e-mail. Walter worried when you took missing, especially since he'd heard you were looking for him earlier, in a bit of a mood." Bo judged Lucky with a sidelong glance.

Lucky sighed and kept his mouth shut.

Bo glanced toward the warehouse door, but the men were still inside. Cruz loitered a respectful distance away. "Walter's got folks following up leads, and Johnson's hanging out with her old crew at Southwestern, to be available if we need her. She's got a lot of connections. I like her."

Trouble was, Lucky did too. Liking people didn't fit in with his standard method of operation. "She'll make a good agent," was all he'd allow.

"The factory can't keep up with orders for Codopure." Bo stood in front of Lucky, blocking the hot morning sun. All cocky grace, long legs, and tight swell pushing out the seat of his jeans. Beautiful. And dangerous. "Even so, we're going to have to start making two runs a day."

Two loads a day? When would they find the time? Walter Smith needed to get off his ass and arrest some damn body. But cases like this sometimes lasted years. Lucky didn't have years. Neither did Bo, if it wasn't too late for him already. "Low dose" Lucky's ass.

"What we need is the closed tunnel. I wanna see the cave-in." The felon in Lucky demanded a return on investment for a tunnel costing upward of a million dollars to build.

The SNB agent in him scratched his head at Stephan walking away from such spending. Anything to do with Stephan needed checking out.

"I can get the guys to cover for us for a few hours." Bo stood in full Cyrus mode, a hard-edged glint in his eyes. If not out of respect, the men would surely obey the sheer command of a man who came across as someone who'd kill for disobedience. At least until the drugs wore off. "We make this morning's run, then break off, have a little look-see, and join up for the trip back. I'll get Cruz to pay the guard to take some time off."

Yeah, and someone might be paying Cruz to keep tabs on Bo and Lucky too. Sooner or later, they needed to get the hell out. An unsupervised tunnel might be their ticket. Once down below, he'd conk Bo on the head if he had to, drag him across the border, leave him with the one person he trusted—Johnson—and haul ass back to Mexico to settle a few scores.

"You want in there as bad as I do, don't ya?" Lucky wiped at the back of his neck with a faded bandana he'd found in the truck. He'd never sweated so much in his life as he had in Mexico. So damned hot even the skeeters stayed home.

"Yep, but it's not the kinda place I'd go alone, ya know? Most of the crew are superstitious, won't go there."

"Superstitious? About what?"

"Rumor has it a devil lived there and was disturbed by the digging. An act of God sealed him into the pit." Bo gripped the edge of his shades and slid them down far enough for Lucky to glimpse of the gold-flecked brown eyes he'd never admit turned his insides to jelly. "The place is constantly guarded on either end."

Fuck superstition. The men would follow Cyrus into the collapsed tunnel or hell itself for salvageable product. Lucky would too, if only to get Bo's body back once Cyrus was done riding it. Bo trusted him to come swooping in like the cavalry, no matter what. May his trust never be misplaced.

Lucky drove the truck alone to the working tunnel, followed by the Jeeps. Bo brought up the rear on the bike.

After three hours of lugging cases, Bo pulled Lucky and Cruz aside. After more eye contact than absolutely called for, Bo clapped Cruz on the shoulder. "Give us three hours. Then come by, just in case."

Bo pulled his shades back down over his eyes and trudged off to the bike, leaving Lucky with Cruz. Lucky growled. Cruz grinned. Maybe he'd like a few less teeth to floss. Easy enough to arrange.

"Lucky, c'mon!" Bo hollered without turning around. Lucky gave Cruz his best evil glare and trotted off behind Bo. He climbed on the back of the bike, dropped his Ray-Bans, and flipped Cruz off while Bo wasn't looking. Ah, the little victories.

Nothing happened of any interest on the way to the collapsed tunnel, except a bug the size of a Volkswagen Beetle nearly knocking him off the Harley. Bo reined in the RPMs and made an unfamiliar right hand turn. Within a few minutes, they pulled up to what appeared to be a rundown factory. The dilapidated block and tin building seemed a poor cousin to the more modern facilities on the US side of the border. A different world. Only a few yards away. Now to get Bo over there.

Lucky held on tight as Bo rode the motorcycle up a steep ramp to the loading dock. He hopped off the bike and snatched a key from Bo's hand to unlock a rusty padlock and lift a bay door. Bo drove the Harley inside of the abandoned warehouse.

Patchy sunlight dappled the floor and broken-down shelves, filtering in from missing portions of the roof. Bo killed the motor, slid his leg over the seat, grabbed two flashlights out of the saddlebags, and stowed his and Lucky's sunglasses. "We won't be needing those where we're going. Ready?"

"Yeah." No. Not that Lucky would tell Bo. No telling what they might find. Snakes, spiders, eyeless white cave crickets. And please, God, not bats. Nasty flying rats.

Oh. And a thousand tons of rock ready to fall on their heads.

Their footsteps echoed on the cement floor, unnaturally loud in the quiet. In the distance, a dog barked. They left the warehouse area with its spray-painted graffiti. Lucky stepped over a stained mattress in the hallway. His misstep sent a can rolling to ping against the far wall. He jumped. Shit. A can. A stupid can. He exhaled and whipped his gaze over to Bo. Good. Bo hadn't noticed.

Traces of other people's lives lay upon the floor: a crumpled cigarette pack, a ragged doll, a shoe. How many hopeful immigrants had sheltered here? Were they living out their dreams in the US? Or would Lucky one day cuff them for hauling drugs across the border? And how much money did the guard make by turning a blind eye, or worse, letting them in?

Piss and decay assaulted his nostrils. The chemical stench of meth. Worse things. The building offered the perfect jumping off point for crossing the border. How many of the folks who'd sheltered here realized the clear shot to freedom that lay buried beneath their feet? Not that Stephan would share his own personal highway. The less folks who knew, the better.

What the hell? Lucky wasn't hardwired to give a flying fuck about other people's problems. Damn, Bo had gone and rubbed off on him again. The man in question booted a toy truck out of the way.

Bo. Cyrus. Whatever. Sometimes dealing with a man with two distinct personalities got too confusing. But the Bo Lucky knew would pick up the toy, repair the dent he'd caused, and try to find the owner. Hard-assed Cyrus provided a buffer for Bo's too-tender heart.

"Here's where the guard usually stands." Bo's voice sounded eerie in the quiet. He stopped before a heavy metal door. Damn, what a sturdy lock. For the early seventies.

"I don't suppose you have the key?" Not that the lack would slow them down much.

"Was counting on you." Bo pulled out a wrench and a length of stiff wire.

Close enough to a key for Lucky. He turned the tumbler to the left and right with the wrench. Ah, more give to the left. He added a slight bend at the end of the wire. Holding the wrench to the left, he slipped the wire in, lifting one pin after another. Great! Only five pins. A quick flip of the wrench to the left, and the lock popped open. Twenty seconds. Give or take. *I've still got it!*

"I guess getting mad and locking you out of the house is never gonna work, is it?" Bo's brief flash of playfulness warmed Lucky's insides.

"I'll teach you. It'll level the playing field."

Bo may have smiled, but his dimple stayed hidden. The pulley mechanism squealed when he slid the door open.

"What does that say?" Lucky nodded toward the red spray paint on the blue door. It couldn't be good.

"The Spanish equivalent of 'Abandon hope all ye who enter here.'"

Without another word, Bo passed through the entrance. The graffiti ended behind the door. A square basin with a drain occupied the center of the space. Similar fixtures existed in other plants Lucky visited, areas set up to clean equipment. Hand trucks and empty carts formed a haphazard ring around the central feature.

Bo crossed to a water tap set in a wall, leaving footprints in inch-thick dust. He studied knobs for a moment and twisted.

Vibration thrummed through Lucky's feet and up his legs, while the dust on the floor shimmered into airborne particles. The basin rose. Bo flipped another switch, starting an engine in the back of the room. "A compressor. We'll need air down there."

Oh, hell the fuck no. No, no, no! On second thought, whatever was down there was none of Lucky's business. Could they go now?

A hydraulic scissor lift raised the concrete rectangle three feet above an opening in the floor. Bo rested a hand on the lip of the hole and hopped down waist-deep. "The lights are still working, but keep your flashlight handy in case."

"Have you been here before?" Bo seemed far too familiar with his surroundings to be treading unknown soil.

"Cruz told me." Cruz? Mr. I-hate-gringos Cruz?

For a moment, Bo Schollenberger peeked out of Cyrus's eyes. "I don't like the tunnels. Without the shot this morning, I couldn't do this." A door slammed shut, sealing Bo behind Cy's hard-assed attitude. With a "c'mon" flip of his fingers, he disappeared downward.

Oh fuck. And he expected Lucky to follow. At some level, Lucky sensed what he'd find, and he'd seen the working tunnel often enough. But the high-tech hydraulics and electric lights hinted at something far more complex. Why in the hell had Stephan abandoned this route in favor of one far less sophisticated? Sure there'd been a cave-in, but it couldn't have collapsed the entire tunnel.

Standing in this room wasn't going to answer any questions. Lucky drew in a deep breath and lowered himself to the edge. The earth didn't open up and swallow him. No, his doom would make him come to it.

Steps led downward. Bo's fading footsteps beckoned. Tons of earth pressing in wasn't Lucky's idea of fun. If he had to be in a creepy place, at least he wasn't alone. And no one else existed on the whole planet who he'd rather be alone with than Bo Schollenberger—or Cyrus Cooper—whoever tended to be driving at the moment. Best to focus on Bo and not any horrors waiting below.

Down and down and down Lucky strode. A PVC pipe served as a handrail, punctured here and there. He held his hand over the holes. Coolness washed over his palm. A crude ventilation system. But what was that ungodly smell?

"You clear?" Bo called from below.

"Yup." Lucky rounded the corner and caught up with Bo. Overhead the hydraulics sealed the hole with a teeth-rattling *thump*. Lucky took a deep breath and let it out slowly. His heart hammered. *Get a grip, asshole.* There were ways out. If not from this end, they'd dig past the cave-in and escape in Texas. Maybe he should arrange that, to get Bo out of Mexico.

The stench of decay nearly knocked him down. His third year with Walter, he'd come across a maggot-covered body in a warehouse. He'd barely kept from throwing up.

"Something's dead down here." Or someone.

"Yeah." How could Bo be so cool?

"If we follow our noses, we'll find out what, I reckon."

The muscles in Bo's jaw worked. He nodded. Oh, yeah, as a Marine he'd seen death. And if it got too much for him, Lucky would haul his ass out of here.

Carts lay abandoned on the floor, one overturned on its side, showing four grooved metal wheels. Rails led into the belly of the man-made cave, and a string of lights cast shadows on the wall.

Breathe in, breathe out. Don't panic. Pushing a hand against his chest didn't slow the frantic thump-thump-thump of Lucky's heart. *And try not to think of how someone, no, something, came to be dead down here.*

Bo stepped between the rails, ducking his six-foot-plus frame. "The cave-in should be two hundred yards this way."

Lucky stood fully upright. All right! His lack of height gave him an advantage. Arms fully extended, his fingers barely brushed the hewn walls on either side of him. *Eyes on Bo's ass. Don't look right, don't look left. Don't let the walls close in.*

He trundled along behind his partner, but only because Bo knew the way. If they met anyone with a gun, Lucky should be in front. In his keyed-up state, he'd pity the bastard.

Shadows gave way to darkness a few yards into the tunnel. Bo stopped and switched on his flashlight. "I guess the collapse broke the power lines." He faced Lucky, determination etched upon his shadowed face.

"I love you." Lucky touched their lips together, a fleeting moment of softness pressed against the roughness of his chapped lips, counterpointed by the scrape of Bo's stubble upon Lucky's two-day whisker growth.

The kiss didn't hint at sex and inspired no desire to slam the guy to the ground and get reacquainted. Lucky's heart ached for this subtle hint that Bo, for all his newfound bravado, shared Lucky's fear of where they were and what they might find.

Bo didn't answer. No, he'd taken refuge in Cyrus. Lucky didn't have an alternate personality for backup.

Lucky's gut twisted, warning him of wrongness, of something sinister lying in wait. He locked gazes with Bo. Did saying the words in tense moments take away from their truth?

Finally the words came, but in Cyrus's brusque manner. "I love you too." Bo swiped his mouth across Lucky's. No time for fanfare now. He bobbed his head in a quick nod and shined his light down the tunnel. Lucky switched on his beam and followed behind.

"There's ventilation down here, but it's sketchy," Bo said. Not that it helped with the increasingly powerful scent of rot.

Lucky pointed his beam at the smooth walls and ceiling, but found no tell-tale signs of weakness. Instead, heavy wooden beams still shored up the ceiling, and plywood braced the walls. Nothing about the walls or floor indicated a cave-in except a pile of rocks sitting off to one side, where they'd likely been left during excavation.

He strode down the passage. Each footfall, each inhalation, was a thunder and an echo. Off to the side another tunnel appeared, extending about shoulder high. He crouched down and aimed his light inside. The hole went about ten feet and stopped against solid rock. Maybe whoever dug this had decided on a different route. And dear God, the smell!

"What's this?" he asked Bo.

"GPS doesn't work down here. The builders have to use compasses. Occasionally, they took a wrong direction and had to reroute. Cruz says there's five or six holes like that down here. They used them for storage, or a place to get out of the way and take a break."

A soda bottle glinted in the feeble light. Yeah. Some break area. For a rat, maybe. Lucky started to rise, but a dark shape appeared in his flashlight beam. "Hey, there's something in here."

He squinted into the darkness, making out the shape of a head, shoulders, back. Fuck. "I think we found what died." Oh great. Not just entombed under the earth, but with a dead body. "How long ago did they close down this tunnel?"

Bo squatted beside a lump of cloth lying prone on the uneven floor. Other than the rock pile, there were no signs of a ceiling collapse. The only "collapse" involved someone with a grudge.

"Six months, give or take."

The overpowering odor assaulted Lucky's nose. He swallowed a mouthful of bile. Still, "He's pretty well preserved for six months." No maggots, no zombie-flesh. The corpse's skin was dried and dark, like a mummy. A man, judging by the short hair. The skin of his neck reminded Lucky of a brown paper bag, but shriveled and leathery. A damp-looking stain spread out on the tunnel floor.

"It stays about seventy degrees down here, but it's dry, and not many insects. A body lasts longer here than in a Georgia alley." Bo flicked his flashlight beam over the body. "On the surface, he wouldn't be nearly as well preserved."

"Any guess who it might be?" The sinking feeling in Lucky's gut offered up a few names.

Bo's shoulder brushed Lucky's when he shone a light on the man's neck and down his body. "Too tall, too well-dressed to be an immigrant who'd found his way in."

His clothes were covered with gore, but they weren't the normal jeans and T-shirt of the locals.

Lucky joined his own light to Bo's, trailing over khakis, a fine leather belt, and a cotton shirt with crease marks still on the sleeves. "It doesn't look like he was hit by any rocks."

Bo eased the man's head to the side in the light. He huffed out a deep breath and dropped his hand. "Lucky, this man was shot."

"What?" Lucky stared at the guy's forehead. No visible gunshot wounds, though too much dirt pressed into his face to make out many features.

"Right here." Bo directed his light near the man's ear.

Oh God. "And that"—Lucky nodded toward the ichor beneath the body—"is his brains?"

"Not necessarily. When a body dies, all the fluids purge out. Without insects to eat the mess or soil to seep into, lots of it stayed on the rock."

Too much information, and Lucky wouldn't dare ask how Bo knew. He'd learned it in pharmacy school. Yeah, that worked.

"Look for a gun."

Lucky fixed his beam on the ceiling. "There was no cave-in, and there's no gun. This man was left here deliberately."

"Yeah, but humor me." Bo held up his cell phone. A bright camera flash momentarily split the dark.

Damn, but Lucky hated when Bo dug his heels in. Sooner or later, he always got his way.

Flicking the flashlight side to side, Lucky searched the floor in the side tunnel. Nothing. He stood and searched the surrounding main tunnel. Chip bag, cigarette butt, beat up ball-cap, and other assorted trash. No gun.

"You can come back now."

"What?" Lucky whipped around to find Bo's eyes glittering in the dimness. The flashlight beam created eerie shadows on his face.

"I needed time to check him out. I wasn't sure if you needed to see."

If any protecting happened, it should be Lucky protecting Bo, not the other way around. Damned, meddlesome, hard-as-nails Cyrus. "Why?"

Bo held up his hand. "I found something."

Lucky made it to Bo's side in an instant. Diamonds and gold sparkled in the flashlight's beam. He held out his trembling fingers. No need to look, he knew what he'd find. He picked his thumbnail against the inside of the band and the inscription: VM.

Lucky's heart tried to crawl up his throat. This ring once glinted off Victor's finger. He'd seen the sparkling diamond a million times. "I think this was Victor's ring." And if this was Victor's ring...Lucky eyeballed the band. *Don't look! Don't look!*

"I hate to ask you this, but is this Victor?"

No, it couldn't be. It simply couldn't. What would Victor's lifeless body be doing down here? Had he managed to escape prison to die alone in this tunnel? Lucky tore his eyes from the ring to study the man's face. Bo brushed away some of the dirt.

High cheekbones, salt-and-pepper hair. Still not enough light to really tell. A familiar ache bloomed in Lucky's chest as it had before when he'd confronted Victor's ghost. Oh God, it couldn't be.

Metal scraped against metal overhead. They both bolted upright. Lucky held stock still. There it went again.

The hydraulic *whirr* echoed down the passageway. His guts turned to jelly.

"Someone's coming!" Bo hissed.

"We run for the border." Dead bodies. Time to get Bo the hell out of here.

"We might not make it. We have no idea what's up there. For sure there'll be more guards."

"Better the devil we don't know." Lucky tugged on Bo's arm. "Run!" He shot toward the unknown end of the tunnel. He'd only gone a few yards when shouting and faint light ended hopes for escape. Oh fuck. Surrounded. He charged back to Bo. "They're coming from that way too."

Pounding footsteps grew closer. A man swore in Spanish.

Fuck! "There!" Lucky aimed his flashlight at the alcove. Not much room, but maybe enough for them to hide in.

Lucky's stomach rolled. To get in the cave, he'd have to go over the corpse. Lights shone up ahead. "Good a place as any."

God, but Lucky didn't want to cram his body into their only escape. "Get in there," Bo hissed. "There's room enough."

A bulge in the corpse's back pocket caught Lucky's eye. Heart pounding, he snatched the wallet on his way into the hole and stole a look at the man who couldn't be Victor. No. Not possible.

He picked his way over the body and through horrible ick. He'd never get the scent out of his nose. Oh shit, oh shit, oh shit.

The side tunnel wasn't nearly deep enough, not even two Bo-lengths. The rear area rose five feet. Lucky slammed his shoulder against a protrusion in the tunnel wall. Pain shot down his arm. Fuck!

Bo scrambled through the opening.

"Watch that..." Lucky warned.

"Keep looking! I know that son of a bitch is here somewhere!" Stephan's voice came from right outside.

They huddled on the floor against the far wall, Bo in the front, Lucky in the back. Only Bo's bulk kept Lucky in place. They switched off their flashlights.

"What a fucking smell. You told me you'd taken care of this! I should have known if I wanted something done right, I'd have to do it myself."

Bo fumbled in his pocket, though Lucky couldn't see his actions.

Someone swore in Spanish. Sounded like Oscar the interpreter.

"Shut the fuck up! You! Get that into a cart. We'll settle this once and for all. You and you! Find Cyrus Cooper. I saw his motorcycle and his footprints upstairs. He couldn't have gotten out.

"He wanted to know what was down here. Let's satisfy his curiosity." That last part sounded too Friday night B-movie for Lucky's tastes.

Stephan had at least three men with him. Oscar and probably the two men who acted as guards and never worked with the drugs.

The air grew thick and dusty. Lucky held his breath to stifle a cough.

Voices sounded in the tunnel outside their hidey hole, the Spanish too soft to make out. Only the snarling gave away

Stephan Mangiardi. Lucky's heart kicked like a mule inside his chest.

"Cyrus Cooper. Meddling son-of-a-bitch. He's down here somewhere. Find him!" Stephan barked.

Another voice yelled back. Flashlight beams flickered out in the main tunnel.

"I should have had him moved a long time ago!" Stephan barked. "If it weren't for the fucking will, I'd bury Lucky Lucklighter's ass here too."

Holy fuck! Was that really Victor's corpse? Had that weasel of a nephew killed him? Why? He'd always been an irritating little maggot, but he'd never struck Lucky as one to bite the hand that fed him. And if Victor had been in Mexico, wouldn't he have contacted his old friend Nestor? *Not if Stephan got to him first.* And now he wanted Lucky dead, if not for a will. What will?

Light shot through the entrance to their cave and the corpse began shifting toward the exit, a disgusting, zombie slither. The beam caught Bo square in the face.

Terror ripped at Lucky's insides. Only Bo's weight held him down.

"Well, well, well. What have we here?" Lucky couldn't see with Bo blocking the view, but heard Stephan loud and clear. "You did have your uses, Mr. Cooper, but I'm afraid you've outlived your utility."

A gun fired. Bo jerked and let out a grunt.

Popping sounded, like someone ripped away one of the wall panels. Lucky caught a glimpse of plywood. The cave went dark.

Rocks slammed to the floor outside their stone prison. Oh dear God. Lucky wriggled out from around Bo. Better to be shot than to die in here. *Let me out! Let me out!*

Bo's arm around his waist stopped him. "No. Wait."

More rocks fell. Finally the din quieted. Lucky shone his flashlight at the sealed hole.

CHAPTER SIXTEEN

Lucky didn't need X-ray vision to imagine the scene outside. The banging rocks, a few hard grunts, followed by the *whumpf* of something heavy hitting a cart. Squeaking wheels led away from the site.

"Bo! Are you all right? Where did he shoot you?" Lucky wriggled around to get past Bo and fumbled for his flashlight. He flicked on the dim beam. No bullet holes. No blood.

Bo's laugh sounded strained. "Do you really think Stephan could hit the broad side of a barn?"

Actually, yes. But now might not be the time to say so. Lucky let out a sigh of relief. Short-lived. They were still trapped. He scrambled back to the entrance of their hole, threw his hands against the plywood, and shoved. Nothing.

Bo joined him. Shoulder to shoulder, they heaved. Dust and grit rained down, but the plywood held. The big-assed pile of rocks he'd seen must all be stacked up outside now.

"Move, damn it!" Lucky backed up and ran at the entrance. Fuck! Bo caught him before he could fall. Damn slippery goo. He launched himself at the door again.

"Don't." Bo grabbed his wrist. "The more you move, the more you'll use up our air. We might be here a while, and sure as shit Stephan turned off the compressor, not that it reached in here."

"What? How can you be so fucking calm? We'll die in here." Lucky braced his back against Bo and kicked at the plywood. Out! Now! Oh, God! He couldn't breathe. Choking sounds came from his throat. Oh God! Oh God!

171

"Lucky! Stop!" Never had Bo sounded more forceful. "You're getting yourself worked up. Panicking won't help. We're buried from the outside."

Once more Bo grabbed him and drew him backwards, into the wider part of their man-made cave. He scrunched down against the farthest wall and pulled Lucky down and to his chest. When Lucky squirmed, Bo held him tight. The warmth of Bo's breath caressed Lucky's ear. "Relax. Don't fight."

What the fuck? "In case you haven't noticed, we're trapped. Those rocks aren't going to move themselves."

"No, and we're not going to move them either, not without using up all our air and energy. Speaking of, turn off your flashlight. No need wasting the battery."

"What?"

"Shh...Don't you trust me?"

Did he? Did he trust Bo with his life? Yeah, but Bo had also gotten shot up with a syringe full of happy juice earlier. "But..." He pulled out his cell phone. Damn. No signal. Not that he really expected one.

"No buts. Lucky, look at me. We're fine. I'm here with you, and I'm not going to let anything happen. I didn't know you were claustrophobic."

"I'm not. I just don't like being in tight places with no way out." Were the walls shrinking?

"Okay. But turn out the light."

Lucky switched off the light and plunged them into absolute darkness. Fuck. Not a damn thing appeared in his vision.

"Isn't that better? We could be in bed at your house, at the cabin, anywhere."

At your house. Not *our house.* And not fucking likely, with the dust and putrid air up Lucky's nose and rough-hewn rock digging into his ass. Why did the "your" and "our" suddenly matter? But the man had a point. With the walls out of sight, Lucky breathed easier. "What's your plan?"

"The guys'll be here soon, and if Cruz can't find us, he'll come looking. He knows this tunnel like the back of his hand."

Fuck it all to hell! Lucky might as well bend over now—if he could—and kiss his ass goodbye. "Cruz? Cruz! You're betting our lives on him? That's it, we're dead."

Bo's low chuckle reverberated through his chest and Lucky's back. "He'll be here."

"I wish I could believe you." Hell, how could Lucky trust anyone when he didn't even know the man hugging him anymore?

"You can. You can always believe me. I've never lied to you, have I?" Bo swiped his lips against Lucky's temple and arguing became a moot point.

Lucky drew in slow, even breaths.

"Lucky?"

"Yeah?"

"Between the two of us, we could easily take over Stephan's whole operation. You know that, right?"

A bucketful of worms wriggled through Lucky's insides. Cyrus was definitely in the house, but how eerie to hear the words in Bo's voice. And alarming. "Why do you say that?"

"You know how things work, and no matter how much you may think you've changed, you miss the old excitement, don't you?"

No denying the obvious. But taking out the bad guys gave its own thrill. "What about his men?"

"Vincent came to live here twelve years ago, and from what I gathered, Stephan visited whenever he wanted something. He hasn't bothered to learn the language or the culture, treats the locals like scum, and has no respect for the competition. Sooner or later, he'll write his own death warrant with or without us. The only reason he's not dead yet is that people respected Victor and his grandfather."

Stone cold Cyrus Cooper, taking over? Yeah, he could. With Lucky's help and Nestor's support. The power, the cash, the fancy cars. They could have it all, and little things like mortgage payments wouldn't be a blip on their radar. And this time Lucky could be a full partner, not just a hanger-on.

But...what about the SNB? If Walter lied about his involvement with Victor, he needed to face the consequences. And the shit Stephan launched on an unsuspecting public—what Bo and Lucky could launch on an unsuspecting public—couldn't go on. Something must be done and soon.

And Bo. Sooner or later, God willing, Mr. Soft Heart would return. What then? "What about work? What making up for your sins and clearing your name?"

"What about it?"

Oh, hell no. Bo Schollenberger rescued kittens from trees and helped little old ladies across the street. He didn't deal in illegal drugs. "You're forgetting something, aren't you?"

"What's that?"

"We're not drug lords." Although Nestor would prefer hard-assed Cyrus and asshole Lucky to loose-cannon Stephan.

"No, we're not."

"Then why are you talking nonsense?"

Bo didn't answer.

Oh. "The drugs."

"Yeah."

"Stephan said you got a low dose."

"I watch, Lucky. I know what I'm given. And I'm a pharmacist. Don't you think I'd know the difference? They've been increasing the dose for the last two weeks."

Two weeks! "And you didn't fucking tell me!" That was it. When they got the fuck out of this hole, *if* they got the fuck out, they'd head straight for the border. He'd drag Bo kicking and screaming all the way if he had to.

"I'm building tolerance. More drug is needed to give the same effect. And what good would it do to tell you? You'd try to get me to give up the biggest case I've ever had to run back home with my tail between my legs."

"You bet your ass I would."

"And that's why I didn't tell you. Would you have told me if our roles were reversed?"

174

No. Lucky wouldn't. Time to change the subject. "Why drug you if he needs you? Why addle the help?"

"Because he's stark raving mad, uses this shit too, and thinks it's an advantage. My question is, why hasn't he given it to you?"

Good point. "What does it do to you?" Lucky laced his fingers with Bo's.

Bo let out a heavy sigh that might have used up a good portion of their air. "I feel good. Really good. Nothing worries me. I'm bulletproof." Bo gave Lucky's hand a squeeze. "I can see why people get hooked. No job? Don't worry, money's gonna magically appear just when you need it. Poor health? All your pains are gone. Insecure? You're suddenly smart, witty, and the life of the party."

Could Bo walk away from what sounded damned near perfect to work at the SNB and be the man who wanted to come home to Lucky? "And if you're facing a wannabe drug lord?"

Bo's light tones deepened to Cyrus's snarl. "You get rid of him and take over."

"You'd really do that?"

"Depends on how high a dose they gave me that day. If it was a placebo, I'd be too busy huddling in a corner whimpering like a scared dog."

"What's it like when that happens?" Best to know all he could about the enemy invading his lover's body.

"You saw Jaime. Nausea, diarrhea, paranoia, excessive sweating, dry mouth..."

"Is that all?"

"Suicidal ideation." Bo's whisper barely registered.

"Suicidal what?" Oh fuck. Not that. Anything but that.

"Withdrawal makes you want to kill yourself."

"If you ever start thinking that way..."

"I promise I'll tell you."

Yeah, right.

Bo's breath beat against Lucky's ear. "So far we've lost two men, one to an overdose. No one counts the other."

"What happened to him?"

"He tried to fly, about two weeks before you got here."

"Oh."

"I've never felt like I could fly, but I've had some pretty strange delusions. How about you?"

"Me?"

"Yeah. Don't think I haven't noticed a difference. He's not giving you the same shit as me, but he's giving you something."

Now came Lucky's turn to sigh. "Chloral hydrate." He scooped up a handful of grit from the cavern floor with his free hand and let it slide though his fingers.

"Aren't we a pair? Bound for rehab the moment we get back. I wonder if Walter will let us keep our jobs."

Walter. Sore subject. "You know we can't trust him, right?"

Bo's snort ruffled the hairs on the back of Lucky's neck. "You'd believe a drug lord before Walter Smith? The man got you out of prison and gave you a new life."

At what price? "Remember what I told you on our first case? Even bad guys have family and friends and buy groceries. It works both ways. Good guys sometimes don't return the extra ten the grocery clerk gave them by mistake." If someone had told Lucky six months ago that Walter wasn't totally law-abiding, he would have laughed. He wasn't laughing now.

"My heart tells me he's a good man."

"Is this the same heart that tells you to put up with my snarky ass?"

Funny how soothing Bo's snicker could be with life hanging in the balance and time slipping away. "The one and only. And it's not often wrong."

Lucky bit his tongue on the one "wrong" he knew of, the ex–boyfriend Bo had pilfered drugs for, earning him a place on Walter's team. The asswipe had deserted Bo at the first sign of trouble.

"Trust Walter, Lucky. If he was in those pictures, you can bet he had a damned good reason."

Damned good reason my ass, stayed locked in Lucky's mouth and didn't escape.

Quiet settled over them. Lucky's back itched from the sweat between their shirts, but if these few moments were all he had left, he'd spend them being as close as possible to Bo.

Bo finally breached the silence. "Wanna hear something funny?"

"Ha-ha funny or weird funny?"

"Take your pick."

"I'm not doing anything else."

Bo bumped his shoulder. "You know the best part about the drugs Stephan gives me?"

"There's a best part?"

"Yeah. On days when I get a full dose, I can't hear my father anymore."

The ragged piece of shit Bo called "father" didn't deserve the title, or a son as good as Bo. "You shouldn't listen to that bastard anyway."

"In my head, I know that. But in my heart, I still hear him screaming, telling me I'm worthless."

Bo, lining cans up just so on a shelf. Bo, stopping to chat with an annoying receptionist. Bo, with a kind word for everyone. "Is that why you try to be so damned good all the time? Are you still hoping to win Daddy's love? 'Cause I'm telling you, he ain't worth it. You're twice the man he'll ever be."

"Do you still think of your dad?"

Fuck. If only someone gave Lucky some magical "forget your pain" drugs. Dad. They'd been so close once. The whole family had dreamed of the day Lucky would follow in his father's footsteps and take over the farm. Instead, he'd hauled ass out of there the first chance he'd gotten. Somewhere, a liver transplant list had Dad's name on it. And Lucky wasn't there to help him. Never would be again.

"I try not to. He wants no part of me. To be honest, my folks are better off without me anyway." Even if their rejection still caused hot tears on occasion. At least Lucky still had his sister. Sort of.

"If we get out of this mess, I want you to make me a promise." Bo's voice was scarcely above a whisper.

"What's that?"

"We try one more time with our folks. Then we never let them hurt us again."

"I can't go home. I'm dead, remember?"

"It's not like there's anyone left *but* your family who doesn't know Lucky Lucklighter is still alive."

Damn. Did the guy have to be right all the time?

Bo wriggled, making slithery sounds against the stone walls. "I'm getting sleepy. Let's lie down."

Lack of oxygen. They'd get sleepy, pass out, and not wake up. At least there wouldn't be pain. And they'd go together. Lucky pushed and pulled until he lay chest to chest with Bo. "Cruz isn't really coming, is he?"

"Yes, he is."

"He works for a cartel. You can't trust him."

"I do. And that started before Stephan decided to use me for a science experiment."

"Cruz? He's an annoying little pain in the ass."

"I know another annoying pain in the ass I'd trust with my life." The softness of Bo's lips met Lucky's cheek. "Tell me. If you could be anywhere but here right now where would you be?"

"What the fuck kind of question is that?"

Bo answered with silence. Lucky filled in the blanks: *A question meant to distract me.*

Lucky could think of better distractions. Butterflies fluttered in his stomach. "I've been thinking a lot about what you said, and I think you may be right."

"Of course I am. About what, in particular?"

Deep breath. Chances were they'd never make it out of here alive, so why not say what was on his mind? "Your lease will be up soon, right?" Lucky stroked his fingers along Bo's arm, teasing the hairs there.

"Already is."

C'mon! Don't make me say it! The silence stretched, broken by the occasional scratch of a rock settling into place. "I was thinking..."

"Yeah?"

The jerk wasn't going to make this easy. Lucky took and deep breath and blurted, "I thought maybewemighttryliving-together." There, he'd said it.

"No."

"What? What do you mean 'no'?" Wasn't sharing a house what Bo wanted?

"No. Right now you're convinced we're going to die. Anything you say to me is under duress. Once we're out of here, you'll feel differently."

What? Now who needed to trust? "Will not."

"Will too."

"No, I won't."

"Yes, you will."

"Won't."

"Prove it."

Prove it? How that hell could Lucky do that? Oh, yeah. "I made an appointment with your Realtor to look at houses."

"Oh. But you wouldn't go with me."

"I was an idiot," Lucky mumbled.

"What did you say? I didn't quite hear you."

Holy fuck. The man wasn't going to let him off easy. "I said I was an idiot, and I'm sorry." No way would he let those be his last words. "But the house you wanted wouldn't do. Too exposed. And besides, it was sold."

"I see. What gives you the right to pick out a house for me?"

"It's not for you, it's for us."

Bo stayed silent long enough to stretch Lucky's already frazzled nerves to the breaking point. After a small eternity, he said, "You mean that, don't you?"

Finally! "I've never been more serious about anything in my life."

"Did you find anything you liked?"

"Yeah. It needs some work, but it's got a big kitchen for you, and a room we could make into a gym."

"Nice neighborhood?"

"Gated community."

"What? Can we afford it?"

"We", not "you". Awesome. Right now, Lucky would take any flicker of hope. "It's a foreclosure. It's got two fireplaces."

"Lucky?"

Lucky strained to see Bo, even though the darkness hid his face. "Yeah?"

"I believe you just got yourself a roommate."

If we live to get out of here.

Bo's solid presence gave Lucky strength. Before he'd been on his own, and while now his brain told him to abandon all hope, with Bo he could face anything.

The words didn't come as easily for him as they did Bo, and normally what popped into his head flew out of his mouth without slowing down. This time his heart spoke. "I guess I don't say it often enough, but I love you."

"I know." Bo shut Lucky up with a kiss. Lucky's heart swelled to the point of pain. Bo deserved better than to end his life in a trafficking tunnel so close to freedom across the border in Texas. And he damned sure didn't deserve to die at the hands of a motherfucking mongrel like Stephan Mangiardi.

And he wouldn't. Not on Lucky's watch.

Bo drew back, took a deep breath and huffed it out. "Now, there's some things I need to say. Don't stop me until I'm finished."

Now wasn't the time for a smart-assed answer. "Okay."

"I said I'd never lied to you. I have."

Oh shit, what now?

"You remember me telling you about the boyfriend who got beat up? The one I stole the drugs for?"

"Yeah." And who bailed the moment Bo got caught.

"I...I didn't tell you the whole truth."

Lucky's terror of bad news screamed, *Incoming!*

"I know you think I'm some sort of do-gooder, but nothing could be farther from the truth. In fact, once I'm finished talking, you'll probably change your mind about wanting to live with me."

Never! "Why do you say that?"

"You know how I told you he got beat up?"

"Yeah."

Silence loomed, save for the steady in/out of their breathing. Finally, Bo said, "I'm the one who hit him."

CHAPTER SEVENTEEN

"Do what? No fucking way! You?" Cyrus maybe, but not Bo.

Bo stayed quiet for a while before answering. "I wasn't always the way I am now. I'm the hotheaded kid who took a baseball bat after his dad, remember?"

Yeah, and it still didn't fit with Lucky's image of his lover.

"I came back home after I got out of the Marines, convinced my four years made me better than everyone else. Hell, half the people I know wouldn't have made it two weeks in combat."

For the second time in his life, Lucky shut up and listened.

"Anyway. We got into an argument, I don't recall about what. Something stupid probably, some guy winked at him or some shit. Who knows? I got pissed, and the next thing I know, he's huddled in a corner, screaming for me to stop." Bo pulled his hand from Lucky's. "I damned near killed him."

Lucky squeezed his eyes shut. No images would come of his mild-mannered Bo beating a man. Fuck. PTSD. Right after they'd met, Bo mentioned Post Traumatic Stress Disorder, what set him on the path to prescription drug abuse and earned him a place on Walter's team.

Here Lucky had hated Bo's ex-boyfriend. Hating a stranger came easier than believing Bo capable of abuse. "The guy didn't press charges?"

"No. Blamed the whole thing on a flashback. Even stayed with me, talked me into counseling. But from then on things weren't the same. Darren walked on eggshells around me, and I avoided him. I couldn't stand to see the bruises, the cuts, knowing I'd done that." He let out a choked sob. "I worried that next time I wouldn't be able to stop."

183

"So he ended things."

"No. I did. Last I heard he'd found himself a nice lawyer from Little Rock. He's happy." Bo's voice slipped back to Cyrus's gruff monotone.

Damn, that had to weigh on Bo's mind. "You had a flashback. You weren't responsible."

Bo jerked back as far as the cave allowed. "It wasn't a flashback. I'd finally turned into my fucking old man."

"I've known you for two years, and you've never been violent." A one-off. That's what it was. Bo couldn't hurt a fly.

"That's where you're wrong."

Okay, time to lighten the mood. "Remember lesson number one? You hit me, I'll kick your ass."

"No, you won't."

"Yeah…"

"No. You. Won't. Lucky. That time in the ring? I held back. You'd pissed me off so bad, it was all I could do not to just let go. But I was afraid if I did, I'd kill you."

"You couldn't…"

"Remember that night in the garage with the Cruisers?"

Bo had taken on several bikers and barely broke a sweat. "Yeah?"

"I was still holding back. If I really let loose, I wouldn't even know what I did until the adrenaline faded. That's why I wish you'd stop your ambushes. One of these days…"

Fuck. "Bo, listen to me. You won't hurt me. You could try, but I'm wiry and I'm mean. I can hold my own. Trust me."

"I do." Bo sighed again. "That's part of the reason I love you. When I went off, Darren took it. He didn't even fight back. You would."

"Damn right I would. But Bo?"

"Yeah?"

"It's not going to happen. I promise."

"I wish I could believe you. You don't want to run now?"

"Just across the border to get you out of this shit." Lucky reclaimed Bo's hand.

"I try so hard now to control myself. After it happened, my aunt quoted some scripture about a man with self-control being more powerful than a warrior. I believe her now. It's not easy. I want kids one day. I don't want them afraid of me. I don't want to live my life worried I'll hurt them. I don't want to be my father."

"Bo, listen to me. We're in this together. We'll get through this. We'll go to counseling. Now that I know I can help you." Lucky paused a moment too long. Reality of where they were hit. "But first we need to get out of here."

Bo pulled away from Lucky and snapped on his flashlight. "Slow, shallow breaths. We'll be all right, but if it makes you feel better, I'll check one more time." He shuffled away, hunched over, toward the tunnel entrance.

"Okay, but watch out for..."

Bo stood upright one moment, the next he'd sprawled on the floor. The flashlight cracked against the wall and went dark.

"Bo! Bo? Are you okay?" Lucky scrambled on hands and knees toward the sound of moaning. He flipped on his light.

"Jesus H. Christ!" Bo lay curled up and clutching his shoulder by the outcrop Lucky had found earlier.

"Oh fuck!" Lucky sank to his knees—right into the goo. *No, not Victor goo. Don't think. Don't breathe too deep.* "What hurts?" Why hadn't he paid more attention in first responder training? He shone the light on his huddled lover. Bo winced and turned away from the beam. No blood—a good sign.

"Shoulder."

Lucky ran his fingers under Bo's to find an egg-sized lump under the muscle that wasn't there before. The egg moved under his hand. Breakfast tried to escape out his mouth. Bo's bones should fit together, damn it! "We've got to get this back in." Lucky had once dislocated a shoulder by falling out of an apple tree. Hurt like a motherfucker when Grandpa set it. What came next wouldn't be pretty. He set the flashlight down.

"It's gonna hurt." The longer they waited, the worse the pain. And fuck. He didn't want to hurt Bo.

Bo's agonized groan ripped at Lucky's heart. "I know. Do it."

Lucky wasn't qualified for doctoring. But without him... He had to fix this, right now. *Gotta pull, gotta get that ball back into the socket before his muscles seize up.* Fuck, he needed leverage. How? Bo was bigger and bulkier. What the fuck ever. Time to drag that joint back together.

If he pulled from this side, yeah, if he jammed his foot into Bo's pit, he could haul a lot more than one bone over another bone that might as well be a mountain. He gripped Bo's wrist and straightened his back. Teeth clenched, he sucked in a breath and prayed, "Lord, let me not hurt him too bad."

Bone ground against bone, but it moved. *Yeah, come on, a little farther, come to Daddy, just hop right over that ledge and back into your nice warm nest, you fucking piece of skeleton that should never have popped out.*

"Mother-fuck!" Bo roared.

What if Lucky wound up hurting him worse? He pulled again, pushing at the lump with his other hand. "Moving, yeah, it's moving, a little more, come on, damn you, get back where you belong."

The sudden jolt of ball meeting socket made Lucky scream. Bo's arm shortened with a crack.

Did it go in? Was that shit-eating piece of arm mated with the shoulder? Was Bo fixed? Lucky flexed Bo's arm every direction; the damned thing swiveled like the joint had never been torn apart. "Bo? You okay? Bo?" No answer.

"Bo? Bo!" Lucky gave Bo's good shoulder a shake. He grabbed up the flashlight and jammed two fingers against Bo's neck. Erratic pulse. Shallow breaths. The lump on the shoulder was gone.

Okay. Just out for a moment. Maybe. Hopefully. Probably a blessing right now. What Lucky wouldn't give for a couple of ice packs. But first, time to get outta here. Now.

He flopped down into something he didn't want to dwell on, put his feet against the blocked entrance, and pushed.

How many times over the years had he counted himself a dead man? Too many to name. He'd claimed he wasn't scared. But now he was. Because now he had something to lose.

He'd never see Charlotte again. He'd never see his nephews again. He'd never get to see Mom and Dad and find out once and for all why they'd finally given up on their oldest boy.

And he'd never spend Christmas with Bo in their own home. Or gaze at a small version of his man—the child Bo wanted one day.

Oh, hell no. They were *not* dying today.

They would have those kids, and the house, and the dog, damn it!

Or Lucky would fucking die trying.

"Unngggh!" He shoved with all his might. Tiny pebbles trickled to the ground. Hands braced, he gritted his teeth gritted, and kicked. *I'm not lying in dead man ick. I'm not covered in gore. I* am *getting the fuck out of here!*

"Move, you motherfucker! Move!" Nothing. He spread his arms further, sliding them across the slick tunnel floor to reach the walls. Something shifted under his hand. His fingers fit perfectly around a molded grip.

He raised his other hand, his fingers hitting a bit of broken blade. A screwdriver. A broken one, but hell, he had a tool.

He maneuvered around in the tunnel. "Bo. I'm gonna get us out of here. And God, if you're listening, I could use a little help here."

Hope in hand, he chiseled.

"Cy-rus!"

Lucky jolted upright. *Bam!* Ow! He grabbed his suddenly wet forehead.

"Cy-rus!" He shook his head to clear the cobwebs. After who knew how long, he'd only bored a hole the size of his fist in the plywood, beat the hell out of his knuckles, and dislodged one small rock. But the tiny opening let in a bit of air.

The yell didn't sound like Cruz, but it sure the hell wasn't Stephan Mangiardi either.

"In here!" He didn't give a fuck who it was, as long as they got out. He grabbed Bo's foot and shook. "Bo? Bo! Someone's here!"

Not a sound answered him. Every drop of Lucky's blood chilled in his veins. Oh, God, no! Especially not now when a thin ray of hope appeared. He squirmed around and lowered his head to Bo's chest. A bit fast, but Bo's heart beat steady.

"Cy-rus!"

"Here!" Lucky yelled. His voice sounded loud in the tiny chamber. Did any of it get out?

He felt his way along the floor. Something moved beneath his palm, and he slammed his shoulder against the wall. "Damn!" He found the errant object. His flashlight! He turned the gadget on and flicked the beam through the hole he'd made.

"Hey! Hey!" He pounded the broken screwdriver against the plywood.

Curses he'd heard many times in prison answered him. Footsteps scrambled away.

"No! Help! Come back!" Tears sprang unbidden to his eyes. "Lord, take me. I deserve it. But if you're as merciful as Mama says you are, please save Bo. He's got to be one of the best men you've ever made. Don't let him die down here."

No. Bo couldn't die. Lucky wouldn't let him.

More shouting, moving closer. Scraping, cursing, groaning. The plywood moved a fraction, enough to let in a breath of air before it fell back into place. Twice more it bowed, only to come back. More voices, a mighty heave, and rocks rolled away.

Lucky caught a face full of dust and backed away hacking. He flashed his light at the two faces peering into what might not be his grave. What a beautiful fucking sight. The Garcia brothers might as well have been angels in white. In a daze, he scrambled backwards to grab Bo by the foot and pull. Alejandro grabbed him by the wrist.

"No! I have to get...!"

The man jabbered in Spanish.

"No!" Lucky screamed.

He aimed his flashlight out of the hole. Cruz's face appeared. "Stop fighting," he said. "We won't leave Cyrus. This I can promise."

Lucky didn't trust the guy—hell, he didn't trust many people. While still trapped probably wasn't the best time to say, "If you hurt him in any way, I'll kill you," Lucky said it anyway. "And watch his shoulder."

Alejandro pulled him out of the hole. Something soft moved beneath Lucky's knee and he grabbed at folded leather. The wallet he'd taken from the dead guy.

Once out of the hole, he glanced back. He and Bo hadn't stood a chance at freeing themselves. Rocks lay in precise angles to seal them in. Stephan Mangiardi was going to die for this. Slowly, horribly. He'd gasp his last breath begging for the mercy he hadn't shown Bo.

Held halfway up by his new best friend, Lucky staggered down the corridor. At last they came to the hydraulics. Jaime helped him. He collapsed on the floor of the warehouse. Someone handed him a cup. It could be poison for all he cared. He chased back a throat full of dust with a mouthful of lukewarm water.

There wasn't enough water in the world to wash away the dead-body stink. He yanked his T off and threw the disgusting shirt away from him.

Rasping, the shuffle of several pairs of feet had him on alert. A moment later, Rafael staggered into view backwards, holding Bo beneath the armpits while Juan carried his feet. Cruz brought up the rear. The men set Bo down and Cruz dropped to one knee.

Lucky stumbled upright, and promptly fell. Damn, but he

weighed a ton. He crawled on hands and knees to Bo's side, dignity be damned.

Bo clutched Lucky's fingers. His eyes fluttered open.

Bo! Oh My God! Lucky snatched Bo up and hugged him for all he was worth.

"Ow!"

Lucky laid Bo back down and patted his shoulder.

Three men crossed themselves. Rafael flumped down on the concrete. All the color had fled his face. If he weren't already down, Lucky might be running to catch him before he fell.

Alejandro knelt beside Lucky and rattled away in Spanish. Tears spilled down his cheeks. He raised his watery eyes, then grabbed Lucky and held him tight.

Aaack! "What now?" Lucky mouthed to Cruz over the man's shoulder.

"He's happy you're alive. But we need get Cyrus someplace safe and figure out what to do next."

Lucky and Cruz loaded Bo into the back of one Jeep. The men stood solemnly to the side. Alejandro cleared his throat and spoke, words punctuated by sniffles. Cruz interpreted. "He says he's glad your friend is okay. Cyrus is a good man."

Lucky took Alejandro in, the sincerity in his eyes, the openness of his face. One day soon he'd have to arrest the man. Damn. How could Bo stand making friends with these guys, knowing what waited down the road?

And every one of them had risked their lives and Stephan's wrath to save Bo.

Alejandro wasn't a bad man. He merely did his job. And he did it well, with all his heart. "Don't make me like you," Lucky muttered. "Bad things always happen to the people I like."

Lucky closed the door after the doctor left.

"Are you sure you're all right?" He tried not to hover over Bo, what with Cruz in the tiny bedroom over the cantina, bearing silent witness, but he wanted to hover. He deserved to hover. Damn it! He tugged at the too-small T-shirt and too-short jeans Graciela had brought. Even after a twenty minute shower with some way-too-floral soap, Lucky couldn't get the scent of death from his nose.

"Yes. I told you Cruz would show up, didn't I? But it looks like game over for me." Bo's bittersweet smile couldn't be more regretful if he tried. He'd loved the game, much as Lucky did during the rare moments of self-honesty.

Did that mean... "You're going home?"

Bo exchanged a glance with Cruz. Sometime soon, those two had some explaining to do. One day Lucky might have to punch Cruz's lights out. But he'd saved Bo and Lucky's asses today. That didn't make them friends, but when the shit hit the fan, Lucky might not shoot him first.

When bullets started flying, the first one belonged to Stephan.

While Lucky and Cruz sat in spindly chairs, Bo leaned back on the bed, arm wrapped in a sling. Voices from the cantina drifted up in undecipherable murmurings. "I'll stay here and work behind the scenes. Everyone thinks I'm dead, and those who know better have a stake in keeping me alive."

"Care to share details?"

Again with the eye contact and Cruz. "Not right now. Soon."

Lucky glowered and gave Cruz the stink eye. He may owe the man one, but hitting didn't count if the fuckwad deserved a good belting.

Damn, but Lucky hated being out of the loop. Anyone else would get a pounding for withholding information, but Lucky had done the same himself on occasion, and might be called upon to make creative use of the truth again. However, he wasn't above using this moment in his next "remember when you..." argument.

He handed over the billfold he'd taken from the tunnel. "Now to find out who Stephan hated bad enough to cut off his supply route to hide the body." He shot a warning glance at Bo and shifted his wary glare to Cruz.

"It's okay, Lucky. He probably even knows the guy."

"Whoever he was, he had on Victor's old ring." No way was Victor found in the cave. Lucky's gut told him so.

And if it did turn out to be Victor? Denial was a beautiful thing.

Bo opened the wallet and checked the bill compartment and slots for credit cards. "Nothing. The son of a bitch robbed the guy, apparently."

Yeah, surely a man roaming around so well dressed would carry money or credit cards with him.

Some tugging got the driver's license out. Bo raised it up to the bedside lamp, squinting as he turned it over. He held the card out to Lucky.

The picture showed a familiar smiling face, specks of white in the man's coal black hair.

CHAPTER EIGHTEEN

Lucky sucked in a deep breath and read the name: Vincent Mangiardi. Vincent. Not Victor. His mouth caught up with his brain. "Vincent. It's Vincent."

"He's supposed to be away visiting family." Cruz's voice held a touch of snarl.

"Yes. That's what Stephan said. He's supposed to be with his sister." Not that Stephan had ever made friends with the truth.

The bastard kept racking up bodies. Time for Lucky to settle a few scores.

"Nestor said Vincent disappeared about six months ago, around the same time Stephan started acting like king of the hill." It all made sense now, or rather, some of it did. At least to Lucky. "Stephan didn't like his father calling the shots, wanted more power and control, yet Daddy owned the rights to the land. He killed Daddy, took over, and now pretends he's Victor mach 2." And doing a piss poor job at it.

"I believe you're right." Bo took the license back and studied the faded plastic with cold eyes. "I say it's time for you and me to get the hell out of Dodge." He eyed Cruz. "You?"

"I'm staying. I have work to do."

Oh yeah, one day these two would pay for their little secrets. Cruz, he didn't trust for a minute, Bo he'd give the benefit of the doubt for now.

"I'm staying too." They had Stephan by the balls. No matter what else local authorities might sweep under the rug for the right price and to avoid involvement, Lucky wasn't going anywhere until Stephan paid for his sins.

"No, it's too dangerous. You need to get out now." Damn. Bo needed to use that commanding tone in the bedroom.

"Cruz? Mind stepping outside. I need to talk to Cyrus alone." The moment the door clicked shut, Lucky growled, "You forget who's senior man on this assignment."

Bo jutted his chin out. Oh, hell. He'd play to win now. "You're not even on this assignment so cut the bullshit. We're getting out."

"If I leave right now, Stephan will know I was there and what I saw and heard. If I go back and play dumb, I just might uncover the truth about Victor." For purely professional reasons of course. Lucky didn't owe the man anything for testifying against him. Really, he didn't.

All he needed to do was tell Nestor what they knew, and the local crime bosses would soon declare war and take care of the Stephan problem without Lucky. Too easy. Stephan had a date with prison that Lucky intended for him to keep.

Lucky met his partner's eyes. Bo's icy resolve softened. "I don't like it, but I understand. Do what you have to do. For God's sake, be careful. I know you and Cruz don't see eye to eye, but you *can* trust each other. Don't go getting shot over some stupid pissing contest."

Graciela knocked and opened the door, greeting them with a sunny smile and a heavenly-scented tray.

Leaving Bo without even a kiss might be the hardest thing Lucky ever did, but with Graciela flitting in and out, bringing juice, food from downstairs, and plumping Bo's pillow every five minutes, should Lucky be jealous or pity the man? Oh, what the hell. When she turned around, Lucky slid his palm behind Bo's head, and dragged him up for a brief but heartfelt lip lock.

Bo's mouth dropped open, but Lucky couldn't take advantage with a witness present. "Hold that thought." Yeah, he was da man! He backed away from the bed with an extra saunter in his step, just in time to regain Graciela's attention.

Oh no. He'd had his share of the *señora*'s fussing over the goose eggs on his head. But the stuff she'd wiped over the cut and his bloody knuckles calmed the stinging a bit.

As before, she reached up and stroked Lucky's cheeks, eyes misty, and spoke what might have been an attempt at English. He understood the same two words: "Son" and "happy."

On the way out the door he asked Cruz, "What did she mean back there about 'son' and 'happy'?"

Cruz snapped off a too-quick reply, "You remind her of a movie actor."

Either Cruz or Nestor lied. Probably both. Lucky had no choice but to follow Cruz outside.

Cruz got behind the wheel of the Jeep and tilted his head toward the passenger door. Okay. Let him have his little win. Lucky intended to ask for Bo's Harley first chance he got.

"Our official story is that we found Cyrus's body, and you were with us. Rafe and Andro are loyal to anyone but Stephan, and enough people saw us at the tunnel to have gotten the word back to Stephan by now." Cruz kept his eyes on the road and spoke like a man used to giving orders.

The asshole in Lucky wanted to call the shots, but the good sense Bo had planted in his brain kept him from spewing out a few choice words. Cruz knew the locals, knew Mexico, and might better understand a Stephan who'd stepped out of his uncle's shadow to become a killer. If Stephan hadn't pulled the trigger himself, he'd definitely ordered the hit.

"Take me back to the house."

Cruz flashed the bright smile normally reserved for gringo-baiting. "You could always come home with me."

"I'd sooner sleep with Stephan."

The grin fell. "If you go back to the house, that might well be the case."

"What the fuck are you talking about?"

"Have you ever wondered why Stephan keeps you around? He didn't need a logistics coordinator. He had me for that. And you've seen Cyrus in action. You have a puffed up opinion of yourself, but even you have to recognize how much better Cy is as a second in command than you."

Yeah, Lucky did, but he wasn't about to make an admission to Cruz. "Do you have a point, or are you just happy for a chance to put me down?"

Cruz blew out a breath, likely the strongest wind to hit this stretch of Mexico in a long time. "Don't you get it? You knew the man way back when, right? Can you tell me he hasn't changed?"

Before Lucky's arrest, Stephan's main occupation had been partying and spending Victor's money. And he'd once called a housekeeper to squash a spider in his room. Hard to imagine such a wuss killing his own father, even for money. "He's changed. He's batshit crazy."

Lucky wouldn't give Cruz the benefit of full-on attention, but noted the man's nod from the corner of his eye. "The local leaders wouldn't deal with him, have no respect for him. Victor Mangiardi is legendary here. Brutal when he needed to be, but very generous to those deserving his time."

Cruz's pause lasted too long. "Well?" Lucky prompted.

"Stephan pretends he *is* Victor, and has somehow managed to convince himself. Those who knew of your relationship see you and Stephan together as your backing him in his uncle's place. Even those who didn't know the full extent knew you as Victor's right hand. Stephan's hoping those who won't accept him for himself will accept him for you."

"And none of this would be necessary if Victor was still around." His insides twisted.

"Exactly. Do you believe Victor Mangiardi is alive?"

That, folks, was the million dollar question. "No. Stephan was too much of a lapdog to piss off his uncle. And what he's doing now goes against everything Victor stood for. He had a huge operation, but kept a low profile, and didn't deal in the kind of instant death Stephan dishes out."

The closer they got to the house, the less sure Lucky was of his resolve to see things through to the end. Why? What possessed him to return? They already had enough evidence to lock the man away for life. What more could he hope to gain?

Him. A gun. A minute alone. Stephan's head. No. No matter how much Lucky wanted to make the bastard pay for what he'd done to Bo, he couldn't murder a man in cold blood. Now if Stephan made the first move...Walter would be pissed.

Walter. Lucky had to find out the truth of Walter's involvement. And if Victor had miraculously survived and was involved in Stephan's trafficking, he'd go down too.

The moment Cruz pulled in through the gates and parked the Jeep, he turned his full attention to Lucky. For the first time he didn't glower, smirk, or curl his lip as though he'd found something disgusting on the bottom of his shoe. "Are you sure about this?"

"As sure as I'll ever be."

"*Vaya con Dios,* amigo." Before Lucky closed the door upon getting out, Cruz added, "If you need me, call. My number's in your phone."

Lucky stood before the house, his mouth hanging open. Was it too late to call the man back?

The house seemed deserted, odd for this hour. The grandfather clock in the living room bonged ten times. Normally Stephan would still be up, or the housekeeper. Even if Stephan had a young man in his room there would be lights on. Of course, no telling where he'd gone to dispose of his father's body.

Lucky showered, shaved, and re-treated his knuckles and the bump on his head. For a man who'd nearly died today, he'd count himself lucky and brace himself for Stephan to be sitting on his bed when he opened the door. Yeah, better wrap the towel really tight around his waist.

Stephan wasn't there, but a glass of orange juice waited on the nightstand. Lucky flushed it down the john. He needed his wits about him.

A chime from the bathroom called him back to his pants and the cellphone in the pocket. A text said, "Get out now. Coming back 4 u." It was from "C".

Oh fuck. Something must have happened. Lucky grabbed his clothes and dressed in record time. He opened the door to his room. A grinning Stephan leaned in the doorway, flanked by Oscar and two guards. "Going somewhere?" He barred Lucky's exit with his arm across the door. "It seems someone reported two men on a motorcycle going into my warehouse today."

"Neighborhood watches are highly overrated."

Stephan's gaze fell on Lucky's battered knuckles. His grin vanished.

A blow from the left came fast. Lucky ducked, rolled, and popped up swinging. Oscar grabbed for him, but fast, small, and mean made a hard target. The guy's hand closed on air.

"Where do you think you're going, you stupid redneck? There's nowhere to run." Stephan's sneer reminded him of old times.

"But stupid rednecks live to fight and run." The guard closed a hand on his arm and immediately let go. Stupid rednecks weren't above biting.

"Tell me, Lucky. Where you there when I shot your lover? I understand my men helped you. They'll be...punished."

Oh shit. And even now Cruz might be pulling up outside, right into a trap. Lucky might not like the guy, but caught between two devils, he'd take whichever one wasn't Stephan Mangiardi.

Shouting from outside created a momentary distraction. One nameless brute ran to the window while the other whipped his head around toward Stephan. Lucky darted for the door.

He wrapped his hands around the door handle, but they were suddenly crushed in the vise-like grip of the first guard. The idiot grinned. Lucky grinned back. He slammed his head against the man's nose hard enough to see stars. *Crack!* The guy let go of Lucky's hand and staggered back, clutching his nose. Blood seeped between his fingers. That'll teach 'em. Lucky wrested the door open and charged across the yard.

A Garcia fought with the gate guard while Cruz decked a man by the Jeep.

Stephan bellowed from the doorway. Oscar translated. Heh. Stephan's prejudice came in handy. One man lunged, and Lucky stooped low. His opponent might be taller, but his over-muscled build cost him agility. Lucky ran for the Jeep.

He snatched the door open and bolted inside. "Come on!" he screeched at Cruz. Cruz smashed another face with his fist. The brothers scrambled inside quicker than such stocky men had any right to. Wiry Cruz hopped in last.

"Where to, my friend?" His bright smile belied his death grip on the wheel.

"Anywhere but here."

The Jeep scraped a fender against the gate, shooting through with seconds to spare. The guards having to re-open the gate to let the others out gave Cruz a head start. He stomped the gas.

"I take it you were seen today?" Cruz asked.

"Yes. Isn't that why you came to get me?" Lucky grabbed the broken "Oh shit!" handle.

"No. Our mutual friend contacted someone in the States. There's something you should know."

Headlights off, Cruz eased down the street and pulled the Jeep into the garage where Bo lived. Alejandro closed the bay doors. Together they rushed to the cantina.

"We'll be down here if you need us. We have work to do. *Amigos*?" Cruz gestured to the brothers to sit. They hopped up onto barstools where a smiling Graciela served them beer. So much for work.

Lucky climbed up the stairs and entered Bo's room. Bo sat upright on the bed, right where Lucky had left him.

"How are you?"

"Fine." Bo crashed his mouth down on Lucky's the moment Lucky sat down on the bed beside him.

"Not that I'm complaining, mind you, but what was that for?" Lucky said when they came up for air.

"Because you're going to need it. I called Walter."

Walter. Either a traitor or one of the two men Lucky trusted at this back.

"And?"

"He's been doing some digging and talking to some people who believe Victor didn't kill himself."

"You mean he's really still alive?" Oh shit, oh shit, oh shit. Lucky heart slammed against his ribs.

"No. The cause of death was listed as suicide. *If* he was found hanging in his cell, according to Walter's source, he might not have gotten there by himself."

He didn't kill himself. His conviction and Lucky's testifying against him hadn't compelled the man to take his own life. Lucky hadn't driven the man to suicide. For twelve long years, he'd beaten himself up, "shoulda, coulda, woulda" following him around like lost puppies. But wait. "If he didn't kill himself, who did? He was under watch with no one else in the cell."

"That I can't tell you. But the word is out that someone offered a lot of money to make sure Victor didn't live long enough to start talking. Walter's still trying to find out more. The man could have put any number of people away for a very long time."

"Couldn't be Vincent. He didn't have the backbone to kill his own brother. And what would he have gained?"

"Who stood to lose the most?"

"Victor dealt with several small fish, but I rounded them up when I started working for the bureau."

"Any big names?"

Fuck. "Nestor." Lucky's gut told him the man had truly loved Victor. "It's business," Victor used to say when his "business" grew unpleasant. "No, I can't believe it was Nestor. He's in Mexico and far too powerful. Besides, I think Victor would have rotted in prison before betraying the man. They used to be close." Real close. "Then there's Stephan."

"Why? Why would Stephan kill Victor?"

"Why does anyone kill anyone else? Money, rage, power, to keep them quiet, a man or woman they both want. The list goes on and on. Pick one. Or, better yet, tell me what he had to gain. It's not like Victor ever turned him down when he wanted something. Trips, cars, clothes. All he had to do was ask."

Bo tapped a finger against his chin. "And a man like Stephan Mangiardi doesn't like to ask for anything. He takes and feels the world owes him."

Stephan, lounging on the beach somewhere waiting for his uncle to die. Stephan, escorted to the VIP room of swanky clubs. Stephan, acting bored when a salesman showed him a car worth more than the farm where Lucky grew up. Stephan, pushing around the servants and glowering at the likes of Lucky. That is, when he wasn't trying to lure Lucky into his bed.

Victor took respect and groveling as his due, but he didn't lord his money and power over anyone. He'd been kind to his housekeeper, Lucky's family, and everyone he dealt with as long as they'd dealt fairly with him. Let someone cross him, though, and his vindictive streak came in force.

He'd handled himself like a businessman, not a spoiled, privileged brat. How many times had Stephan begged the man to use his influence to settle personal grudges? *"That man sneered at me. Make him sorry he ever lived."*

One morning when Victor wasn't home, Lucky had found Stephan in the dining room, sitting in Victor's chair, naked. *"One day all of this will be mine, and you'll be sorry you ever rejected me. So, I'm generously giving you another chance to get in my good graces."*

Lucky glared at the asshole, ignoring what rose between his legs. With his dilated pupils, he must have taken something.

There would be no reasoning with him. Lucky nodded toward Stephan's tiny erection. "Ask me again when that's a bigger dick, and you're a smaller one." He turned on his heel and bolted.

Two days later Victor asked, "My nephew tells me you tried to seduce him while I was gone. Is that true?"

"What the fuck? No way in hell would I want that bastard!"

A smile curved Victor's lips. "I thought not." The smile fell. "Remember, that bastard is my nephew. No one else would dare lie to me. Maybe I should teach him a lesson."

"Stephan used to brag that when he inherited all of Victor's wealth, I'd be out on my ass unless I kissed up." Lucky shuddered. He wouldn't fuck Stephan Mangiardi, no way no how. Not even with someone else's dick. Only to save Bo.

"So Victor left everything to Stephan."

"As far as I know. At least that's what Stephan said. It wasn't none of my business. I didn't ask. And right before he died, Victor started selling off properties, in the US at least. He never told me about other countries." And yet in the tunnel, Stephan had mentioned keeping Lucky alive because of a will.

"Everything he didn't sell got confiscated at his conviction?"

"Again, all I know about is US holdings." Like Lucky's car and Victor's North Carolina mansion.

"But not down here." Bo stared at the crucifix on the far wall. "Stephan might not have realized how much the government would take, or maybe he didn't care. Maybe by that time, Victor had shifted the bulk of his wealth offshore. Only, why leave Mexican properties to someone who hated the place?"

"Nestor said he didn't, but he's not sure who the beneficiary was. I can't see Victor running off the mother of his half brothers and sisters. He wasn't that type of man." If anything, he'd buy them off with another house. Never let it be said that Victor didn't take care of his own. "Besides, Nestor said only Mexican citizens can own certain properties down here. Even if Stephan did inherit, he couldn't own the land, only lease. Victor would have wanted the land to stay in the family."

But, if Victor hadn't left his holdings to Stephan, that would explain why the bastard insisted Victor lived. To acknowledge his death meant no more money, hacienda, or factory.

"He planned to leave and take you with him."

"That's what I've been led to believe." By a group of Feds who'd lied to Lucky to ensure his cooperation. And Nestor.

"Would you have left? If you knew the heat was on, and y'all had to leave the country, would you have willingly left your family?"

Would he? Back then, the Lucklighter clan had been thick as thieves. Lucky wouldn't have left them behind. Not even to save his own sorry hide. "It's a moot point now. Right after my arrest, my folks stopped speaking to me except for Charlotte."

Bo didn't say a thing, but the expectant look in his eyes spoke volumes.

Holy fuck. "They never said why they disowned me, they just did. If they put up with my thieving and drug dealing ways, what the hell could be so bad that they'd turn their back on me?"

Victor must have said something, done something, that caused Lucky's family to finally wash their hands of their wayward son. And Victor would have pulled it off, too. To get his way. He wasn't above manipulation, excelled at it, even. Especially when he justified his actions as "taking care of his own." Like snatching Lucky away from prison time.

"When this is over, you need to find out. But for now suffice it to say there's a reason Stephan hasn't had you killed, but we don't know when he might change his mind. My guess is he needs you for something, and won't think twice about taking out the trash once you've served your purpose, like me. But I got a picture of a corpse on my phone, and Vincent's wallet. Plus..." a sheepish, somewhat guilty look crossed Bo's face. "I recorded what Stephan said in the tunnel. We have enough evidence to build a murder case."

Except for one thing: the guilty party. "I just have to go and get him."

"No, Lucky, *we* do. You're not taking him on alone. I'm going."

"No, you're not. You're hurt."

Bo snorted. "This?" He nodded toward his arm, still nestled in a sling. "Like being shot stopped you a few months ago."

"That was me, this is you. And an injured man is a liability in a fight." Lucky wasn't above fighting dirty.

"Cruz will be there too."

"I don't trust him."

"I do."

"He belongs to Nestor."

"He no more belongs to Nestor than you do to the SNB. Ever since you started questioning Walter, you've acted on your own. The moment I called him, I got answers we needed. You say I'm too trusting, yet you don't trust enough. Do you even trust me?"

Bo's eyes, those guileless dark depths, bore into Lucky's. Did Lucky trust the man? Knowing the Cruz connection might help. "Why won't you tell me the truth about Cruz?"

"Because I don't know anything for sure, like he doesn't about me. Agents don't just announce themselves, and anyone can lie. But it's not like you didn't *know*. Tell me you hadn't pegged him about five minutes after you met."

Lucky averted his eyes and scratched his head. "Well..."

"You knew, Lucky. I didn't have to tell you a damned thing. And you don't like him. Normally I'd say to listen to your instincts, but your instincts tell you not to like anyone."

"Not true. I like you, don't I?"

Bo could have melted lead with his scowl and glare combo.

Lucky wasn't that much of a hard ass, was he? Okay, maybe he was.

"Promise me that if anything happens to me, for real this time, go to him. He'll help you get out of this in one piece."

"Nothing's going to happen to you." Lucky wouldn't let it.

"You didn't answer my question."

"What question?"

"Do you trust me?"

With my heart, with my soul, with my measly bank account. With my life, which isn't worth much without you. "You're the man who switched me to decaf without my knowing."

"I was doing my best to take care of you."

Victor would do whatever it took to take care of his own, justify anything. Scary how much he and Bo had in common.

Bo was right. It wouldn't take a lot to wrest control of what was left of the Mangiardi empire from Stephan. The dark hair, the dark eyes, the merciless streak he conjured when he needed to. Deep down in the soul of sweet, kindhearted Bo Schollenberger lived a brutal man who'd rule the underworld with single-minded determination. Never before had Lucky been afraid of Bo. A shiver raced up his spine.

What would it take to push Bo over the edge from good guy to bad? Not money. Not power. His previous downfall had happened when he'd tried to right a wrong.

If Stephan shot Lucky tonight, tomorrow the world would have a new drug lord. But could Lucky trust Bo? Being switched to decaffeinated coffee had nothing on this. "I believe you'd die to save me."

Bo never flinched. "I would."

"If it comes to that, don't. Dying to save someone is the easy part. Living after someone's taken a bullet for you is harder." Lucky kissed Bo if for no other reason than the man was there and alive. This conversation was heading nowhere Lucky wanted to go.

Bo pulled away first and lifted the covers. "It's almost morning. Cruz is going to make a few calls. The Garcias are watching the house. Once we find Stephan, we go after him. Right now, though, we need some rest. This afternoon Walter wants you to meet with Nestor."

God help them, they were going after Stephan. But first, a night in Bo's arms.

CHAPTER NINETEEN

"Well, Mr. Lucklighter, I see you're still in one piece." Nestor relaxed in his chair in the upper room of the cantina. Graciela bustled about, placing plates and a sizzling platter of meat and veggies on the table.

"I've been told I'm a hard man to kill. Or rather, I don't seem to want to stay dead."

"So it would seem."

Lucky rolled his eyes upward to glare at the man from under lowered brows. The *señora* quietly excused herself.

"No, I had no part in what happened to you, and had I known, my men would have freed you." Nestor's jovial tone disappeared, and he placed his hand on top of Lucky's on the table. Lucky fought not to flinch. He reserved touching for people he cared about. "You found Vincent's body."

"Yes."

"I knew the engineer who designed and built the tunnel and didn't for a moment believe there'd been a collapse. But I never would have dreamed a ..." Nestor paused, face scrunched. "What is the word...?"

Lucky supplied, "Dipshit, dumbass, shithead, puke-for-brains, peckerhead?"

The corners of Nestor's mouth twitched. "Those will do nicely, thanks. I never dreamed an, as you say, 'all of the above,' like Stephan capable of killing his own father."

How much should Lucky tell this man? How much did he already know?

Nestor pursed his lips and puffed out a breath. "And he might have killed Victor too." Okay, so no news flash at eleven.

The guy reminded Lucky of Walter the all-knowing. "Had him killed. I don't think Vincent gave the order. He was too dependent on Victor. It had to be Stephan." Telling Nestor he'd been under suspicion, however briefly, wouldn't be a good idea.

"What do you intend for our *friend*?" Nestor's gaze burned into Lucky's.

No need in keeping up pretenses and lying. Nestor might know more about Lucky than Lucky did himself. "I plan to arrest him. Extradite him to the US."

"That wouldn't work. Either he'd buy his freedom or die in his cell. A suitable ending, don't you agree? Poetic justice for him to die alone in jail?"

Yeah, but Lucky wanted the man to face a jury trial, like he and Victor had. And come out the loser. "I can't haul him across the border."

"No, but you can make him go willingly. Either he goes with you, or he dies here. That's his choice." In any other circumstances, the man on the other side of the table might appear to be a kindly old grandfather, discussing nothing more threatening than Graciela's salsa. He'd played judge and jury before. One day he'd cross the line, and someone would deal with him. But not Lucky. Not today. The enemy of his enemy and all that. Right now.

"If all goes well, he'll be out of your way tomorrow."

A smile crept across the man's face. "I could end his life now with a single word."

"I figured that. Why give him to me?"

Nestor took his hand from Lucky's. "Victor was a businessman. He did things your laws don't allow. He was also a good friend, and more, once." A flicker of regret pulled Nestor's mouth down at the corners. "But he loved you. Wanted to make a life with you. If Victor is dead and Stephan stole my friend, you still suffered more. You've danced the edge of saint and sinner as long as I've known you." He barked a laugh. "And you do it well. Who would have thought Lucky

208

Lucklighter would reform? You were so good at what you did. But you have a flaw, and your heart wasn't in the work."

"But—"

"No buts. You considered yourself a criminal, but Victor spoke often of your kindness. How you'd do anything for family, and you didn't seek to take advantage of him. He called you a good man, I trust his opinion." Nestor paused to take a bite of grilled peppers. "I've met many men over the years who'd sell their souls for money and power. Not you. You were a thrill-seeker, you loved the adrenaline flowing through your veins, but you were never vicious, never cruel."

Lucky waited. He was *not* a good man. Bo was a good man.

Nestor took his time in biting, chewing, and wiping his mouth on a napkin. "You should have your revenge. Whether you choose a bullet or your courts of law, who am I to decide? As long as you honor Victor's memory."

If Lucky failed, a bullet might bear his name too. "He'll pay."

"Other coyotes wait in the shadows, but they dare not cross me in this. Stephan is yours, unless you say otherwise."

Lucky could put a bullet in Stephan's brain and likely get away with murder. But..."I'd never do that."

"Good. Now eat up before your fajitas get cold."

"Rafe says Stephan is at the factory." Cruz waved a hand at Rafael, perched at the cantina bar like he'd never even moved from the night before. Alejandro pulled out a chair and sat with Cruz, Lucky, and Bo at a table. He turned adoring eyes to Lucky. Someone needed to stop. Now.

Bo stifled a laugh, then grasped the arm wrapped up in a sling. Lucky shot him a dirty look.

"How does he know?" If Lucky didn't trust Cruz, he sure as hell wasn't going to trust the guy's henchmen, even if one of the henchmen did have the hots for Lucky—which only proved his insanity.

"He called his cousin, who works there."

Lucky glanced at Bo, who nodded. "Who else is with him?"

"His guards."

"What about the factory workers?"

"Only a few remain at this hour."

Old Western showdowns happened at sundown or high noon. Lucky would rather have had high noon, but at least there wouldn't be as many workers around to get caught in the crossfire.

"Okay, Cruz, Cyrus, you called the shots up until now, but I've got more experience when it comes to confrontations." Cruz couldn't have been with an agency for more than three or four years. "The fact he's still in the country tells us two things: either he's up to something, or he's waiting. He doesn't know Cyrus is still alive." Damn, how easily Lucky'd nearly slipped up and said "Bo". Three nights of restless, unaided sleep left his brain fuzzy. "It's me he's waiting for."

"We could call in the cops," Bo offered, sounding more like his by-the-book self than let's-make-our-own-fucking-rules Cyrus.

"We don't know which ones he owns." Cruz? The voice of reason?

Yeah. Lucky figured. "We take care of business ourselves. Who else do we have?"

"Rafael and Alejandro are good men to have at your back." Cruz patted Alejandro's shoulder. "They also openly defied Stephan. They have a lot to lose if he's not taken out."

Okay, desperate men might work. "They can watch the perimeter. Yesterday, Stephan had at least three men with him. No telling how many he has now."

"Still three. If shots get fired, only one man loyal enough to stay." Cruz shrugged. "Oscar isn't a very popular guy. Others might be outside. There are usually two factory guards on duty at any given time. How much cash you got on you?"

"What?"

"You heard me. How much cash do you have? They can be bought off if they believe Stephan won't be back."

They sure didn't make henchmen like they used to. "How much will we need?"

"I'll take care of it," Bo said. "You worry about getting Stephan." Oh yeah. Cyrus likely had stacks of cash. He'd been getting paid. Lucky hadn't.

"And no one will fault you if you decide dead works better than alive." Cruz spoke the words offhandedly, with a mere touch of inflection betraying his preference. He carried a personal grudge. Best to remember. If he'd set his heart on seeing Stephan dead, he might a problem.

"What does our uncle say?" Lucky asked Bo.

"That by the time he rounded up the necessary troops, Stephan could be anywhere. We need to handle this."

"We do?" The SNB's reach didn't extend past the border. Lucky nearly missed the quick, silent exchange between Bo and Cruz.

Cruz. It all hung on Cruz. Lucky gazed at the wiry Mexican with new eyes. Or was he Mexican at all? He sure as hell reeked of DEA or maybe one of those new international drug task forces. Probably a lot older than he looked too. But if he had the power to take Stephan down, why hadn't he already?

Ah. Stephan was a little fish who'd been promised to Lucky by Nestor. Cruz had a larger target in mind. Maybe even Nestor himself.

Lucky would have to deal with the Bo and Cruz Show later. "Okay. Let's move out. The dead man takes the rear!"

"Lucky?" Bo's voice wavered. "There's something I need to do before we go. And I'm going to need your help."

Bo held his back straight, and didn't double over until he slammed his room door behind them.

Lucky grabbed his arm and eased him down on the bed. "What's wrong?" Oh God. He should have taken Bo to the hospital the moment they'd crawled out of the cave. What if his shoulder was hurt more than the doctor said?

He never should have let Bo talk him into this. He shoulda conked the man on the head and left him with Graciela.

Bo moaned and let out a shaky breath. "Look under the sink."

Lucky dug through rolls of toilet paper and bottles of who knew what. "What am I looking for?"

"The kit."

The words barely reached Lucky's ear. "The kit? Are you—?"

"No. Close. Something else."

Lucky found a syringe and a vial. Shit. Stephan's new wonder drug. He glanced over to Bo, who shrugged.

"After what happened with Jaime, I thought it best to keep some around. Two cc's ought to do the trick." Bo leaned over, clutching his middle.

"You shouldn't be taking this shit. Let me get you to a hospital."

"No! You think Stephan can't find me there? Let's end this, tonight. But I can't function in withdrawals. Damn it, Lucky. Please!"

Lucky wanted to balk, but the "please" and the pleading big brown eyes did him in. He filled the syringe.

Bo grabbed a belt, tied off his arm, and inserted the needle into the crook of his elbow. He pushed the plunger, and left the empty syringe on the bed. "This is fast-acting. By the time we get to the factory, I'll be okay. But, Lucky?"

"Yeah?"

"Don't let on there's anything wrong. The men listen to me. We need them to listen. When all this is over, I promise I'll get help."

When all this was over, they'd both be picking up pieces. "How do you feel?"

Bo's smile didn't summon his dimple. "Like warmed-over shit. Let's go."

***

Stephan's Jaguar sat inside the fence, near the front of the factory. He'd either holed up, or he'd placed himself strategically to lure Lucky out of hiding.

Lucky and his team of misfits huddled in the Jeep far enough from the gates not to be seen.

Rafael murmured into a cell phone before handing the device to Bo, who sat sandwiched between the Garcias in the back. Bo lowered the field glasses he'd been looking through and fired off more words than one mouth should hold, quieted, and nodded so hard his brain probably rattled.

His face grew grim when he ended the call. "He still has three guards with him in one of the front offices, and a man outside. Cameras are there," he pointed to the edge of the roof, "there"—he pointed again to the other side,—"and there." Lights in the parking lot illuminated the walkways up to the doors, except for the darkened loading area.

The perimeter fencing posed another problem Lucky didn't want to deal with. "Is the fence electrified?"

Cruz shook his head. "No, but remember the razor wire at the top."

Razor wire. Fuck. Lucky had forgotten. "Weaknesses?"

Even in the gathering darkness, Cruz's teeth gleamed when he smiled. "I thought you'd never ask."

The sharkish expression made Lucky wish he hadn't.

The *snick* of a gun being cocked sent chills up his spine. Lucky hiked his thumb toward the backseat. "Do I even want to know what those guys will be packing?"

Cruz's grin widened, appearing far more sinister in the dim Jeep interior light. "Probably not."

"Asshole."

"Like your reputation doesn't precede you." Cruz snorted.

"I don't like it," Bo muttered. "Playing into the bastard's hands."

Cruz twisted around in the driver's seat to stare into the back. "Listen, my friend, he thinks you're dead. That's the biggest advantage you can have right now. You're our secret weapon."

Bo folded his arms across his chest. "I take lead with Lucky. You watch perimeter."

"And get us all shot. If Stephan didn't want Lucky dead before, he will now. You, he's already killed. He wouldn't think twice about doing it again. Besides, you're in no condition to confront anyone." Cruz reached into the back to tug on Bo's sling. His voice softened. "You're not one hundred percent."

"I still don't like it." Bo's eyes glittered in the semi-dark.

If someone died tonight, it wouldn't be Lucky. And it damned sure wouldn't be Bo.

"Stephan has killed before. It's too dangerous." There Bo went, digging his heels in again. "I need to be there."

"Would you say that to anyone else but me?" Lucky growled low. No wonder the department put an anti-fraternization policy into place, if off-duty relationships led to one partner being overprotective of the other. It's not like Lucky stopped Bo's stepping into the line of fire—much.

"Probably not." Bo's sigh announced defeat.

"Here. You'll need this." Cruz passed Lucky a Glock and two magazines. "Thirteen rounds each. Make 'em count." The familiar sounds of locking and loading filled the quiet.

Lucky slapped a magazine into place, pulled the slide back and let it go. "Time's a'wasting. Let's get moving." Shielded from view of the factory, Lucky hopped out and stood beside the Jeep, gun cradled near his chest. It wasn't his .38, but it beat the nothing he'd been carrying the past few weeks.

Bo didn't say a word when he got out, but gave Lucky's arm a nudge, the closest thing he'd get to a kiss for luck under the circumstances. They trudged single file up to the rear gate.

The gate slid open. Cousins on the inside were wonderful things.

"Get down," Bo hissed. He snatched a shotgun from Rafael. The attached suppressor wouldn't kill the sound, but would kill the location-revealing muzzle flash.

214

Only how the hell did he intend to shoot one-handed? Bo snugged the butt of the gun against his shoulder and sighted.

Lucky hit the ground. *Pop, pop, pop, pop, pop.* Damn! The boys were packing some serious firepower. Semi-automatic. Mr. Marine sure as hell knew how to shoot. The cameras and lights shattered in an explosion of tinkling glass. All grew dark and quiet.

"You didn't learn that from your aunt," Lucky groused.

Bo slid on his belly over to Lucky. "No, she only taught me handguns. The good old United States Marine Corps taught me the rest. You ready?"

"I reckon? You?"

"Yeah. Rafael? Alejandro? Cruz?" A "yes" and two "¿*Sí?*" answered him.

"The shoulder good?" Lucky squinted into the gloom, but he couldn't see anything moving in the yard. Surely the guards would come running any minute now. Unless they had a sense of self-preservation. What he wouldn't give for a pair of night vision goggles.

"Yeah."

"Let's move!" Lucky kept to the shadows, zigging and zagging his way to the front of the building. Bo, Cruz, and the brothers followed behind. Another round of *pop, pop, pop*, took out the lights and single camera by the door.

"Come out and play, Stephan," Lucky taunted under his breath. Keeping his voice low, he laid out his plans. "Cruz, you know this part of the building?"

"Yes."

"We need the Garcias out here watching for that guard and if anyone comes in. You, me, and Bo go in." Lucky would rather go it alone, with Bo hurt and Cruz still an unknown. Just because he hadn't screwed Lucky over yet didn't mean he wouldn't. "I take it you've done this before?"

Lucky directed the question to Cruz, but both he and Bo answered, "Yes."

Good. That made two out of three. Lucky knew the drill and had practiced many times, but hadn't taken active part in an organized building raid with the SNB since earning the right to carry a gun. Still, Bo was injured, which meant Lucky took lead. If Cruz turned traitor, Bo could take him out as easily as he had the lights.

Lucky counted to ten. Then he counted again. On the fourth round, he crept up the steps to the main entrance. The door was unlocked. Lucky stood to the left. Cruz darted to the opposite side of the door. Bo pressed himself flat against the wall a few feet way.

Lucky slipped inside, hugging the wall to make a smaller target. The lobby was dark, as was the hallway. A square of light in a door marked the first office.

He crept down the hall, his heart sounding a bass beat to rattle every bone in his skull. Just a little more...As before, Lucky took left and Cruz took the right, the light from the inset window painting his face with shadows.

Turning the knob slowly, Lucky strained his ears. No sound from within. He shoved the door open and jumped back, heartbeat loud in his ears. Nothing. He peered through the crack behind the door. Glancing up to meet Cruz's gaze, he crossed his fingers and put hope in Cruz not lying about knowing the drill. Cruz nodded. Good. Once, twice, Lucky bent and straightened his knees, silently counting to three.

On three, Lucky shot through the door, Glock at the ready. Cruz crisscrossed his path. They both spun. Bo slipped inside the door and hovered in the doorframe, swiveling his head to the left and then the right to study the hallway.

With a double-handed grip on the Glock, Lucky swung around the lone desk and jerked a chair away while Cruz stood by, his own gun at the ready. At Lucky's nod toward another door, Cruz grabbed the handle and pulled. A closet. Stacked with papers. If they took the time to look, they might find something useful. Stephan came first.

With the first office clear, they retreated back into the hallway, Lucky taking point, and Bo bringing up the rear.

One by one, they cleared three more lighted offices. The fourth was dark. Stephan lurked somewhere within this building, as did three or four henchmen. Lucky's heart pounded harder with each footstep. He murmured, "Stephan has his faults, but he's damned good with a gun. Used to target practice with V... his uncle." At what distance had he shot his father? The man hadn't lost his head, so it couldn't have been too close. And he'd never let Bo know how lucky he'd been back at the tunnel. Stephan didn't often miss. Must've been the drugs. They served a purpose after all.

No matter how good a shot he was, Stephan still wasn't a match for a North Carolina redneck who'd learned to shoot before he could tie his own shoes. Last office. Unless they'd moved on, Stephan and his crew might be waiting inside.

"Cy-rus!" The main door slammed open. A wild-eyed Rafael barreled down the hall. "Cy-rus!"

Oh fuck. What now? Rafael slammed into Bo, jabbering away in Spanish. Bo lowered his weapon.

Rafael stiffened and drew back. At the last minute, he snatched the shotgun. His horrified expression slowly melted into a grin of pure evil. He aimed the muzzle point-blank at Bo's heart.

"Well, well, well. Look what the cat dragged in." The voice of Lucky's nightmares. A pinprick at his neck made him freeze.

Stephan's toady interpreter clonked Cruz. Cruz crumpled to the floor. Oscar grabbed his fallen gun, then came for Lucky's. Lucky held on.

"Drop it, or I'll tell our friend over there to finish what I started with Mr. Cooper."

Lucky's heart dropped to his stomach. Damn that motherfucking, double-crossing Rafael. Where the hell was Alejandro?

Lucky glared at the traitor, who had the good graces to pale. One day soon. He'd get his. Lucky dropped the gun and jerked when something sharp bit his flesh.

"Ah, good. You know what I'm holding." Stephan slipped out of the office, urging Lucky along with an arm around his chest and a needle to his neck. "I've never tested this on you. Don't make me start now." He kicked the door open wide. Two of his guards sat before the desk.

Stephan rounded the desk and all but threw Lucky into a chair. He aimed a gun straight at Lucky's head and placed a filled hypodermic syringe on the desk blotter. "There's your reward, Rafael, but if you release Mr. Cooper to take it now, I'll shoot you myself."

He stared into Lucky's eyes hard enough for Lucky to see the crazy inside, and murmured, "I would have made you a full partner, you know."

Lucky didn't have time for bullshit. "Half of nothing is still nothing, dipshit. You think men like Nestor will let you piss in their sandboxes forever? You've only lived this long because they're scared of Victor." Best not to let on the intel he'd gotten earlier. Daddy always said, *"When all else fails, read the instructions."* Lucky's motto was, *"When all else fails, play dumb."* Over the years, he'd made being underestimated into a survival skill.

Stephan had had a fit when Lucky mentioned Victor before. Best to keep him off balance. "You can't make me a partner when your uncle owns everything, including you."

Stephan narrowed his eyes, his brows nearly forming into one. Ah, a direct hit. No matter what he'd done or who he'd killed, he still wasn't satisfied. Interesting. But if he hadn't yet gotten all he wanted, why not?

"Tell me, Lucky. Why did Cyrus take you to the tunnel? I told him to stay away."

Why did someone discover my colossal fuckup? would have been a better question. "It didn't add up. That tunnel was closer, better built, and came out in a better area. It just made sense to try to clear the rubble if we could."

"I've never known you to think so logically." Cold calculation shone from Stephan's eyes. "And you're lying."

Rumor said that with a look Victor could see one's soul. Lucky had believed it once before meeting Walter Smith and figuring out both men were experts at reading body language. Stephan? He played games. He guessed. And like a blind dog sniffing for a bone, sometimes he got lucky. But he'd never get Lucky with a capital L. Heh. Time to shake him up a bit, make him think he'd gotten something right. He probably didn't even realize he'd dropped his guard, and the gun.

One quick lunge, and the .38 would be Lucky's. But at this range, Stephan might get a shot off first. Just once it might be nice to complete a major assignment without winding up in the hospital. "You're right," he said.

The momentary surprise on Stephan's face made the confession well worth the effort. He raised the gun a bit, enough to shoot Lucky in the knee. As long as the muzzle didn't come near vital organs. "Why were you really there?"

Lucky gave an "oh please" grimace. "It's not good business sense to close down that tunnel without trying to fix it." *Believe that, you son of a bitch!*

Stephan's smugness made Lucky want to slap the bastard. "Mr. Cooper should be dead now, and he's not. I want to know the truth about why you went to the tunnel. Who else knows what was down there?" He aimed the .38 at Lucky's head again.

"We went down the tunnel to check things out, but some guy ran past us, heading for the US side. We found the body, but someone else got there first and was going through the dead guy's pockets. I went to chase the man. He dropped a wallet, and stopped to pick it up. I got a good look at him, so he brained me one." Lucky rubbed his hand over the goose egg on his head.

"He took the man's wallet?" Stephan's face puckered like he'd swallowed a bug.

Serves you right for leaving ID on a body, dumbass. "Yeah."

"Who was it?"

Time to throw someone under a bus.

"Looked like one of Nestor's men."

CHAPTER TWENTY

LUCKY TWISTED the knife. "Who was the dead guy? Someone who got in your way?" If only boss man was here, they'd have Stephan on his knees confessing all to Uncle Walter. Lucky would have to do in a pinch. It might buy them a little time to keep playing ignorant.

The flush on Stephan's face told just how close to the mark Lucky hit.

"He interfered in my business. I couldn't allow that."

And just like that: a murder confession. Damn. Why the hell hadn't Lucky set his cell phone to record? "And you didn't think anyone would ever try to use the tunnel again?" Especially not the migrants who'd obviously camped in the warehouse. If they knew the road straight to Texas lay under their feet, a little thing like a dead body likely wouldn't have stopped them. "Did you think no one would miss your father?"

Their eyes met. This time, Lucky saw into the black pit his enemy had been given in place of a soul. He let Stephan see everything and know Lucky'd held Vincent's wallet in his hand, had seen the bullet hole and the fancy diamond ring. Why the hell hadn't Stephan taken those identifying markings? *Because he'd left Vincent's body where it wouldn't decay, and where it could be found at the right moment.* Surely Vincent wasn't the first casualty to lie in the dark for months.

Stephan planned to point the finger at someone else. Perhaps another man who'd amassed too much power to let live, and who might have reason to cull the herd a bit when it came to who ran the show. Someone who'd been seen with Nestor and with the defector Cruz.

So many good targets existed. Bo, or maybe even Nestor himself. No doubt Stephan would go whining to the neighbors, hat in hand, seeking vengeance for his slaughtered father.

Holy shit. And slaughtered father would take the rap for Victor. Vincent had taken over Victor's business, even wore his ring. Damn. Lucky's policy on being underestimated backfired. The Stephan he used to know and avoid hadn't been so damned clever. Perhaps he'd learned something from his uncle after all.

Or maybe he'd just shot his father in anger, left the body, and buried himself in denial, with nobody left to fix his messes.

Stephan stepped closer, resting the gun muzzle against Lucky's cheek. Lucky jerked back as far as the chair allowed. His pulse thudded fit to drown Stephan's voice, but he couldn't let this asshole see him sweat.

"My uncle was rich and powerful. He could have had anyone he wanted for the taking. And he wanted you."

Panic squirmed to life in Lucky's gut. Jealousy. Stephan was jealous. But why? "I was just an employee with benefits."

"No. He planned to retire, spoke of traveling the world. With you."

"Victor never mentioned retiring. Of course, he never mentioned what a nasty piece of work you were either. He let it be a surprise." Lucky didn't dare glance away from Stephan to find out how Bo fared. His vision went dark around the edges, tunneling down to a man with a gun and nothing more.

Stephan's hand shook, jiggling cool metal against Lucky's cheek. No telling what the fucker might do.

His maniacal laugh wouldn't be out of place for a late-night movie villain or a psycho ward. "I think I might see more of your appeal after all." Stephan stroked the gun barrel over Lucky's jawline. "I had a friend who owned a tiger once. I asked why he wanted an animal around that might eat him. Know what he said?"

"'I taste like chicken?'"

"He said, 'True power is being powerful enough to control a wild animal's instincts.'"

"As we say back home, your friend is dumber'n a bag of hammers."

"Was." Stephan unleashed a wolfish grin. "The tiger ate him, you see."

"Don't worry. No way in hell would I eat you. You'd taste like rank asshole."

Stephan smashed the gun against Lucky's face. Stars erupted. A brilliant flash of pain followed. That'd leave a mark. The gloves were off. He glowered at Stephan as the tiger must have glowered at its master the moment before taking the killing bite.

Eyes every bit as feral stared back at him.

The door slammed open, driven by a pissed off Garcia. Alejandro grabbed the shotgun from his brother's hands, screaming at Rafael.

Stephan turned and yelled. Lucky kicked him square in the crotch. The yell turned into a scream.

Cruz sailed through the doorway, knocked Oscar to the floor, and wrestled the gun from the translator's grip. At his barked order, the two lounging guards raced out the door.

Stephan made a grab at Lucky. Lucky kicked against the desk, tumbling over along with the chair. He rolled straight into Oscar's kick. Damn it! He curled around his injured ribs and gasped.

A shot rang out, then another. The Glock! There! On the floor! Lucky snatched the gun and shimmied back over behind the desk. Cruz had Oscar pinned to the floor. Alejandro held a gun on Rafael; Bo aimed his shotgun at Stephan. Oh, for one of them to sneeze about now.

Lucky took aim. Just one shiver, one false move, and he'd happily put Stephan out of the world's misery. Only...until recently he'd never even shot a man, let alone killed one.

Once his pulled the trigger, life would change. He'd shot enough deer in this life to see firsthand how a one-second decision had lasting results. One minute the animal would be grazing, the next minute, it'd be thrashing on the ground. And then the light in its eyes would go out for good.

As much as he hated Stephan, could he take the man's life?

He spared a glance at Bo. So calm, so cool. Stephan had tried to kill him. Would try again if given the chance.

Lucky squared his shoulders. Yes. Yes, he could kill the man. It might mean tons of paperwork, and a full investigation. To save Bo, he'd dance through fire.

Stephan slowly raised his hands, left palm out, right loosely wrapped around his pistol. He smiled and shot.

The shot went wide. Bo loosed a primal scream and tackled Stephan to the floor.

Lucky took aim. The moment he found the target, the men rolled. Oh fuck. He might shoot Bo.

Another shot rang out, chipping out a hole in the wall behind him. He glanced up to find a man standing in the doorway, chambering another round. Fuck! Another guard. Lucky's brain switched off. He aimed and fired. Time slowed. Shock registered on the man's face. He grabbed his chest and lifted his bloody hand. His mouth dropped open, and he stared at Lucky a moment before crumpling to the floor.

Rafael broke free of Alejandro and charged the desk to grab his payment for selling out. Lucky whipped around. Bo had Stephan's arm, bending it back, trying to get Stephan's gun. If Lucky aimed just right...

Stephan's gun went off. The lights went out in an explosion of glass.

Flesh smacked against flesh. The door opened and closed. A scream of rage ripped the night. "Go, go, go," sounded like Cruz.

Something heavy hit the wall with an "Oof."

Lucky rolled to his stomach and cradled his gun. Inch by inch, he crawled across the floor. A body blocked his way, too thin to be one of the Garcias, too tall to be Cruz, and too smelly to be Bo.

"Wait a minute, I think I got it." Yeah. That was Cruz.

Bap, bap, bap, came from outside. The gate screeched open, and a few seconds later tires squealed in the distance. A shadow raced for the window. "He's getting away!" Lucky didn't know the voice. Light drove back the darkness from a lamp in Cruz's hand.

Rafael and Oscar lay sprawled on the floor, along with the man Lucky had shot. Alejandro was nowhere in sight.

Bo lay on the floor, an empty hypodermic sticking out of his neck. "Lucky?" He grabbed at the needle.

One of the guards who'd deserted Stephan earlier stared out the window. "He took your Jeep." Lucky crawled over and grasped Bo's hand. His fingernails were blue.

"The kit," Bo whispered, dropping his head back.

Oh, God, no! "The kit! The kit's in the Jeep!" If the syringe held what Lucky thought it did, combined with what Bo had earlier, he'd be dead soon. They kept the drugs in here. Surely the lab had what Lucky needed.

"Get Stephan."

"No," Lucky growled. "You come first."

"No!" Bo might have meant to shout. It came out as a hoarse yell. "Go get Stephan. Don't let him get away!" He pulled out the empty syringe and flung it away.

If Lucky left the room, he might never see Bo again. He wanted Stephan. Wanted to see him bleed. Wanted him to rot in prison. He wanted Bo alive more. Bo breathing or Stephan bleeding? Not even a contest.

"Cruz." Lucky met Cruz's gaze. "He took something earlier. To fight the withdrawals. That along with this might kill him."

No telling how much shit flooded his system. "Help me pick him up!" Lucky ordered the guard. "Get him into the lab." He glared at Cruz, daring him to say no. He wasn't letting Bo or Cruz out of his sight.

"Do as he says," Cruz said.

The guard nodded and lifted Bo's feet while Lucky grabbed Bo under the arms, doing his best to avoid the injured shoulder.

Cruz picked up the needle. "We might need this if we can't find another." He checked the body blocking the door, lying in a pool of blood. "Oh, Rafael." He crossed himself and let out a sigh. "Come. We see to Cyrus, then look for this one's brother."

They rushed down the hall and into the lab, Cruz leading and Lucky bringing up the rear.

A woman wearing a lab coat squealed and disappeared through a door. There were no flat surfaces in the lab large enough to hold Bo. "There." Cruz pointed to a chair next to a blood pressure cuff. "This is where the men are injected every morning." He curled his lip.

Lucky and the guard set Bo down, and he dashed to the far side of the room to rifle through cabinets. Saline, saline, saline. Damn, no wonder the US didn't have any. Saline, acetaminophen, hydrocodone in an open cabinet, where anyone had access.

He tossed aside vial after vial. Finally, naloxone. "Got it!" He rushed to Cruz's side. Holy fuck!

Bo barely breathed, a blue tinge creeping into his skin. He opened his eyes and stared out at nothing. "You need to work fast. And once it's in me, I need a doctor within an hour."

Cruz punched a needle through the top of the bottle while Lucky wriggled Bo's jeans down to expose his thigh. "Anyone around here you trust?" Lucky asked. Not that he trusted Cruz.

"No. We gotta get him to the border. The clock's ticking."

Lucky winced along with Bo when needle pierced flesh. Trapped between the devil he knew and the devil he didn't left him no choice. Lucky took out his phone to call Walter.

A body lay face down in the parking lot. "Alejandro." Cruz knelt by the wheezing man and rolled him over. Oh fuck. Not Alejandro. Lucky leaned Bo against a railing and dropped down beside Cruz.

Alejandro cupped Lucky's cheek with his fingers. He smiled through bloody teeth. "Lucky," he said. *"Mi amigo."* His hand fell, and he stared at nothing. Once more Cruz crossed himself, as did the guard.

Lucky stared at the man who just might have died for him, had fought his own brother. A vise tightened around his heart. Fuck. Why Alejandro? Why? "I'm sorry," Lucky whispered, hand against the man's jaw.

"You stay here," Cruz told Stephan's former guard. "Be my eyes and ears." Money changed hands. "See that Alejandro and his brother are cared for."

No time to stop for the dead. The living needed him. Lucky stood and resumed his grip around Bo's middle. "Sure you can walk?" He led the way across the parking lot.

"To the nearest car? Maybe. Up the side of Bear Mountain? Not on your life." Lucky had no idea of the whereabouts of Bear Mountain, but Bo's weak attempt at a smile fell short, a mere twitch of the lips quickly tightening into a grimace. No telling how much shit was in that syringe, or if the antidote even worked.

"Here. Stephan's car." Cruz rushed to the Jaguar. "Damn it! Locked!"

Oh, how Lucky loved classics. "Stay right here." He propped Bo against the car's hood. Popping the lock took sixteen seconds. What could Lucky say? He'd gotten rusty. He lost twenty seconds hotwiring the engine, but still it was good to be the redneck.

Cruz settled Bo into the area not big enough to be called a backseat. "I'm driving," he said.

"Now wait a damn minute—"

"I know the way and the car. You don't." Cruz dropped his voice. "Your man needs you." Lucky wedged himself in back and pulled Bo against his chest, careful not to jostle him. Cruz took the wheel.

They'd only gone a few miles when headlights appeared behind them. "Oh shit, we got company."

Cruz sped up, but the other car still gained. Lucky braced for impact. The car whipped around them. A Mercedes E250. Nestor's Mercedes. Another car rode their ass while the Mercedes took the lead. Neither made any move to stop them.

"Our escort," Cruz announced from the front seat.

"You okay?" Lucky asked Bo.

"Would you believe me if I said yes?"

"No. But you can try."

Bo gave him a weak smile. "Did you mean what you said about living together?"

A year ago, Lucky would have screamed and run at such a suggestion. Not anymore. Not from Bo. "Yeah."

"Tell me about the house again."

"It's got a big kitchen with two ovens. It's even got a grill so you can cook portobellos to your heart's content."

"Nice."

"A fireplace in the living room." And by God, Lucky meant to see Bo stretched out on a rug, enjoying the blaze. "And another in the dining room."

"That'll be great around the holidays, if we ever manage to spend Christmas together."

Every Christmas since they'd met, they'd been separated by the job or circumstance. Last year, Lucky allowed himself to dream of the family Bo wanted one day, neatly inserting himself in the picture. "The house has three bedrooms and another room we could use as a gym." No need telling him one had been outfitted as a nursery.

"How's the yard?"

"Fenced. Ready for a dog."

"I'm tired." Bo got quiet. "And cold."

"Rest. I've got you." Lucky rocked Bo in his arms and crooned a song Bo had once sung to him, an old country tune about needing someone. He couldn't lose Bo, not when he'd finally found enough of himself to appreciate the man, and could possibly find a way to make Bo happy too. He'd never been big on relationships, but Bo hadn't run screaming yet.

Coffee, bacon, steak, hell, sacrifice every vice, just leave Bo. "Bo?"

"Yeah?"

"Stay with me, hear?" Lucky planted his lips against his lover's forehead.

"Not going anywhere. My stomach's starting to cramp. The naloxone takes the drug out of my brain. Expect withdrawals."

Fuck. "Cruz? How much longer?"

"See the lights up ahead?"

A fuzzy glow appeared in the distance. "Yeah."

"That's the border crossing."

"Hang on, Bo, we're almost there." Each minute stretched to hours. So close. So close. Strobe lights flashed ahead, a Brownsville police car and an ambulance coming into view. Damn, Walter came through.

The escort car in back dropped away, and the Mercedes pulled off on the shoulder. Cruz stopped the car and opened the door. "Here's where I get out. Take care of yourself, amigo." He fist bumped Bo.

Lucky scrambled through the opening between the bucket seats. Cruz held the door open a moment. "Take care of him. He's worth it. *Vaya con Dios, hermano.*"

Eyes trained on the flashing lights ahead of them, Lucky didn't look back. "I know he said 'Go with God,' but what did he call me?"

Bo replied, "Brother."

CHAPTER TWENTY-ONE

The jitters weren't bad enough to slosh the hospital coffee out of Lucky's cup. The eight-on-the-Richter-scale tremors would come later. He took a sip of bitter brew and stared down at his partner, sacked out on a hospital bed. The openness on Bo's face had gradually faded since he was a rookie, even while sleeping. Or maybe Lucky'd only imagined it in the first place. So many layers to the man. Just when Lucky thought he'd figured all the pieces out, Bo showed some new facet of himself, sometimes good, sometimes scary, but all part and parcel of the same unique man.

Lucky was no prize himself. Hell, he'd killed a man. Taken a life. Which meant a mandatory psych evaluation and another death on his conscience. But he'd saved a life too. Several. Bo's. His own. Cruz's. But not Alejandro.

There'd been no word yet on Stephan, though Nestor would likely follow through on his threat now to handle things the old-fashioned way. Unless Cruz got there first. Cruz. The guy reeked of DEA, but not the desk types Lucky normally dealt with. No, Cruz was a "roll up the sleeves and let's get dirty" kind of guy. *Hermano.* Yeah. *Hermano.*

The door opened, and Walter Smith blocked out the light from the hallway with his bulk. The moment of truth for a long overdue conversation. When morning came, Lucky would be out of a job one way or another. Maybe they could still get the house on Bo's salary, if Bo didn't lose his job too. If Lucky bargained right, that wouldn't happen.

"How is he?" Most people would call Walter's whisper demanding. They should hear him when he *meant* to talk loud.

231

"Sleeping. His hell starts tomorrow." As would Lucky's if things didn't go as he hoped. Even if it wasn't his fault, Bo had become drug dependent, the one thing he'd sworn never to be again. Withdrawals and rehab lurked in his future. No telling what the long-term effects of Stephan's poison might be.

And the deathbed confession in the cave now would meet the light of day, to be dealt with by Bo all over again.

"Can we go somewhere and talk?" Walter held himself stiffly, keeping a distance between them. Either Lucky had an ass chewing coming, or Walter read body language better than even Lucky gave him credit for. He had some explaining to do, and he'd better start talking.

After another quick peek at Bo and a pat on the hand, Lucky dropped his empty coffee cup in the trash can and followed Walter out the door. The man sitting alone in the waiting room jumped when Walter approached. Landry. The last person Lucky wanted to see. Lucky's sometime trainee nodded. "Mr. Harrison, Mr. Smith. I'll wait in the car." Damn. Somehow the waste of skin had picked up some manners. Two big Starbucks cups sat on the side table.

How do you make a jerkoff more tolerable? Have him guard coffee. Lucky grabbed a cup and lifted the lid. Plain black liquid—the drink of the gods, not the frou-frou, whipped cream, caramel, and everything but the kitchen sink crap Walter drank. Lucky took a sip. Damn, but Starbucks made good coffee. Still, a cup of coffee wasn't a big enough bribe to make him believe Walter's sweet talk.

"Spill," Lucky said, barely containing a snarl. "And this better be good." He flopped down into an uncomfortable chair, likely designed to make patients' loved ones keep a vigil at home instead of here.

Walter eased down into another chair and lifted his cup to his lips. Asshole. Quit stalling. After what seemed like hours, Walter put the cup down and sighed. And sighed. And sighed. The big man held an ungodly amount of air. "Where do you want me to start?"

"How about coming clean about why I found a picture of you and Victor having lunch and laughing like two old friends."

Both of Walter's bushy eyebrows shot up toward his hairline. "What picture?"

"Didn't you search my house after I left?"

"Yes, and we found both your phones. But I didn't find a picture of me." He shook off his shock. "I'd have been most flattered."

Jerk. "I found an envelope in my mailbox, with a note that said careful who I trusted, and a picture of you and Victor munching pizza." And the more Lucky considered it, the more convinced he was that the picture hadn't come from Stephan.

Walter never hesitated before answering. "I assure you, I didn't know of any pictures, but I did have lunch with the man on several occasions."

A confession? Really? "Care to explain?"

"In my early days with the SNB, I spent a few years as an inspector, quite similar to what we do now in helping pharmaceutical companies spot their weaknesses and protect their supply chain." His brown-eyed scrutiny sent a shiver up Lucky's spine, like the man knew all of his numerous secrets. "Victor Mangiardi started out as a legitimate businessman, Lucky, working for his grandfather. When I came for inspections, he took me out for lunch."

Walter sat slump-shouldered, bringing him down more to Lucky's level. He appeared harmless with his hands clasped together around his coffee cup, but the rumpled suit he'd probably thrown on at a moment's notice didn't hide the predator the man could be when he wanted to. He wasn't Lucky's boss for nothing; he'd earned his place at the top of the food chain.

Nothing about his stance said he lied. No niggling little doubts warned Lucky of danger. Maybe he spoke the truth. This time. "You said you hadn't made any deals with him. I have it on good authority that you were in negotiations." Or rather, someone was. Nestor had never said who. "I also saw a picture of you following him down the courthouse steps after his arraignment." There. See him squirm out to this.

Walter stared at his hands. "I was afraid you'd find out one day. Only, I didn't lie. I didn't make a deal with him, not for his own sake anyway." Lucky barely heard his boss's normally booming voice.

"Then who did you make a deal for?"

Walter rolled contrite eyes upward to meet Lucky's hot stare. "You. He wanted a deal for you."

"What the fuck? And I testified against the man." What he wouldn't give for a beer, or some of what Stephan had supplied these last few weeks. Let him sleep. Let him forget. Even while Lucky kicked his former lover in the teeth, Victor had still looked out for him. Sainthood didn't suit men like Victor.

"Don't you understand? Your testimony didn't matter. The evidence was clear. And Victor Mangiardi had no intention of staying in prison. You better than anyone should understand. Men of his means, with his cunning, didn't stay confined for long. His lawyers were working on his appeal the moment the guilty verdict came in." Walter scrubbed a hand through his black and white speckled hair. "It's you he was concerned for. For all your bluster, he worried what prison might do to you. He offered names, schedules, you name it, to clear you."

Fuck, even with the man gone, Lucky kept racking up the debt. "So you hired me because a drug lord made a deal."

Walter shook his head. "No, I didn't. What I presumed was his suicide cancelled any deals. I'd gone to bat for him, and he left me high and dry. By that time, I'd already spoken to the top brass about recruiting former traffickers, and I went through hundreds of names. No matter my criteria, you always were the best man for the job." Again with that piercing gaze. "I didn't hire you for Victor's sake, but in spite of him."

"You told me he was dead. Was that a lie?"

"I didn't lie about that either. I saw the coroner's report. Cause of death: asphyxiation due to hanging. Yet, after your disappearance, I requested copies, to find the originals have been *misplaced*."

Chilling fingers traced up Lucky's spine.

"It also seems the guard on duty the night Victor supposedly hanged himself was found dead in his apartment a week later. An autopsy showed heroin in his system. He'd just passed a drug test the week before, and yet he died of an overdose.

"I've launched an inquiry into the missing records. We'll see what happens." Walter's dejected tone said, *Don't hold your breath.*

Bo overdosed and laid up in the hospital, Stephan on the loose in Mexico, and more and more evidence piling up for something screwy about Victor's presumed death. "Killing me off and renaming me Simon didn't help for a hill of beans, did it? Everyone I'm hiding from knows exactly where I am, even if they don't know I work for SNB." At least, Stephan didn't seem to. Nestor probably knew what Lucky'd had for breakfast.

"I'm sorry, Lucky. I truly am."

Should he stay or go? His cover with the SNB offered some protection, or at least the illusion of safety. But to protect Bo, Lucky couldn't stay. Bo's probation would be up soon, if it wasn't already, and he'd spoken several times about wanting to continue on with Walter, make a career out of taking down drug dealers.

Then again, not too long ago he'd been ready to take over Stephan's outfit. *Please, God, let it just have been the drugs talking.*

Now for Lucky to find out where he truly stood with Walter and the SNB. He took a deep breath and let it out slowly. "Stephan killed his father, Vincent Mangiardi, and I believe he planned to frame a convenient scapegoat."

"Do you have proof?"

"I found a wallet in the victim's back pocket. And it sure as hell was Stephan who carted the man away. Besides, Stephan had one of those evil mastermind moments when he confessed. I thought that shit only happened on TV." He pulled Bo's phone out of his pocket and handed it over. "Pictures, recordings. It's all here."

Lucky paused to down a mouthful of coffee and stall for time. Right now exhaustion fuzzed his brain, and he didn't know what to believe. But he owed the man sitting next to him one hell of a lot. And now was time to part ways. He needed to get the words out before he changed his mind. "Boss, I think this is the end of the line for me and the SNB. I thank you for the chance you gave me, no matter how it happened. But it's time for me to leave."

Walter narrowed his eyes. "You're not thinking of going vigilante on me, are you? Or searching for Stephan? Don't make me regret my decision."

"No, it's nothing like that. It's a matter a little closer to home." Fuck, he gave himself away by peering down the hallway toward Bo's room with more than worry for a coworker in his eyes.

"Oh, I see. How long have you been involved with each other?"

No matter how badly his instincts told him to lie, Lucky had to get everything out in the open. "Since our first case staking out the Ryerson Clinic in Florida."

"Is it serious?"

Lucky nodded, not trusting words.

"How serious?"

Damn the man for not leaving well enough alone. "Moving in together serious. Me quitting my job to see him through the next few weeks serious." *Would cut my heart out and give it to him serious.*

"You know the department's rules against fraternization?"

"Yes." Shit, meet fan.

"And you also know that Virginia falls within The Southeastern Narcotics Bureau's jurisdiction."

"What's that got to do with anything?" Virginia, nice state. But Lucky'd seen enough tobacco fields for one lifetime. If he looked hard enough, he might still see the blisters and stains on his hands from hours spent in his parents' fields.

"A woman in a domestic partnership works for our Virginia office. Taking a nod from the Supreme Court's decisions, the SNB granted her the same rights as in her home state, and that was before our president took steps to insure non-discrimination."

"I still don't see what that has to do with me."

"Even a few years ago, if you and Bo lived in a domestic partnership state, and you needed time off to take care of your partner, I'd have to grant you leave."

"We live in Georgia."

"Yes, but I couldn't treat any member of my team differently than the other states we cover. And besides, the SNB falls under government guidelines."

Lucky's hope tried to rise, but like him, it was too damned tired. "We're not living together yet."

"I take it you slept in separate beds in Orlando? How about that cozy cabin by the river near Athens?" Walter raised one brow.

Oh, no! No way would Lucky consider what Walter might be picturing right now. "Fraternization on the job, remember?"

"The rules were written to prevent married team members from having affairs with coworkers, and conflicts of interest from developing. The way I see it, Simon Harrison and Bo Schollenberger had a preexisting relationship when I hired you, like Jack in Accounting and his wife Laura in Human Resources."

Jack? Laura? Who were these people? Lucky heard "Told you so" in Bo's voice, loud and clear.

"You're not going to fire him? And I don't have to quit?"

"No, I'm not, and you don't. You may catch flak at work, but you're more than capable of taking care of yourself." Walter relaxed back into the world's most uncomfortable looking chair.

"You knew all along, didn't you, you smug bastard?" A weight lifted off Lucky's chest.

"I suspected, but I've been wrong before. I think it was in 1972." Walter's weak attempt at one of Lucky's patented smirks appeared worn-out but sincere. "But promise me you won't go after Stephan on your own."

"I doubt he'll be a problem anymore." If Nestor had his way, even now Victor's asshole nephew could be dead or pleading for his life. Damn it, Lucky wanted to watch him pay for what he'd done to Bo and so many others. Hell, the bastard had to pay for Alejandro, who'd proven himself a good man with his life. Or maybe Cruz would get to Stephan first and finish whatever he'd started with Nestor.

Not Lucky's problem now. His problem was a house in serious need of work, if a For Sale sign still hung in the yard, and getting his partner through rehab while weeding out Cyrus Cooper from Bo's personality.

Walter's expression hardened, and a crease between his eyes deepened. "You do know that Bo might not want to come back after his ordeal. He's been undercover for nearly a year. That's a long time. What then?"

"We'll cross that bridge when we get there. Now, excuse me, but I need to go see about my partner." Lucky stood. Time to check in on Bo.

"Of course."

"And Walter?"

"Yes?"

"If you ever withhold information from me again, I'll shoot you myself."

"Wouldn't dream of it."

CHAPTER TWENTY-TWO

The crisp scent of fall swept the hospital smell off Bo, or maybe Lucky'd only imagined the disinfectant when he'd picked Bo up this morning.

The day had started off cool, but had warmed—the perfect late September day in Georgia. Best to enjoy being outside while he could, on a blanket on the ground by the river. With Bo. No better place on earth existed, even if Lucky had lied to Walter and everyone else about where they were.

In the back of Lucky's mind, a clock ticked off the minutes until five p.m. would separate them again. He'd make the most of each moment and put their parting out of his mind completely until four.

"Did you take your medicine?" Not that Bo would forget, but withdrawal symptoms could really screw over their afternoon.

Even Bo's eyerolls tugged at Lucky's heartstrings. "Yes, mother."

"How's your shoulder?"

"Fine." Bo rolled his shoulder and didn't quite hide a wince.

"Need..."

"Lucky?"

"Yeah?"

"Would you stop your fussing? You're getting on my nerves."

"But—"

"The only butt I wanna talk about is under your jeans."

Okay, so apparently Bo wasn't in danger of dying anytime soon. Still..."Sure I can't get you anything?"

"If you ask me that one more time, I'm getting up from here to kick your ass."

Now wasn't the time to remind the man how he'd been bested in the ring by a cocky bantam rooster. One day soon they'd hit the ring again with spotters and orders for Bo not to hold back. "Okay. I've got a surprise for you. Close your eyes."

Instead of obeying, Bo raised a skeptical brow. "What am I? Eight?"

"'Bout that, yeah. Lucky me." Lucky plastered on his most annoying grin, the one he used to piss off coworkers.

Face twisted into a scowl, Bo closed his eyes.

Lucky opened the cooler and pulled out the cake he'd run to town for earlier. "Okay, you can open your eyes now."

Bo opened his eyes and opened them some more. "You remembered!"

How could Lucky forget? "Under the circumstances, I didn't have time to get you anything."

"You got me cake."

"But I didn't get you a gift."

"I'll take it out in trade. Now, what kind did you get me?"

Lucky smiled. "Carrot." On top of the cake, along with "Happy Birthday, Bo", was a frosting image, half carrot, half penis, harking back to the first meal they prepared together when Lucky had carved carrots into penis shapes. "I had to pay extra for the artwork." Not to mention sign a disclaimer with the bakery, promising he'd never tell anyone who'd made the thing. But someone who avoided sugar and white flour like the plague made exceptions for birthday cakes, right?

Bo swiped a finger through the cream cheese frosting and popped it into his mouth. He sucked in his cheeks, giving a darn fine impression of a blowjob. "This tastes really good on my finger. I'll bet it tastes better on you."

"Oh, you sweet talker, you. Must be the sugar." Lucky peeled off his T-shirt and flung it to the ground. He needed distraction from what waited for them at the end of their private celebration. And nobody did distraction better than Bo.

240

Bo stuck his finger into the frosting again, and this time smeared the gooey confection across Lucky's chest. "I'm not usually one to eat sugar, but I'll make an exception today." He followed the trail with his mouth.

Lucky took care removing the sling from Bo's arm, and they both wriggled out of their clothes. Bo loved outdoor sex. Lucky wanted Bo any way he could get him.

Then the vision of so much skin, after weeks of intermittent sightings, and all else fell by the wayside. Lucky sealed their mouths, tasting frosting on Bo's tongue. He peppered kisses across Bo's whiskered jaw, down his neck, and to the hollow of this throat. Bo's moans vibrated against Lucky's mouth and tongue. Now this would be a really good place for... He scooped cake to spread across Bo's Adam's apple and feasted off warm skin.

"You make a great plate." Bo made a pretty great everything.

"Yeah? Well, it's my birthday, so I should get the first piece." One handed, Bo rolled Lucky onto his back on the blanket, keeping the arm with the injured shoulder close to his body. With an evil grin, he decorated Lucky from neck to balls with birthday cake. He dug the carrot decoration out to place on the head of Lucky's erection.

Smile never fading, he proceeded to lick off the sweetness. Oh, hell yeah! Lucky lay back, stared at the puffy white clouds overhead, and enjoyed his tongue bath.

"You like that?"

"Sure do. Can't you tell?"

"Then you're gonna love this." Bo engulfed Lucky's cock. The sugar carrot fell to the side.

"Oh, sweet mercy!" Lucky arched off the blanket. Damn, damn, damn, damn, damn, but the man sucked him just right. But Lucky wanted to play too. "Turn around."

After a little shuffling, Lucky lined up for a mouthful of more than cake. Out here, where anyone could see them. A two-twenty current shot straight to his groin. Oh yeah. Maybe Bo brought out the exhibitionist in him.

Hands on Bo's hipbones, he guided Bo's cock into his mouth, thrusting up in perfect tempo with his own sucking. A light breeze raised goose bumps on his arms. Bo's foreskin slid up and down under his lips, and he licked away a drop at the end of Bo's cock.

Bo jerked away like Lucky'd bitten him. "No!" He dropped back on the blanket, hands in his lap.

"What do you mean no? No, you don't want to come in my mouth, or no, you don't want to come at all?" What the hell had gotten into the man?

Bo dragged his jeans across the blanket by one leg and fished in the pocket for two items: one they needed, and one they didn't. He lowered his gaze.

"Look, Bo. We've been over this. I agreed we didn't have to use those anymore." He stared at the foil packet in Bo's hand. Surely this wasn't a confession. When had Bo been with someone else? Oh dear God, no. "Stephan didn't..." Once Lucky killed the son of a bitch, he'd find a way to bring him back and kill him all over again.

"No. He tried, but eventually gave up when you got there." Bo still didn't look up. "I used a condom the day you came to my place, remember? The needles. The drugs. Lucky, you *have* to practice safe sex with an intravenous drug abuser."

"You ain't no abuser." And Lucky would take a fist to anyone who dared accuse Bo of such.

"It was drugs. I got them IV. Every morning they lined us up, and I can't be sure they used clean needles." Lines formed around Bo's frown.

An image Lucky didn't want stuck in his head. Bo, left with no choice but to roll up his sleeves or walk away from a case empty handed. "Okay, yeah, but don't call yourself an abuser."

"I dunno, Lucky. That was some mighty fine shit." Bo stared at his hands. "I can't be sure, you know? Actually, neither of us can be sure after Aureo."

Lucky knee-walked over to Bo's side. "Can't be sure of what?"

242

"What if...Between HIV and Hepatitis C, you need to get tested. They took my blood at the hospital, but I haven't gotten results back yet. And even when I do, I'll have to wait a bit and retest."

Stephan would die three times. Painfully. Maybe four. Lucky took a minute to pry the condom out of Bo's hand. "Bo, look at me." Shimmering brown eyes met Lucky's. "Good. Don't ever avoid me. If we have a problem, we need to talk about it." Where the hell had that come from? It sounded good, felt even better, and tasted like the truth.

"It's not your problem, it's mine." Bo tried to glance away.

Lucky caught him by the chin. "It's not *you* or *me* anymore, didn't you get the memo? We're in this together. I say we don't need this." He tossed the condom to the blanket.

Bo picked it up again. "No. Not in this. I won't expose you. Bad enough you may have been already."

Sometimes words weren't enough. Lucky wrapped his arms around his man and kissed him. They fell to the blanket, Lucky above, Bo beneath. "Where were we now?" He decorated Bo's nose with cake and kissed the crumbs off. Bo blinked hard but forced a smile.

Lucky would kill for an appearance of The Dimple.

They came together chest against chest, mouth against mouth, groin against groin. Lucky picked his battles and didn't comment when Bo unrolled the condom onto his cock. He found the discarded lube on the blanket, squirted the contents against Bo's hole, and slid his finger inside. Tight heat welcomed him to the wonders of his lover's body. He worked the muscles into pliancy, reaching deep to caress Bo's gland.

Bo's whiskers scratched Lucky's face as they moaned into each other's mouths. There was no urgency this time, no stolen, hurried moments, no one lurking around the corner. Just the two of them, in their own little world.

Lucky rolled Bo over onto his back and eased inside, closing his eyes against the pleasure.

"Look at me," Bo whispered.

He gazed down at the man he'd once criticized for being too perfect. Now, all his known flaws made him far more amazing, beyond simple perfection.

Slowly Lucky worked himself in deeper, watching Bo's face. Bo lifted his legs and hooked his feet over Lucky's thighs. They rocked together, picking up the pace.

Bo dug his fingers into Lucky's biceps. "I missed this so damn bad."

Lucky didn't want to dwell on missing with more time apart looming. He shut off his brain and focused on the cadence of their loving, the breathy sounds Bo made, his own throaty groans. And in the background, birdsong.

"Oh God, oh God," Bo chanted. He bucked up to meet Lucky's strokes with each chant.

Lucky reached down to cup Bo's ass in his hands, hoisting him up for a better angle. The ecstasy on Bo's face made the loss of kissing distance worthwhile. "You're gorgeous," Lucky grunted out. "I can't get enough of you."

Bo's babbling became more sounds than words, until... "I'm coming!" He reached down and grabbed the base of his cock with one hand, stroking with the other. "Ah, ah, ah!" His face contorted and every muscle seized. The cords of his neck stood out. Splatters hit his stomach, and his internal walls squeezed Lucky tight.

Lucky let go, burying himself as far as he could go. Weight braced on his arms, he rode out the storm. He opened his eyes to find Bo's wide smile, though his eyes were misty.

"I..."

Chirping sounded from the vicinity of Lucky's jeans. Bo's smile vanished. He rolled his head toward the offending clothing and barked, "Not fucking now!"

Lucky sagged down over Bo. *Not now, not now, not now.* "Fuck."

"We *were*. Can't we get any peace at all? He doesn't make a move on us in months, and now he can't damned leave us alone for two seconds."

The phone stopped ringing. Lucky pulled Bo close. "There, it must not have been important. Where were we?"

The phone rang again.

"Motherfuck…"

"You reckon he'd believe that it fell in the lake by accident?" The hint of Cyrus peering from Bo's eyes said he'd do it.

The ringing stopped and started again. Why couldn't the world go the hell away?

"Damn it!" Bo sighed. "I reckon you better get that."

"Ignore it, maybe he'll get the message."

"It's the boss. He wants you. He's not going away."

"We could try."

"Lucky, that's your work phone. You're required to answer." Yeah, and couldn't Walter have waited a damned day or two before giving him back his phone?

Now was not the time to tell Bo about requesting a partnership leave. Or about coming out to the boss.

The phone continued to chirp. Bo continued to stare.

"This is more important."

"Yes, it is. But he's more annoying."

The phone stopped chirping.

"See? He'll probably leave a message."

The phone started chirping again. Lucky sighed. "Oh, all right." He grabbed his jeans leg, tugged them over, and fished the intruder out of his pocket. "Harrison here." For the moment.

"Ah, good. I caught you. Are you busy?" Walter Smith was the last damned person Lucky wanted to talk to right now.

"Just enjoying a bit of birthday cake with a coworker. What's up?" *And it better fucking be important.*

Lucky pulled out of Bo and folded a blanket edge over him. As discreetly as possible, he rolled off the condom and stashed it in a paper napkin.

"I know you had plans for the weekend, but I need to see you Monday morning."

"I thought I didn't have to do that." No way in hell would he let Bo in on the leave.

"You have paperwork to sign. Your leave was approved, and we need a complete report of what happened in Mexico. Also, I'm told that if you don't report to Human Resources within a week, they're issuing a warrant for your arrest. Accounting is trying to close out the fiscal year, and I quote 'Simon Harrison is single-handedly responsible if we can't.' End quote."

"All right, all right. But it better not take long." No telling what the bean counters wanted. Maybe he'd forgotten to sign a tax form or something.

The upbeat tone left Walter's voice. "And there's another matter for us to discuss."

Oh shit. Maybe Walter had somehow found out about the man Lucky shot. He'd deal with that, he really would. One day. "What's that?"

"The inquiry into the missing coroner's report."

"You're not going to tell me over the phone, are you?"

"No. I haven't received the report yet but have been assured I'll know something by Monday morning. I'll expect you in my office at nine o'clock. One more thing?"

"Yes?"

"Wish Bo a happy birthday. But Lucky?" Walter's voice lost its humor. "He's scheduled to check in at Magnolia Center by five. Please don't make me call out a search party."

"I won't."

Bastard.

"Are you sure about this?" The squat brick building brought to mind the Durham Correctional Center, for all its hoity-to-ity name. Lucky shivered. He couldn't drive off and leave Bo here. He simply couldn't. Magnolia Center his ass. Lockdown Central was more fitting.

"We've been over this. I need to prove to myself and the boss that I'm not going to relapse." It wasn't Bo's fault he'd been forcibly injected at the whims of a madman—a madman whose days were numbered if Lucky had any say on the matter. *Just you wait, Stephan Mangiardi. Just you wait. One day you'll turn around, and I'll be the last thing you see, for Bo and all the others you hurt.*

Victor may have prized family, but being disowned created a whole new definition of the word. Family now revolved around a sister and nephews Lucky never saw, and the man at his side.

Bo got out of Lucky's Camaro, taking Lucky's heart with him. He rounded the hood, arm still in a sling and a packed duffle over his good shoulder. He stopped when Lucky rolled down the window. "Take care of yourself."

Bo leaned down through the window. "You too. And no going after drug lords without me."

"Would I do that?" Lucky faked innocence.

"Not if you value your life."

When Bo touched their lips together, Lucky wouldn't have pulled away if the whole damned department watched. "Sure you don't want me to walk you in?"

"I have to take this step on my own. There's twelve of them, you know." Bo's half-hearted smile stopped well short of his eyes. "You should have checked yourself in too."

"I'll deal with my problems on my own. Been there, done that." Now wasn't the time to mention Lucky's issues would be a walk in the park compared to Bo's.

Bo kissed Lucky again. "I love you." He stepped away, eyeing the ground. "If you don't mind, I'd rather you not visit. I...I might not be myself."

"Half the time you're not yourself, you're Cyrus." And if Cyrus got Bo through the bad time, then Lucky owed the guy a favor. "That hasn't stopped me yet."

"That's different."

No. Lucky couldn't stay away. No way, no how. "I don't care who you are. I love you, and I'll be waiting."

Bo's wavering smile blossomed into something more genuine. "I'm counting on it."

Lucky sat in the car watching long after Bo lumbered up the walkway and disappeared into the building, fingers against his chin where the rasp of Bo's stubble lingered. "I'll be waiting. Waiting to take you home." Lucky picked up his phone and dialed the Realtor's office, ignoring the trembling in his hands. This year he'd get Bo something for his birthday the man would never forget.

A home.

ABOUT THE AUTHOR

You will know Eden Winters by her distinctive white plumage and exuberant cry of "Hey, y'all!" in a Southern US drawl so thick it renders even the simplest of words unrecognizable. Watch out, she hugs!

Driven by insatiable curiosity, she possibly holds the world's record for curriculum changes to the point that she's never quite earned a degree but is a force to be reckoned with at Trivial Pursuit.

She's trudged down hallways with police detectives, learned to disarm knife-wielding bad guys, and witnessed the correct way to blow doors off buildings. Her e-mail contains various snippets of forensic wisdom, such as "What would a dead body left in a Mexican drug tunnel look like after six months?" In the process of her adventures she has written fourteen m/m romance novels, has won several Rainbow Awards, was a Lambda Awards Finalist, and lives in terror of authorities showing up at her door to question her Internet searches.

When not putting characters in dangerous situations she's a mild-mannered business executive, mother, grandmother, vegetarian, and PFLAG activist.

Her natural habitats are airports, coffee shops, and on the backs of motorcycles.

For more information about Eden, please visit her website at www.edenwinters.com.

***

Want to hear about Eden's news and special offers? Join the Rocky Ridge Books newsletter for Eden's doings here, Dreamspinner Press, and wherever her muse takes her.

If you enjoyed Bo and Lucky's adventure, you'll want to read the others.

DIVERSION (BOOK 1)

Ex-con turned narcotics agent Lucky Lucklighter has a new-bie agent to train. Bo Schollenberger has a few things to teach the old hand while they take a corrupt doctor's pill-mill down.

COLLUSION (BOOK 2)

Bo and Lucky go undercover in a children's cancer hospital where some heartless bastard's profiteering from tragedy. Heartbreak and disaster may catch them first.

CORRUPTION (BOOK 3)

Breaking the pipeline on a psychosis-inducing designer drug puts Bo into motorcycle leathers and a new persona. Lucky'd better save his worries about who Bo's becoming for after they survive.

REDEMPTION (BOOK 5)

A dangerous man from Lucky's past calls, asking the same terrible question as his bosses: "How well do you know your partner?"

REUNION (BOOK 6)

Families are a fraught subject for both Bo and Lucky. Now Lucky's father needs something only Lucky can give, and has something that may destroy all he believes. The truth.

SUSPICION (BOOK 7)

Something stinks at the Southwestern Narcotics Bureau. The Boss is stricken just when he's revealing an investigation gone wrong, and only Bo and Lucky can find the enemies in their ranks.

Also from Rocky Ridge Books:

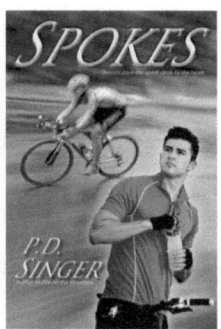

SPOKES BY P.D. SINGER

Pro cyclist Luca Biondi is more scared of loving journalist Christopher Nye than he is of the 200 riders pursuing him and the yellow winners' jerseys. The danger isn't where he fears: can Christopher help him through it?